A Reasonable Man

A novel by

Stephen F. Medici

A Reasonable Man

Published by Thea & Golf Publishing

For more information contact:

Stephen F. Medici at sfmedici@hotmail.com

Printed in the United States

A Reasonable Man

Stephen F. Medici

1. Title 2. Author 3. Fiction

ISBN 13: 978-1658088091

Other fictional novels

by

Stephen F. Medici:

Adverse Selection, 2007

A Walk Around Cold Spring Pond, 2011

The Girls In Pleated Skirts, 2014

Wellington Redemption, 2017

Dedicated to

my children

Paul, Lauren, Christian, Philip, Bryan

Preface

The manuscript I am about to share with you was written by Leo Monday, between November 2018 and January 2019. The original document was discovered in his Manhattan apartment and, per the instructions on the manila envelope in which it was contained, was given to his son, Stephen Monday upon Leo's death. It was intended only for his children; Stephen, Veronica, and Paula.

However, a digital version of the document was also contained on Leo's laptop computer. None of his children had use for the aged computer and, unaware it contained another copy of the private manuscript, they donated it, along with many of Leo's other personal possessions, to a local church thrift shop.

Six month later, I purchased the laptop for seventy dollars and discovered the document you are about to read. Understand, I am sharing it with you in its original form. That is, I've made no changes to the document whatsoever. All the grammatical imperfections, misspellings and typographical errors were Leo's and have been maintained to preserve the original work's authenticity. Like a fine piece of leather, its blemishes are what make it beautiful.

I

"Time weighs most on those with it least."

I'm not sure who first said that, but they were sure right. It's only when something is taken from us that we appreciate the value it once held. Perhaps, that's what makes life so precious; the fact that it is... finite. Everyone, no matter how rich or positioned, has a finite life.

The tropical fish in the colorful tank to my right seem not to care. A neon tetra weaves its way through the plastic plants in the tepid water and hasn't a care in the world. Why? Because he has no idea that someday he will no longer exist. I envy that tiny fish for his naivete.

My name is Leo Monday and I am sitting in my doctor's waiting room, doing what I'm supposed to be doing; waiting. As the seconds tick off the wall clock just beyond the fish tank, I can't help but appreciate the irony of the scene; a man with only six months to live, is wasting so many of the few precious minutes he has left, waiting for his doctor to tell him once again, that there is no way out of this. That all the tests have come back, and they all say the same thing: "You're a sixty-six year-old man with pancreatic cancer. It's not fair, but you're fucked."

This nightmare started just a few weeks ago. More correctly, my awareness of this nightmare started just a few weeks ago. I'm told, by the same doctor who is currently wasting much of my remaining time, that I may have been walking around with this parasitic cell mutation for twenty years, or that I may have been born with the mutated cell back in 1952. They don't really know, and it doesn't really matter. The grim fact is that it's now in its final stage which means so am I.

I haven't told anyone yet. I don't really know what to say. The thought of telling my son and two daughters terrifies me. And how can I sit down with my grandson and explain that I won't be around to pick him up from kindergarten on Tuesdays? He won't understand any more than I do. Peter and I have an unusually close relationship. I fear he, more than most, will be hurt by my passing. And the thought of hurting him makes me angry; angry at the doctor who keeps me waiting, angry at fate, angry at my body which, for the first time in my life, has betrayed me.

Where do you begin? I mean, is there a list of stuff you're supposed to cover when you have six months left? Are there things I should be doing to protect my family's future finances? I have a will but haven't updated it in fifteen years. Should I make a list of things I want to see and do in my remaining days? I'm not sure what's expected of me. Though I went through this five years ago with my wife, Annie was so organized about the end of her own life, the details were lost on me.

I suppose I'm expected to compile a "bucket list"- the things I want to do before I die. Again, the cruel irony here is that

I actually put my bucket list together over twenty years ago. I listed fifty things I wanted to do in my life and began working on it immediately. Back in my early forties, I was smart enough to realize there were things on my list that required significant physical ability; like skydiving and running a marathon, and then there were things that could be done much later like reading the bible cover to cover. So, I set out to check off the items that were most physically demanding and accomplished several before getting sidetracked with Annie's illness. Now, I guess I'll need to dust the list off and pare it down a bit.

I remember that one of the things on my list was to write a book. Well, I'll consider this the start of that one. I'm sitting in my doctor's waiting room, observed only by a few tropical fish while pecking at my laptop using my best two-fingered typing. My goal is to write the story of my life in the hope that after I'm gone, my children will use it to better understand the man they've only known as "dad".

I mean, how hard can it be to write a book? As you will quickly realize, I'm not overly concerned with proper grammar or fluid sentence structure. I'll type the way I think. And if I have time, and that's a big if, I'll go back later and clean it up to make it more readable. Since I'll be writing the story of my life, I don't need to do any research or create fictional characters. All the players will be real; people I've known, worked with, played with and some I've loved.

That will be the hard part- telling the story of the people I've loved.

Wait... I finally heard my name called to go see Dr. Romaro. I'll write more later.

Two hours later....

I'm looking out the window of my fifth-floor apartment and reflecting on my afternoon with Dr. Romaro. Although it's still raining, I can see the last few leaves clinging to their branches as a cold November wind tries to shake them loose. My view of the park never lets me down. There's always something new and wonderful to see. Particularly, since I learned my life will be about twenty years shorter than I'd expected, I seem to appreciate subtle nuances in the way the park looks each day.

I live on the corner of Fifth Avenue and 70th Street in a hundred-year-old brownstone. I have the top two floors of a very narrow brick building that some say was the first on the street to have telephone service. Now, I rely completely on my cell phone, having abandoned the traditional landline due to the barrage of robotic calls.

As I said, my view of the park is spectacular. I wish Annie could have seen this. Although she never wanted to live in the city, she would have loved the view. And she would have loved the local markets on 70th and 71st Streets. She always liked to shop at neighborhood places. I miss her. But I'll tell you more about Annie later.

Right now, I'm thinking about how my doctor wasted too much of my precious time today. He said the third round of MRI's confirmed what we already knew, and that the most recent blood reports were consistent with the last. That means everyone who has prodded or poked me in the last few weeks is now on the same page. And that page is the one that says, "You're fucked Leo!"

He did have one piece of good news. He confirmed that if I don't start the treatment he suggested; that being, an aggressive course of chemo and radiation, that I'd surely be dead within six months. That wasn't the good news. The good news, if there was any to be gleaned from my visit, was that if I don't go along with the treatment plan, I may still have two good months before the debilitating atrophy of my guts begins.

The way I see it, why exchange sixty days of relatively good health for several months of nausea on the one-in-fifty chance the treatments will buy me an extra year. That's the simple math behind it; there's a slim chance the treatment will help at all and a less than remote chance it would lead to remission, a word Dr. Romaro has never used in my presence.

The good doctor and I had this conversation about a week ago. "As your doctor," he said, "I will tell you that your best chance at life is to begin the treatments as soon as possible. I say that because chemo offers the only hope you have. But as a man and a father, like you, I will tell you that I would use whatever time I have left to embrace life."

So, I've chosen to embrace life. I did think about it for a short while, but once Dr. Romaro said that to me, I knew I'd come to the correct decision. Now I just need to hope my children don't give me a hard time about it. With less than six months of breath left, I don't want to waste any of it arguing with the people I most love.

Today is Friday. My short-term plan is to fly to West Palm Beach on Monday to see my twenty-nine year-old twin daughters and tell them, face to face, that I will soon cease to exist. That will be difficult for me. I'm sure we'll all cry a lot. Then on Wednesday, I'll fly back to New York and give my son Stephen the same grim news; also very difficult. But the conversation I most dread is the inevitable one I'll need to have with Peter, Stephen's only son and my only grandson.

But first I plan to spend one whole night, tonight, getting really drunk and feeling sorry for myself. I know the perfect neighborhood bar on 72nd Street for such catharsis and my poison of choice will be thirty-year-old single malt Scotch. The bar, *Bona Notte*, usually has a brisk Friday night crowd so I can quietly plant myself on one of the leather stools and get lost in the crowd. From there, and with dozens of otherwise happy people around me, I can be alone and spend some time reflecting on my first sixty-six years and how I plan to spend the next few months.

Tomorrow, I'll continue making plans and writing. I am overwhelmed by the sense that there is so much to be done, but I know that if I am methodical, making lists of things to do, that I can get control of this emotion. Right now, it just feels like there are ten thousand things to be done and so little time to do them.

I find that typing helps calm me. The simple act of telling my story to someone, even someone I'll never meet, brings me a little peace. So, I'll keep writing. And if you chose to endure me and share a bit of my journey, I'll tell you about my life and the wonderful people I've loved. But, if you read on, don't feel sorry for me. I seek not your pity nor your tears.

My life has been very blessed. I am a fortunate man. But, like all men, I am very far from perfect. My faults run deep and have haunted me nearly all my life. If you'll listen, I'll tell you about my wonderful life, about the highs and lows, and about my most buried secrets. You see…, I've done some terrible things. In the course of my wonderful life, I've killed four people.

And before I am no more, I'm going to kill one more.

II

I woke up Saturday afternoon with an understandably painful headache. My own fault; never mix colors of liquors. Eileen, the shapely bartender warned me but there were a bunch of college kids at the bar doing shots and they asked me to join them. I think I did three shots of Tequila. I remember there were limes involved so it must have been Tequila.

I do remember walking home and passing out, fully clothed, on my couch. While an unhappy prisoner of this happy state, I had one of my usual nightmares. I have several recurring nightmares. This one is the one about my older sisters, Lucy and Jane. Fraternal twins and a bit less than two years older than me, I don't think two sisters could be more different than Lucy and Jane; Lucy the tall blonde while Jane, the tomboy, was stocky with a darker complexion. But, as different as they were in appearance and personality, they were inseparable.

Now that I think about it, I'd bet what triggered the nightmare was a poster hanging behind the bar last night. I spent almost five hours sitting in the same spot and looking in the general direction of that damn poster all night. Eileen even mentioned it once, saying she had never been there but wanted to go. It was a picture of a deep blue lake nestled between two mountains. I have no idea where it was supposed to be, but it reminded me of Lake George; a place I went a lot when I was a kid, and the place where my sisters drowned when I was eleven.

If it hadn't been for that family vacation in 1963, Lucy and Jane would have been sixty-eight next week. I can't believe it was so long ago and that they've been gone so long. I miss them even today. They were wonderful and so full of life. They made our family happy. And after they were gone, so was the happiness. My parents never recovered. The twins' death eventually wound up tearing the family apart. My mom started to drink too much, and it didn't take dad long to catch up. They divorced while I was in college. More about my parents and sisters later.

Today, as soon as my head feels better, I hope to start on my short list of things to do. The first thing on my list is to do a little more research on what's killing me. After my preliminary diagnosis, I did the usual Google and WebMD search and learned a few gruesome facts, but if I'm going to put my life in the hands of a few doctors I didn't know three weeks ago, maybe a more extensive exploration is warranted.

Two and a half hours later:

So, I learned quite a bit about pancreatic cancer. Turns out, the internet has a very sobering way of explaining bad news. Unfortunately, what I learned is in complete agreement with what my doctors have told me. Many of the terms they've been throwing around, like "Non-functioning NETs", now make a little more sense to me. Bottom line is that I have exocrine pancreatic cancer, which is definitely not the type you want to get. The problem is, doctors can't really be sure you've got it until it's too late. Basically, they can't tell you've got it until the cancer spreads to other organs nearby. Apparently, for some reason, once it's in your stomach or bladder it is easily detected.

In my case, according to my doctors, it has spread to my stomach, bladder and liver; all organs within a stone's throw of the pancreas. Hence the grim prognosis. By the time I showed any symptoms, it was already in the other organs and too late for surgery. The whole process may have occurred in a few weeks or over several years. No one can say for sure and It doesn't really matter. I've got inoperable cancer. I'm going to die pretty soon. That's just the way it is.

Well, at least I confirmed that thirty years of combined med school wasn't wasted on these guys. They got it right. Good for them. Bad for me.

But I didn't start writing this to wallow in self-pity. I'm writing to set the record straight on my life. Hopefully, one day, in the not too distant future, Stephen, Paula, or Veronica will find this and share it with one another. I'd like my children to read it first. They need to understand. After that, I don't really care who sees it.

III

Every year, as my dad's Ford station wagon crested the top of the last ridge hiding Lake George from the outside world, the shimmering blue of the lake would overwhelm me. The three of us, me and my twin sisters, would play a game on the long ride to our annual week-long vacation. We would have a contest to see who spotted the lake first. We all knew it appeared as we came over the top of a hill, but there were so many hills on that five-hour ride, knowing which hill is what got you the prize.

We'd been making this trip every year that I could remember, and my parents talked about trips they'd made to the same cabin, long before any of us were born. So, I guess it was a family thing. We all loved the lake and the tiny one-bedroom cabin. For Lucy, Jane and me it was a week of pure fun. For my folks, I think it was a way to relive the way things were before they saddled themselves with a mortgage and three kids.

But in 1963, the ride was different. I remember it was a hot August day. We were just getting on the New York thruway when the news came over the tinny dashboard speaker. President Kennedy's wife was hospitalized because her third pregnancy had ended in a miscarriage. My mom was in tears and dad didn't say a word for at least sixty miles of the trip north. I had to ask what a miscarriage was and one of my sisters gave me a thirteen-year-old's explanation.

What I didn't understand was why my parents cared so much about these people we didn't know personally.

But, like us, the Kennedy's were Catholic and that meant we had adopted them as if they were our own. Wiping tears from her face, mom explained that losing a child was something no parent ever recovers from. She said it was something we couldn't understand until we had a family of our own. Little did she know she'd be standing over the caskets of her own daughters the following Friday.

* * * * * * * * * * *

I won the lake-spotting contest that year, mostly because everyone else was preoccupied with the radio. As we descended the final hill, Lake George came into view. I should be clear. I'm talking about the shimmering lake itself, not the horrible town that bears its name. Even as an eleven-year-old kid, I knew the town was a shithole; a tourist trap filled with bad restaurants and dirty arcades. They never should have allowed the town to be named after the lake.

Don't get me wrong; for a kid, the town was a lot of fun on a rainy day, which was the only time we ever went into town. There was a "House of Horrors" complete with a guy dressed convincingly like Frankenstein's monster walking out front. The arcades had rows of skee ball machines and riffle ranges where you could shoot at mechanical bears that rotated back and forth. It had pizza and dozens of ice cream parlors, commodities in scarce supply back at our cabin.

But the lake itself was pristine. In hadn't changed much in the 10,000 years since the receding glaciers of the last ice age to cover North America carved its deep canyon. Almost four hundred feet deep in some places and almost thirty miles from its southern tip to Fort Ticonderoga in the north, its waters were as clear as anything I'd seen on postcards from the Caribbean. To me, it was the most beautiful piece of nature I could image. Towering green mountains surrounded the lake like two large hands. Much of the adjacent land was part of the Adirondack State Park and completely undeveloped. And this natural paradise was only a four-hour car ride from New York City.

As he did every year upon our arrival at McNulty's Cabins, dad would get out of the car and go into the office to pay Mrs. McNulty the balance due for our weekly rental. The McNultys had sixteen dilapidated cabins they rented in the summer to families like ours. We'd all wait anxiously in the hot station wagon. Then dad would emerge from the home they used as the front office holding a key hanging on a large green piece of wood shaped like a maple leaf. Because we rented every year, dad was usually able to get us one of the few cabins directly on the lake. And when I say, "on the lake", I'm not exaggerating. The lakefront cabins literally hung over the water's edge. The only remaining mystery was which one of the cabins would be ours for the week.

"Number six!" He said proudly as he got back in the car dangling the maple leaf and attached key.

"That's the best one, the one all the way on the right." And mom's favorite. Her happiness was evident, and I was glad to see she'd taken her mind off the Kennedys for the moment.

Dad drove us down the steep half-mile dirt road that led to our little slice of paradise. The dusty road ended at the boathouse, about fifty yards past our cabin, but we jumped out of the wagon in front of cabin number six and unloaded our supplies for the week. Then dad drove the car down to the parking lot at the boat house, the only place you could leave a car.

Nothing had changed or been repaired since last year. The torn screen on the porch door was still in tatters and flapped as Lucy opened the door. The porch, which hung over the shallows of the lake, contained only a small table, two chairs and a refrigerator that had to be WWII surplus. The ancient planks that barely kept us from falling into the lake had enough spacing between them that I could see the glistening water below. It looked cool and was calling me.

But before we were allowed to head for the lake, we all had jobs to do. Mom brought our duffle bags into the cabin and sorted out the few articles of clothing we each brought. Dad unloaded the Scotch cooler into the dingey refrigerator while the girls set up our clothes line, extending a rope from the porch to the nearest tree. And I had to gather dry wood for our daily campfires.

"Gotta get as much wood as we can on day one in case it rains. Need to have dry wood." Dad made the same speech every year. But he was right. By gathering wood while the ground was dry and storing it under the back of the cabin, we had fires every night. Other campers struggled to build an acceptable campfire after a late afternoon shower, but they were always welcomed to join us at ours and usually brought marshmallows to reciprocate.

My search for twigs and small branches lying about was a task I enjoyed. It allowed me to walk in the deep woods that surrounded the McNulty property and along the lakeshore. And since the McNulty's owned about 200 acres, basically everything from the main road down to the lake, I had plenty of space to roam.

In forty-five minutes, I had enough kindling and small logs to get us through the week and probably leave a supply for the next week's tenants. As I pushed the last of it under the cabin Lucy and Jane emerged from the porch in bathing suits and headed for the boat house carrying beach towels.

"Hey, wait for me," I yelled.

"Put your suit on," Lucy yelled back. "We'll wait for you on the dock." Then they ran bare-footed over the pine needles blanketing the path from our cabin to the boathouse and its docks.

I quickly changed into my swim trunks and by the time I joined them, Lucy and Jane were sitting on the edge of the farthest dock with their feet dangling in the crystal-clear water.

"What took you so long Leo? The water feels warmer this year," Jane said.

I dropped my towel on the wooden bench in front of the boat house and raced past them along the creaky wooden dock. I did my best cannonball into the lake just as my sisters realized what was happening. The splash from my grand entrance soaked them both.

"Hey creep! That wasn't fair. We waited for you!"

'Creep' was Lucy's favorite name for me. She'd been using it so long, none of us could remember its origin. I tend to think it was based simply on my behavior. I used to like needling my older sisters and resented anything they were allowed to do that I wasn't, just because of our age difference. To be honest, I probably deserved the nickname. Although I loved my sisters, I was always razzing them, just for being girls, a gender I completely misunderstood.

So, on that warm August day, as I floated away from the dock, I looked back on the boathouse, the cabin and my two beautiful sisters. It all seemed so perfect. But nothing would ever be the same after that day.

IV

I'm writing this from somewhere over North Carolina; about 35,000 feet over North Carolina to be exact. So far, the flight has been, as they should be, uneventful. I'm on my way to see Veronica and Paula, both of whom live about ten miles from West Palm Beach Airport, in a place called Lake Worth.

Fortunately, the woman sitting next to me has finally gone to sleep. The gaggling Jesus-freak talked my ear off for nearly an hour while we were delayed on the tarmac. She had the nerve to complain she was going to be late for some horse show she was attending. Although we were both detained the same sixty minutes, I bet that wasted hour represents a bigger chunk of my remaining life than hers. Like I said before, people don't appreciate the precious commodity called time until they have little left.

It must be raining in the Carolinas because, from my window seat, I can see spectacular clouds glistening below in the afternoon sunlight. The sky that separates the sun from the top of the clouds is a glorious deep sapphire. It's quite beautiful and a reminder of so many scenes like this I never stopped to appreciate before.

To be honest, I'm very nervous about my visit with Veronica and Paula. Ever since their mom died, they have clung to me in a desperate attempt to avoid feeling like orphans. I guess it's normal that people want to hold on to their childhood. It's a way to feel safe and protected. If mom's not around to do it, there's always dad. And, up to now, I've been there for them. I'm afraid when they learn of my impending demise, they'll feel frightened; reminded of their own mortality. So long as a parent is alive, you're still a kid, right?

Neither of my beautiful daughters are married, although Paula has been getting serious about a male-nurse she met at the hospital where she works. Paula is an emergency room RN. Veronica, the kindergarten teacher had a serious boyfriend for two years but was devastated when he dumped her for a pole dancer. At least, that's what Veronica calls her.

It does surprise me that neither are married at this point. They're twenty-nine and both very pretty. And that's not just their father's opinion. In high school they had dozens of guys interested and, as a sophomore, Paula was homecoming queen. Although they look no more alike than any other sisters, both my twin daughters have their mother's facial features. Paula has the dark brown hair and eyes. Veronica has her mother's pouty lips and porcelain skin. They both have Annie's petite frame and bubbly personality.

I've given a lot of thought to how I should break the news. I tried to put myself in their position and asked myself, "How would I want to find out my father was dying?" Do I get right to the point? Or, should I settle in first? Maybe enjoy one more normal night with my girls and then talk to them over breakfast.

Should I do it at Paula's condo, where we'll all be staying for the weekend? Or, would it be better if I broke the news in a more public forum; a restaurant maybe? They'd both be reluctant to make a scene in a restaurant but is that a good thing? Or should I let them vent and cry as much as they want? I just don't know how to do this. It's all frighteningly new to me.

More to follow.....

****

I'm back at the airport. Paula just dropped me off on her way to her regular Wednesday morning Orange-something exercise class. I don't know why she needs to exercise. She weighs one-o-five dripping wet and is in great shape. Paula- if you're reading this someday; "No one thinks you're fat. Relax."

So, the last two days weren't as bad as I expected. The girls met me at the airport on Monday and we drove directly to their favorite Italian restaurant. I decided to hold off on the bad news until Tuesday morning, so our dinner was delightful. My daughters got me all caught up on their lives; not that I don't hear about it all on our weekly phone calls. But it's wonderful to hear it in person.

Did I mention that I love my daughters. Now, that sounds like something any father would say, right? But what I mean is that these two women are so delightful, I would love being in their company even if we weren't related. They take a genuine interest in other people and are able to empathically listen to others. When I'm with them I feel like all they want to hear about is how I feel about this or that; what do I think about some recent event in the news; or how do I feel about the latest school shooting? They couldn't care less about the facts. They want to know how I feel about it.

So, other than my rigatoni being a little limp, dinner was fun. On the drive back to Paula's, she had some big news of her own. This was news I really didn't see coming.

"I'm glad you're staying for a few days, dad." She started without taking her eyes off the road.

"Why's that, honey?"

"Teddy's coming for dinner tomorrow night. I'm going to cook."

"That's the guy you've been seeing? The nurse?" I pretended I hadn't been listening during all our phone conversations.

"Yes, you know who he is. And I'm excited for you to meet him. I think you'll really like him."

Veronica leaned in from the back seat to hear what was coming next.

"I'm sure I will. Just as long as you like him."

"Well, that's what I wanted to talk to you about." Her voice was softer now. "We've been seeing a lot of one another for about three months now. Actually, since just before Labor Day."

"Sounds like it's getting serious."

"It is, dad. We're, um… we're talking about maybe moving in together. You know, to see how it works."

That caught me off guard. I could tell she was nervous about telling me. To the best of my knowledge, neither of my girls had ever lived with a guy before. And, I have to say, at first, I was taken back by the image of some thirty-something man walking into my daughter's bathroom to take a leak while she's at the sink brushing her teeth. I know, it's an odd first image, but that's what I envisioned.

"Wow! That's big news." But I tried to sound controlled. "Are you sure about this?"

"I'm completely sure about Teddy, yes. I'm not completely sure about living with someone. That's all new to me."

"Well, that's good to hear," I said a bit sarcastically.

"Stop! You know what I mean."

"No. Actually, I don't."

I could tell this conversation wasn't progressing as Paula had thought it through in her head a hundred times. My daughter always rehearsed life. She wouldn't make a move without first studying it from every possible angle. When we used to play chess together, I could read the Reader's Digest while Paula contemplated her next move. Literally, sometimes fifteen minutes would pass between moves. So, I knew she had a plan for this conversation and maybe I wasn't following the script.

I offered, "What is it you're concerned about honey?"

"I don't know, exactly. I guess I'm worried that Teddy will start taking me for granted if we're always together. Or maybe I'll take him for granted." She paused for a moment as she made the right onto her street. "It's just that things between us are so good now, the way things are. I mean, we never fight. We never even have arguments."

"Well, first of all, there's nothing wrong with arguing once in a while. As long as you respect each other's positions."

"That's exactly what I told her." Veronica chimed in from the rear seat.

I continued, "Honey, you can't script your whole life. As much as you'd like to, you can't determine how others are going to behave. You just have to feel comfortable in your response to that behavior." I was getting way more Dr. Phil than I intended.

Then I said something that even surprised me. "Look honey, if you love him and if he loves you, it will work. Most importantly, don't be afraid of failing. Be afraid of not trying hard enough."

"So, you're okay with us moving in together?"

"Of course, if that's what will make you happy. Being happy is the most important thing. Life's too short not to be happy."

As I reflected on the fact that I was probably thinking more about myself and my abbreviated stay on planet earth, it occurred to me that I'd just been manipulated by our driver. She'd gotten exactly the response from me she wanted. Probably the one she'd scripted for me in her head weeks ago.

****

Veronica and I both stayed at Paula's condo that night; Veronica on the living room sofa and me in the guest room that looked like Laura Ashley threw up on the walls, curtains and bed. I guess when Ted moves in, they'll butch it up a bit, but right now this room wreaks of estrogen. Then again, I doubt he'll be sleeping in this room.

And as if the thought of some guy defiling my little girl in the room next door wasn't disturbing enough, what kept me awake most of the night was how I was going to break my news to the girls. After much tossing and turning and mentally rehearsed monologs, I came to the conclusion that I'd do it at breakfast. I hated to rain on Paula's parade; she was so excited about Ted. But, it had to be done and it had to be done early in the day so they'd have time to process it and then move on to her big dinner. After all, Ted was coming to meet me, and although our journey together would be brief, I would like to get to know the guy who might be taking care of my daughter, potentially, for the rest of her life.

As I finally drifted off to sleep, a really odd image forced its way into my head. In it, I was looking up from my grave at a cold grey sky and the people who'd come to bury me. Now first of all, I want to be buried and I'll make that very clear to my kids before I go. But the point of this morose image is that as I looked up at the people looking down on me, I could see Paula and Veronica, but it wasn't Stephen, my son who was at their side. It was a faceless man dressed in green hospital scrubs. His arm was around Paula's shoulder and it was clear, he was comforting her. I assume this was my brain's way of telling me Ted, whatever he looks like, will be the guy taking care of my little girl. And the first family crisis he'll need to deal with will be my demise.

I awoke to the fabulous smell of sizzling bacon drifting up from the kitchen. If it's possible to miss something when you're dead, I'll miss bacon.

I wanted to pull myself together before the girls called me down for breakfast, so I jumped in the shower then shaved. As I was shaving, I studied my face in the steamy mirror. I have to tell you, I think I looked pretty good for a sixty-six year-old guy with less than six months to live. I mean, the ravages of the cancer had not yet manifested themselves on the surface. All the killing was going on inside. The skin on my face was still fairly tight and, although my hair was completely grey, at least most of it was still where nature put it. Sure, I had to pluck hair from my ears every so often, but I think that's par for the baby-boomer course.

I think there was a time when women found me handsome, at least in an aging Tom Hanks sort of way. You know, not the perfect proportion of facial features but a face covered with enough boyish enthusiasm that you were happy to overlook the flaws. Annie often told me I looked like David Janssen, the T.V. Fugitive. And she adored David Janssen so that was good enough for me.

Anyway, I wanted to look my best this morning. I didn't want my daughters staring at me, searching for the first signs of atrophy on the outside after they learned how sick my insides are. I wanted to look youthful, alive, and strong. You see, I'd decided not to tell them everything. Not just yet.

As I bounded down the narrow stairs I shouted, "I can't believe how wonderful that bacon smells."

"Actually, this may be the first time I've cooked bacon since I moved into this apartment," Paula said as she spooned a half dozen scrambled eggs onto a platter. "I never eat bacon, but I know you love it."

Veronica was already sitting at the round wooden table, sipping coffee as she scrolled through her emails on her laptop. "I don't think I've had bacon since we were all at cousin Jimmy's wedding and we had that huge buffet breakfast in the hotel. That's got to be six years ago. I remember because mom spilled milk on my plate, and I had to go back and..."

The mention of Annie made us all pause. It seemed that just about everything in our lives was relative to Annie; everything was either before she died when memories were happy, or after, when everything went black for a while. And whenever someone mentioned her name or said the word mom, we all got this strange feeling. It was as if we were remembering for the first time that she was no longer with us and we were reminded of the emptiness.

Veronica immediately realized she'd set off the reverent silence and quickly added, "... and get a whole new stack of pancakes. But, by the time I went back the buffet was closed so, if I remember correctly Paula, you actually shared yours. Probably the first time in your life you didn't eat like a hundred pancakes on your own."

I appreciated the effort, but my daughters needed to stop protecting me from the memory of their mother. What they didn't realize was that I loved it when one of them brought up some pleasant story about Annie.

For some reason, I saw this as my chance to drop my bombshell. I launched into it without thinking it through. That turned out to be a mistake.

"Hey girls," I started. "I have something to talk to you about. And it's not the best of news."

Paula turned from the stove. "Sounds serious," she said in a mocking way.

I pushed away from the table a bit and clasped my hands in from of me. I knew if I hesitated, I'd never find the nerve to continue, so I just kept going.

"So, I went for my regular annual physical about a month ago and my primary care guy didn't like some of the results from my bloodwork. At first, he told me not to worry, that it was probably nothing, but he wanted to redo the tests just to be sure."

Veronica and Paula were now seated at the round table and I clearly had their attention. They said nothing so, after a short pause, I continued.

"When the second bloodwork came back it showed high levels of some enzyme in my blood. Dr. Levin explained that usually meant something was going on in the pancreas. I guess your pancreas is supposed to produce enough of a certain hormone to kill the bad enzyme, but in my case, it wasn't. So, he sent me to a bunch of specialists to have a bunch of tests done. I had a CAT scan and an MRI. I also had a sonogram."

"What's going on Dad?" Paula asked. Her voice was shaky.

There was no point in dragging them through all the test results. It was the final answer that was of consequence. I decided to just drop it.

"I have cancer. It's in my pancreas."

I knew that Paula, the nurse, would immediately want more details. And I was right.

"What stage Dad?"

I lied. "They're not really sure. They say it may not be too far along yet."

"Is it exocrine or endocrine?" Paula said a bit too loud.

I could only whisper the word, "... Exocrine."

"Jesus Christ Dad. How long have you known about this?" Now Paula was holding her head, as if that would keep the message from getting through.

"I just found out for sure on Friday. All the specialists wanted to rerun their tests to be sure. Then I had a meeting on Friday with Dr. Romaro, he's my main guy now. He confirmed the results and we discussed treatment options."

I saw Paula glance over at Veronica and I knew she was checking to see if her sister grasped the gravity of what I was saying. I'm sure Paula understood more about the options for those of us with exocrine pancreatic cancer than even I did. And she certainly understood them far better than Veronica. Now she was checking to see if her kindergarten-teaching sister was as upset as she was.

"Look, Dr. Romaro gave me a bunch of options," I lied again. "He told me to take some time and think about it. I'm supposed to go back to see him next week and we'll figure out the next steps. Maybe surgery, maybe not. Chemo-therapy could be all it takes. We don't know yet."

I could see that Paula saw right through my bullshit. "What stage, Dad? They had to give you a stage."

Veronica interrupted, "What does that mean? What's a stage?"

Paula decided to just rip the bandage off, "It means how far along has it progressed. Stage one is not so bad. Stage four is terrible. So, what stage, Dad?"

I lied this much, I figured I could lie a little more. "Maybe stage three. They're not sure. He said two or three." My mouth was suddenly getting very dry.

"Have you got any orange juice, sweetie?"

"Dad," Paula said very firmly. "Has it spread to your liver?"

I assumed Paula would know that after all those tests, the good doctors would have a pretty solid idea if the cancer had invaded any other critical organs, so I fessed up. "Yes sweetie. They're pretty sure it's also in some of the adjacent organs."

Silence enveloped the room for close to a minute. At least, it seemed that long. I could hear my heart pounding. Funny, that was one of the few good organs I had left, and there is was, thumping away.

Finally, Veronica spoke. "So, what does this mean Dad? Are you telling us you're going to die?"

"Hey, we're all going to die honey. But nobody's talking about dying just yet. Hey, even if the worst case happens, I have no regrets. I've lived sixty-six wonderful years, most of them shared by the most wonderful woman in the world. I've been given so many amazing gifts, like you and Paula," I gestured. "I've been blessed in ways I don't deserve."

Paula broke in, "Dad, we need to get you to the guys at Wellington Regional. They have a cancer specialty that's the best in Florida. I can set up…"

I cut her off. "No sweetie. No more tests. I've done them all at Sloan. There's no place better." I swallowed hard. "And don't say a word to Stephen yet. I haven't told him. I'm flying home tomorrow and will talk to him on Thursday. I'm meeting him for racket ball Thursday night."

More silence. So, I offered, Hey, we're all going to be together in two weeks for Thanksgiving, right. Hopefully, by then we'll have this sorted out and I'll know what we're going to do about it."

V

The first leg of my flight back from West Palm Beach was smooth. Unfortunately, in order to get back to JFK, I had to change planes in Atlanta, usually a nightmare. This time was no exception. My flight from Atlanta has been delayed three hours. So, I've got time to do some more typing here in the Delta terminal.

I was able to sleep about a half-hour on the first leg of this odyssey. Regrettably, while sleeping, I had one of my recurring dreams about my sisters. It probably happened because I'd just spent a few days with my daughters. Veronica and Paula always remind me of my sisters, Lucy and Jane.

When I awoke from the dream, I sat, staring out the plane window and reliving that day in 1963 when I lost my innocence and my sisters. As the puffy clouds whisked by, my mind's eye could see the azure sky hanging over the green Lake George mountains on that hot August day so many years ago. I could see it like it was yesterday.

I remember I was the first to awaken that morning. It was our first morning in the cabin and I laid on my back, looking up at the pine ceiling boards for almost an hour before anyone else stirred. We were forbidden from leaving the cabin until a parent was awake. That was partly a safety issue; I'm sure my parents didn't want us out on the lake without their knowledge, and partly because the cabin was so small, there was no way I could extricate myself from my cot without stepping on at least two other people.

In a way, I enjoyed those silent mornings. I used to look for patterns in the grain of the knotty pine and pretend the longest lines of grain were rivers. Then I'd pretend I was a tiny sailor navigating the river and trying to avoid falling off the edge of the earth. The tricky part was sailing around the large knots that speckled the planks. Those were the perilous islands in the river, filled with pirates. The rules of my game said you couldn't hit one of the islands.

The other wonderful thing about lying on my cot in the morning before anyone else was awake was the smell. The smells in the cabin penetrated me. The cabin itself had a unique and pleasantly familiar smell. But it was the scent of the dewy woods that filled the morning air that day.

Finally, I heard dad rustle. That meant it was okay to start talking. Once dad was up, the day officially started.

"How long you been awake?" He whispered in my direction.

"About an hour."

He silently motioned for me to get up and join him on the porch. I carefully slipped out of my sleeping bag, unzipping as quietly as possible, then tip-toed over my sisters. I held the screen door so it wouldn't slam behind me. Once on the porch, my father threw a towel in my direction and pointed toward the steps leading down to the lake.

I hoped he intended to go for an early swim but, once we were far enough from the cabin to allow full voices, he said, "We could both use a shower, kiddo." I knew he was referring to the shower house behind the boathouse. It was little more than a lean-to with three stalls, but it did have hot and cold water and a sign outside that allowed the current user to indicate male or female inside.

The flooring of the shower house was aged wooden planks that were spaced about a half-inch apart to allow the water to run off. Sometimes, when you were the first to use the shower house, there would be small frogs sitting on the floor who would quickly retreat to the shadows below when the hot water began to fall. Once, I walked into the shower and found a small snake curled up in the corner. We never took showers at night.

That morning, we were alone. I showered quickly and wrapped myself in the coarse towel. My father needed to shave so he told me, "Don't go back to the cabin yet. Wait for me in front of the boat house." I knew he was referring to the wooden bench facing the docks and I was happy to oblige. That was a great place to watch the day begin. The sun was still over an hour from cresting the towering mountain tops on our side of the lake, but its light had already filled the sky and I could see the promise of a sunny day beginning on the opposite side. The highest points on the mountain across the lake were painted in warm, bright sunlight. I liked to sit and marvel at how the line of light would slowly creep down the hill until it eventually hit the lake. But our side of the lake wouldn't see direct sunlight until after eight.

When he'd finished shaving, Dad came and settled next to me. We both sat silently for several minutes, taking in the lake's majesty. One of the many things I learned from my father was how to appreciate the simple beauty of nature. And to do so without searching for meaning or purpose. In other words, nature is what it is. It's been doing its thing for millions of years without our intervention or need for attaching purpose, and it will continue to do so for millions more. I wonder now, what dad would have thought about global warming and climate change.

In the distance, the aspens shimmered in the morning light and the lake began to show small ripples caused by the gentle breeze.

"You know why the lake is always dead calm in the morning, then starts to ripple as the sun comes up?" He asked me. I had no idea. I was eleven.

"It's because at night, usually, there's very little breeze, especially just before dawn. Then, as the sun rises and gets higher in the sky, it heats up the air over the mountain. When that nice warm mountain air meets the cool air over the lake, it gets pushed up and creates a breeze. It's the breeze that causes the ripples."

My head was filled with more basic questions like, "What makes the sun come up in the first place? What if there are clouds in the way? Or, what's for breakfast?" But I loved when my father tried to teach me something. And today, for some reason, I sensed a particular importance to our conversation. Not because of the lesson about thermal warming, but because I felt his warmth. I felt it was important for him to pass on his body of earthly knowledge, maybe because he sensed everything was about to change. Or, maybe that's just my imagination in hindsight.

My dad explained several of nature's mysteries to me that morning. He taught me why clouds form, why it's good to go fishing early in the day, and how to know which direction is north when walking in the woods. We sat on that bench for almost an hour and by the time we returned to the cabin, mom and the girls had set up the red gingham tablecloth on the picnic table outside the screen door.

The smell of coffee caught us as we approached, and I could see the twelve-pack of Kellogg cereals on the table. I always went for the frosted flakes on the first day. By the second day only the healthy stuff was left.

"I thought maybe you guys went fishing already. Where have you been?" Mom liked to keep tabs on everyone.

Dad hung our wet towels on the cloths line and explained, "The men needed showers." I liked it when he referred to us as "the men." It provided me a special place in the family where women outnumber the men. I took enough ribbing from my sisters, so any chance there was to align myself with the guy who really ran things, the better.

While we cut open our cereal boxes and carefully poured milk into the opening, dad laid down the rules for the week. "Nobody leaves the property." That meant we weren't allowed to go past the road we came in on. "If you take a canoe out, make sure there are at least two of you and make sure you bring life jackets." My father referred to the square cushion/flotation devices the McNulties provided as life jackets. We didn't actually know what a real life jacket was although I did remember seeing them in a World War II submarine movie. And finally, "Nobody goes in the water alone. You want to swim…, you take a buddy." This was the hardest one for me because it meant I'd always have to coax at least one of my sisters to swim with me. If I could, I would have spent the entire day in the lake. I loved the water. And, although they were both very competent swimmers, neither of my sisters ever wanted to stay in the water longer than fifteen minutes.

Dad announced he was going into town to get more ice, our only way of keeping our precious supplies cold. Mom said she planned to take her book down to the beach after breakfast and read, something she rarely had time to do at home. I volunteered to go with my father, a maneuver that sometimes resulted in a stop at Stewart's for a root beer.

The girls were happy to stay at the cabin and look through the magazines they'd brought along. I don't remember what they were called but they were filled with stories that appealed to teenage girls; stories about Elvis, Fabian, and Ed Burns, the guy with the hair from 77 Sunset Strip. Being thirteen, I guess I couldn't blame them for being boy-crazy, but since I was only eleven, I hadn't yet developed an understanding as to why they fawned over these guys. It was one of the many silly things we always teased each other about. I'd razz the girls that they were boy-crazy, wore ridiculous amounts of make-up, and wanted nothing more than to be kissed by Troy Donahue. They'd give it back to me in the worst way possible; they'd say I was too young and immature to understand these grownup things. It made me crazy to be told I was too young for anything, yet I got that a lot. After all, I was the youngest in a family of five.

There was to be no stop for root beer on this trip to town. But we did stop at the bait shop to pick up a dozen blood worms.

"Leo, are you sure you packed the small hooks, the ones for Perch?"

"Yeah dad. It's all in my tackle box."

Fishing with my father was the best thing about our trips to Lake George. Not just because I loved to fish, but mostly because it gave me a chance to be his focus of attention for a few hours. It was man-time; no women around. As Lucy and Jane had gotten older, they demanded more and more of my dad's time, something that had previously been reserved for yours truly. But, because my mom didn't drive, it was dad who chauffeured the girls to cheerleader practice, parties, and the biggest time-killer, dance recitals.

So, fishing was the one thing he did exclusively with me. Even if they wanted to, my sisters couldn't possibly go fishing. They were terrified of the worms. This gave me one more way to torture them; dangling an unexpected blood worm in front of Lucy would always get a scream.

When we returned to our cabin, I rigged my rod and raced down to the dock with the cardboard box filled with worms. The water at the end of the dock was crystal clear but only about six feet deep. I could see the Yellow-bellies swimming beneath the dock. It almost didn't seem fair to fish where you could watch your prey. Also, I wasn't interested in Sunnies or Yellow-bellies. They were fine when I was a kid, you know, six or seven. At eleven I was a seasoned fisherman and sought more exotic game, the sort that patrolled the waters as far from the dock as my Zebco would allow me to cast. That's where the Perch or maybe even a Lake Trout lived; in the wispy sea grasses hidden beneath twenty feet of water.

It was turning out to be a very warm day; the kind that made you love being in the mountains. The air was dry and the gentle breeze on my bare back felt wonderful. I cast my line as far as I could and watched the red and white bobber create a series of rings when it touched down, the tempting worm just ten inches below the surface. And I waited. And waited.

After fifty minutes, I sat down on the warm planks and dangled by bare feet in the cool water, but never taking my eye off the bobber. After a while, a Yellow-belly came out from the shadows beneath the dock and began harmlessly nibbling on my toes. Even at eleven years old, I saw the irony in that.

I heard my mom calling me for lunch, which was about the only thing that could distract me from fishing, and I reeled in my line. The worm was still hanging there, although a bit more pale and limp than when I'd tossed him in.

To be honest, I don't remember much about lunch that day. There's no reason why you'd remember a lunch from fifty-six years ago. I don't even remember where we ate. It could have been at the cabin or at the beach, as we sometime did. What I do remember is that at some point Lucy announced, "Jane and I are taking a canoe after lunch and going across."

"Take one of the big canoes and bring Leo with you," dad said.

"Aw, come on dad! Do we have to?" Jane was quick to add, "Can't we ever have some time without him?"

"This is a family vacation. It won't kill you to take Leo with you. Besides, you'll get there faster. He's a better paddler than you Jane."

I wasn't even sure I wanted to go on their lame canoe ride, but once dad told them they had to take me, I wanted to be there just to annoy them.

"Are you going to Salamander City?" I asked. Salamander City was a small cove directly across the lake. We'd been there many times because it was very sheltered from the rest of the lake and had a sandy bottom under about four feet of water. In the center of the cove was a huge rock protruding above the lake's surface. It was big enough for the three of us to stand on at the same time. And we had done just that once when dad took us all over there in a rented motor boat. We snorkeled all around the rock. But the cove got its name because of the numerous salamanders along the water's edge.

"Yes. And actually, it's okay if you come. I want you to take a picture of me and Jane on the rock with my Brownie. "

"Why, so you can give it to Brad, your boyfriend?" I said in a teasing way with special emphasis on the words Brad and boyfriend. I loved to razz Lucy about her boyfriend.

"He's not my boyfriend you little twerp!"

Dad put a quick stop to the bickering with, "Good, then it's settled. Take the three-seater and make sure you have life jackets."

Mom added, I've got a plastic bag you can put your camera in, so it stays dry."

So, right after lunch we all put on bathing suits and headed over to the boat house to select our canoe. The aluminum canoes were stacked upside-down just in front of the boat house. Dad said this was to keep out rainwater, but it made it difficult to pull one down and drop it in the lake, especially the big ones, the ones with three seats. Once we had ours in the water, Lucy jumped in and held it close to the dock while Jane and I retrieved three paddles and seat cushions from the boat house.

Salamander City, on the opposite side of the lake was over a mile away. Even with three of us paddling, it would take about forty-five minutes to get there. So, this wasn't just a canoe ride. This was an adventure, and for an adventure you needed supplies. Supplies like a sleeve of Oreo cookies and my boy scout canteen filled with water. We also brought Lucy's camera, secured in mom's plastic bag, and a length of cloths line so we could tie the canoe to a tree once we got there. Clearly, this was not our first expedition to Salamander City. In fact, we usually made the trip twice each season. And for the last two years, we were allowed to go without adult supervision, a fact that pleased the three of us. Up until two years ago, dad would always come along either in a motorboat, or in another canoe with mom.

As we shoved away from the dock to begin our journey, I could see mom waving to us from the beach. "Be careful," she yelled in our direction.

I sat in the stern seat because I was the most competent paddler. I would be responsible for steering the canoe. Lucy was in the bow seat because, although she was a girl, she could handle a paddle better than Jane. And Jane was relegated to the middle seat because, well Jane wasn't much of a paddler.

We were only about fifty yards from the dock, and still in clear sight of mom still waving from the beach, when the color of the water changed from light green to deep, dark blue. The depth of the lake dropped off dramatically to over one hundred feet. And, although the color wouldn't change again until we nearer the other side, the bottom would continue to plunge beneath us. Dad said the lake was over four hundred feet deep in places. Even so, the water was crystal clear, and I could plainly see the face of my paddle as I thrust it deep into the dark lake with every stroke.

After just a few minutes my shoulders were hot from the afternoon sun and I regretted not bringing a tee shirt. Jane and Lucy didn't have shirts either. They were preoccupied with getting the perfect tans. So much so, they'd lathered up in baby oil before we left the cabin and whatever skin wasn't protected by their lime green bikinis (they always wore the same bathing suits), would soon be golden brown. Or, at least, that's what we thought back then.

The lake was calm, and our canoe cut through the water with ease thanks to me being in the stern position assuring proper steering. After just thirty minutes we were approaching the mountain on the west side of the lake. A red and white buoy became visible on the horizon and we knew that marked the entrance to our cove. We paddled with renewed enthusiasm.

"I see the rock," Lucy yelled.

Sure enough, the huge boulder protruded above the water nearly six feet. It was majestic and I often wondered how far down it went. After all, this was only the tip we could see. How much of this behemoth lay hidden beneath the bottom of the cove? I remember making a mental note to ask my father, the guy who seemed to always have an answer for my questions.

As we glided pass the buoy and entered the cove, Lucy said, "Let's tie the canoe to the rock and swim from there."

"And what do you plan to tie to, birdbrain? It's a rock." I offered.

She immediately saw the flaw in her plan so we headed for the shore where there were plenty of trees to which we could secure the cloths line and the other end to a cleat on the bow of the canoe. We stowed the paddles, cushions, camera and Oreos, then swam the twenty yards from shore to the rock. The bottom was visible through the clear water and shallow enough for us to stand. But because the salamanders were on the bottom, the girls swam directly to the rock. The thought of accidentally stepping on a salamander freaked them out.

If I lived to a hundred, which I now know I will not, I would never forget how I felt that day lying atop that rock in the warm August sun. It may have been the last time in my life I was completely happy and at peace.

After a while, Lucy volunteered to swim back to retrieve the Oreos and canteen. Lying in the sun on the granite behemoth we feasted on the delicious cookies and when we ran out of water, we just refilled the canteen with lake water. It was a glorious day. The water was cool and refreshing and the rock was warm on our sun-soaked skin. My sisters laid on the huge stone and giggled about things only teenage girls could giggle about while I swam tirelessly around them, occasionally splashing enough to make them yell at me.

"Leo, could you do us a big favor?" Lucy asked.

I dove once more just to let them know I was indifferent to her request.

"Come on, Leo. Please get my camera from the canoe. I want you to take our picture on the rock."

I rested my elbows on the edge of the rock. "How do you propose I take your picture from in the water, birdbrain?"

"No. Paddle the canoe back this way and take the picture from in the canoe. Then you can just pick us up and we'll go home."

"You're going to get in the canoe from the rock?" I asked incredulously.

"Sure. Why not?"

"This I gotta see." So, I swam back to shore, untied the canoe and paddled back toward the rock. Lucy and Jane were primping for the picture. I assume they planned to show the picture of themselves in their bikinis to their boyfriends when they got home.

"Get about fifty feet away and take the shot. Take a couple of pictures."

Lucy did her best to pose in what she must have thought was a provocative way. Jane was more reserved and sat with her legs crossed. I took several shots, maybe five. I put the camera back in the plastic bag and to my surprise, the girls were able to move from the rock into the canoe. It was a little shaky, but they did it.

"Why do we have to leave?" I whined.

"Dad said don't stay too long."

Jane added, "And I have to pee."

"Are you kidding me?" I screamed. "Pee in the lake!"

"Oh, gross! We drink this water. You don't pee in the lake, do you?"

"Of course I do!"

"You're disgusting!"

I knew arguing about the fact that fish pee in the lake all day long would get me nowhere, so I let it go. My sisters had really strange bathroom rules anyway. Especially since they turned thirteen. At the time, I was blissfully unaware of women's cycles and all that goes with them.

And so, we began our fateful trip back to the cabin. I wish I had known it would be the last time I'd ever visit Salamander City. As we paddled out of the cove, I might have looked back for one more glimpse of this beautiful place.

****

From the back of the canoe, I watched Lucy stroke her paddle with surprising skill. Sitting in the middle seat, she had the most difficult position. She was the power behind our movement while Jane and I were the front and rear rudders. Together, we were working surprisingly well and began the crossing with a light breeze at our backs, a fact that may have contributed to our early success.

I watched Lucy's shoulder muscles strain with each stroke, and I marveled at how well-formed her back muscles had become. Hidden only by the string-strap of her bikini top, her well- tanned skin covered impressive lats and shoulder muscles. I had never thought of my two older sisters as anything but gaggling girls, but I could see they were becoming women. If I were a bit more mature, I would have noticed that earlier by looking at the front of them. None the less, it occurred to me for the first time, there on the lake, that they were changing, and I was being left behind. They were becoming adults leaving me the only child in the family. The realization chilled me.

The breeze, which up till now had been an asset, grew increasingly more gusty, and now came more from the south and hit us broadside. At the same time, I noticed dark thunderstorm clouds behind us. The hot, humid August day was suddenly becoming something different.

"Hey ladies," I called out, "Don't look now but we may have a thunderstorm coming from over the mountain."

Lucy turned her head and saw the ominous clouds. "Oh, shit," she said in a rare use of the word. "Paddle faster twerp!"

"Hey, I'm doing my job." I yelled back. I hated being called twerp.

We all put a little more into each stroke. For a while, with the wind at our side, we continued to make good time. We were about a third of the way across, in the deepest and bluest part of the lake. Lucy kept looking over her shoulder at the approaching storm. We could all feel the rapid drop in temperature, and I was reminded of my father's lesson on weather and how wind develops when there are two opposing air masses.

The little bit of blue sky that had been holding on now surrendered to the dark clouds. Rain began to ping on the floor of the aluminum canoe. Within minutes we were all drenched, not that we cared. We were in bathing suits. But after a few more minutes, there was almost an inch of water sloshing around at our feet.

Now it was raining so hard, it actually hurt. My visibility was limited both because I had to continually wipe the water from my eyes and because we were in the midst of a squall; a blanket of water that surrounded our canoe on all sides.

"Keep paddling," I yelled. "We need to keep going forward."

But forward was a concept, not a direction. I now had no idea which direction was forward. Because we couldn't see much beyond the front of the canoe, there was no way to tell if we were heading in the direction of the boat house. I was concerned that we might have been pushed around by the changing direction of the wind, and now headed in the wrong direction. For all we knew at that point, we might have been paddling directly away from our destination.

For the first time in my life, I was genuinely concerned about my safety. Not just that; I was concerned for the safety of my two sisters, for whom I felt responsible.

A strong gust of rainy wind now hit us from the right, and it felt like we'd been turned around. But without a reference point of land, it was impossible to tell.

Again, I yelled out to my sisters. "Hey, if we get swamped, just grab a cushion and stay with the canoe. Hang on to the canoe, even if it fills with water." I remembered that lesson from Boy Scout camp. Always stay with the canoe. It won't sink.

The sheets of rain were so strong, I got a mouth full as I yelled my instructions. From her seat at the bow, Jane turned and seemed to be looking for more direction. Her face was filled with worry. It was my job as the man to calm my crew.

"Just keep paddling straight!" More rain in my mouth.

"What the hell, Leo? Which way is straight? Maybe we should stop paddling for a while." Jane was losing it.

"No. Keep moving forward. The storm came from our left so keep paddling straight ahead." My instructions made no sense at all.

Lucy called out to Jane, "Just paddle. We'll get there." But I could barely hear her. The sound of the massive raindrops crashing onto our canoe and on the surface of the surrounding water was deafening.

Then, just as quickly as the storm came on, it began to subside. Within another minute the rain had completely stopped. The sky was still an ominous grey, but the wind died down a bit and the far side of the lake began to come into focus. I could see the mountain. I could make out a few buildings. We were still headed in the direction of the boat house, although we'd been blown a bit to the north. We had about a mile yet to go, and although the lake was still very choppy, there was a palpable sense of relief that it was no longer raining.

But now there was a bigger issue. The swells were hitting us broadside. So much so that lake water was slopping over the gunwale and adding to the rainwater already accumulated in the canoe. With each slap of a wave, the aluminum canoe would make a thunderous and eerie sound. My sisters were freaking out and I didn't blame them. The noise was scary.

I did my best to angle the canoe into the waves and, even though we were heading in the wrong direction, at least we wouldn't be swamped by the increasingly violent swells.

"Just keep paddling," I yelled. "We need to head into the waves."

I have to admit my arms were beginning to tire from the strain of paddling and I was grateful my sisters were still at it. Doing this alone would have been impossible. Although Jane's strokes were shallow and weak, she was trying. Lucy was the powerhouse. I don't think she ever took a break. It was only because of her effort we were making any headway at all.

Just then, a huge swell crashed onto the front of the canoe, drenching Jane and nearly knocking the paddle from her hands. She screamed. Not the kind of scream a girl would make on a roller coaster ride; this was a scream of true terror.

More water flowed into the canoe with each swell we breeched. The water at our feet was now six inches deep and starting to weigh us down. But there was no time to bail. We needed to keep paddling or we'd never be able to keep the bow into the wind.

Though my shoulders ached, I dug deep and with each stroke, pushed as much water as I could. Despite the crashing waves on our bow, we were making headway. I started to get the feeling we'd be okay. Our progress was slow, but it was progress. Unfortunately, our slow progress was against the wind and waves, and in so doing, we were getting farther and farther from our intended destination. Eventually, we'd need to cut back toward the land. But that meant taking the waves broadside again. For now, we were better off heading directly into the waves.

I looked to my left and saw whitecaps all over what had been a bucolic surface only twenty minutes earlier. The water looked more like a raging sea than a quiet mountain lake. It looked angry.

"Just keep paddling straight." I yelled again.

We held our own for another ten minutes and the waves and wind began to subside. We were no longer taking on water at the bow and the horrible metallic noises that came with each crashing swell were lessening. We could now hear each other without yelling.

I decided this would be a good time to change our course and angle more toward land. If we turned to the right, we could take the waves on the stern and keep a forty-five degree angle to the land. Eventually, if the waves didn't start breaking over my back, we'd get home.

"Everyone paddle on the left," I said. "We'll turn and have the waves pushing us instead of killing us."

The girls did as I said, and the canoe made a sharp turn to the right. I steadied us using my paddle more like a rudder than a paddle.

"Okay. Now try to keep us pointed at…" I looked for a landmark. "Try to keep us headed for that big field." I motioned with my hand toward a large green field on the side of the mountain. I assume it was some kind of farm.

The field was a long way off but aiming at it would keep us going in the right direction for now.

And it worked. The swells were now following us, pushing us a bit, and, although I kept getting slapped in the back with spray, we were doing well. There was far less noise. There was much less panic. I could tell from their posture my sisters were finally relaxing. Their bare shoulder muscles were far less tense, and they could now paddle with, instead of against the lake.

As if an omen that our situation was improving, the skies began to brighten. It was still very cloudy but not the dark grey clouds that hung over us just a few minutes before. These clouds gave us hope there was still a sun somewhere above them.

"Well, that was pretty freaky," I offered.

Lucy put on an air of disinterest. "That wasn't so bad."

"Not so bad?" I screamed. "Are you kidding me? You two were screaming like babies."

"You're crazy. We were just fine."

"Are you nuts? The two of you were scared to death."

"We were not."

"Jane screamed like a little baby when that wave hit her." I couldn't believe they were denying having been frightened.

"You're nuts. I didn't scream. I just didn't expect it." Jane chimed in.

"Bull!"

"Actually," which was one of Lucy's favorite words, "Actually, I think we did very well. If anything, we could have used a little more paddling in the rear."

In retrospect, I know this was just harmless sisterly teasing. I should have let it go. But, at the time, I was incensed. I was livid. I wanted to scream. And I should have.

But instead, I did something I will regret for the rest of my life. I put down my paddle, grasped each side of the canoe with my hands and threw my weight to the right. My intention was just to shake the canoe to scare them and maybe elicit a scream. But just as I was doing this, Lucy turned to her right to say something to me, and also leaned right. At the same moment, we were hit with a swell on the left side of the canoe. The combined effect was to capsize us to the right.

We were all thrown into the water. The canoe turned completely over. Then, now being empty, it caught a gust of wind and was thrown to the right once more. This time it hit me on the head as I treaded water searching for my sisters and a seat cushion. The blow was painful but not serious. I looked up and could see the canoe had done a complete revolution and was now right-side-up but rapidly drifting away from us. The wind was blowing the canoe away from us!

I called out for Lucy and Jane. "Hey it's getting away. Swim to the canoe as fast as you can!"

But there was no response from my sisters. I yelled again, "Lucy! Jane! Where the hell are you?"

Still nothing. I could see the canoe was already fifteen feet away and getting farther from me every second. With no one on board and sitting high in the water, it drifted with the wind faster than I would possibly swim.

I suddenly felt something hit me gently on the back of the head. It was a seat cushion and I grabbed it before it too was windswept out of my reach. As I turned back to look for my sisters, I caught a mouthful of water as a wave broke over me. I gagged and choked but held tight to the cushion. I could see the other two cushions drifting quickly in the same direction as the canoe.

"Lucy! Jane!" I screamed again.

Where could they be? They were both better swimmers than me. They had to be somewhere. Could they be holding on to the canoe and drifting with it? Maybe that was it. Maybe they were both in the water, on the other side of the canoe and holding on to the side as I'd told them to. If that was true, the canoe was already too far away for them to hear me.

I tucked my arms through the cushion's two straps and tried to elevate my head as far out of the water as possible. I wanted to see if there was any sign my sisters were hanging onto the canoe. Another wave broke over my head momentarily blurring my vision. When I was able to look up again, I could see the canoe had turned into the wind.

Although it was now at least fifty feet away, I could see both sides. No one was holding on.

I screamed, "Lucy! Jane! Lucy! Jane! Where are you?"

They were gone. I was alone.

VI

They just announced my flight will be delayed another forty-five minutes. I've been sitting here in concourse C of the Atlanta airport, on a very comfortable chair, typing for almost two hours now. I've gotten pretty good at balancing my laptop on my lap. But tears are rolling down my cheeks.

It occurs to me that I've never told anyone about what happened to my sisters. I mean, what really happened. I've never said the words. I've certainly never written then down. Through all the family counseling and individual therapy, I never told anyone I caused us to capsize; that my stupid attempt to scare my sisters caused them to drown that day. And now that I finally typed the words into this silly metal box, I can't stop weeping.

The canoe drifted completely out of sight. I held onto that faded red cushion with all my might. There was no point in swimming yet. The lake was still too rough. Oddly, I never thought I would die out there. I knew the lake would calm down eventually and I had confidence in my ability to swim, with the cushion, to safety. I just didn't know how long it would all take. But I didn't want to be out there in the dark.

After an hour, I was exhausted. After about two hours, I heard a motor. Someone was in a motorboat and coming toward me. The sound was definitely getting louder. Then, I saw it. A small powerboat with two men standing at the windshield. The boat was being thrown around by the waves but cutting through the chop and coming directly at me. The man driving the boat was Mr. McNulty. When I saw the man standing next to him was my father, I wanted to let go of the cushion and sink to the bottom of the lake as fast as a hundred pound anvil.

But I didn't. I guess there's a part of everyone that wants to live no matter how painful you expect life to be. But the thought of explaining to my father what had happened, what I'd done, was overwhelming. I began sobbing uncontrollably. Then, I must have passed out.

The next thing I remember was lying on the floor of that runabout. My dad was shaking me and saying my name. Then, when he saw me come to, he hugged me so tight I thought he'd crush me.

"Oh Leo, when we saw the storm coming, mom and I were frantic. We watched from the dock with my binoculars. We couldn't see much, and we weren't even sure it was you, but we saw the canoe capsize." He hugged me again and was talking so fast I could barely understand the words.

"When I saw you capsize I went crazy. I ran up the hill and got Mr. McNulty. We called the police. We've been looking for you. Oh, thank God you're okay Leo."

He squeezed me again.

"We found the canoe about an hour ago. It was all the way down near town. We've been looking for you, but the waves are so high, it was so hard to see anything. Oh, thank God you're alive Leo."

He hadn't mentioned my sisters, so I asked, "Were the girls with the canoe?"

Suddenly his face was ashen. "No. We've been searching for the three of you. It's so hard to see someone floating on the lake because of the swells." His voice trailed off.

I sat up on one elbow. "Well, you found me. They have to be nearby somewhere."

"The boy's right," Mr. McNulty said. "We need to keep looking while we still have light."

But we searched for hours with no sign of them. We did find the other two cushions, which diminished hope of finding my sisters. And as the sun was setting over the mountain, Mr. McNulty's boat was running low on gas. The lake was finally calming but darkness took over and we needed to return to the boat house. We held hope that upon our return Lucy and Jane would be standing on the dock, having been rescued by the police boat.

That was not to be. When we returned to the boat house, mom was standing on the dock. When we were close enough for her to see three people on the boat, she nearly fainted with happiness. I stepped off the boat to a barrage of hugs and kisses.

"Any word about the girls?" Dad asked.

Mom shook her head slowly.

My father turned to Mr. McNulty, "Jim, I have to keep looking. Can I...?"

But Mr. McNulty was way ahead of my father. "I've got a good spotlight. Let me fill the gas cans and we can get out in about a half hour."

"Dad, I want to come. I want to look for them."

But my father would not hear of it. He insisted I go back to the cabin with mom. He knew she needed to be with me. So, he and Mr. McNulty set out again, this time armed with a powerful spotlight, my dad's flashlight and two full cans of gas. They were not alone. We later learned there were also four police boats on the lake that night. But no one had much hope. Unless my sisters had been able to swim to shore somewhere along the rugged lakefront, without the cushions, they had very little chance of treading water throughout the night.

Because the storm had been so severe, no one ever asked me what had occurred. Everyone assumed the storm was the sole cause of our dilemma. And I wasn't about to challenge that assumption. Sudden storms were common on the lake and the police were accustomed to vacationers getting stuck out on the lake. The Park Rangers who had also joined in the search for Lucy and Jane, reported they rescued three boys earlier that day who were clinging to a capsized sailboat.

As mom heated a can of Campbell's soup for me, darkness settled over the Adirondacks. The skies had cleared and filled with stars but there was no moon to light the way for the searchers. I stared at the vast surface of the lake and tried not to think about my sisters. I tried to focus on my hot soup, but it was impossible, and I wasn't hungry.

I guess because I was so tired from treading water, I was able to fall asleep. I don't remember dreaming that night. I'm grateful I didn't.

I remember waking to the sound of car tires crackling against the pebbles behind the boat house. It was light out, but just so. I was alone in the cabin.

I threw on a tee shirt and went to the porch to see what was going on. My father and mother were walking toward me. They were wrapped around each other in a tight embrace. Something was terribly wrong. I could tell just by looking at them.

I glanced toward the boat house, just beyond my parents and could see the taillights of an ambulance disappear up the hill. I later learned the bodies of Lucy and Jane were in the ambulance.

Their bodies had been found at 3:30 A.M. by one of the Park Rangers who was searching the west side of the lake. He reported their bodies were found together, entangled in the cloths line we used to tie the canoe to shore. Even in death, my twin sisters stayed together.

My parents were inconsolable. Mom was teetering on the edge of a breakdown and dad was like a zombie I remember seeing on T.V. He was walking but he wasn't there. His body was moving but there was no one inside. It terrified me.

They'd spent the last ninety minutes giving the police all the details they could about what had happened. I found out when I was older that they had to identify the bloated bodies right there on Mr. McNulty's dock. The police had to physically wrench my mother away from the bodies. She wouldn't leave them. Seeing the coroner zip up the bags that would cloak my sisters, was more than she would withstand. She'd fainted dead away, which was probably for the best.

And that was it. We silently packed our things in the cabin, loaded the car, and drove home. Not a word was spoken for the first three hours. No one ever asked me specifically what had happened. Everyone assumed I was just a lucky survivor of a horrible accident.

No one ever accused me of killing my beautiful sisters.

VII

It's a rainy Friday morning. The sheets of wetness are driving against my bedroom window. Cold wind has ripped the last remaining leaves from the Central Park Elms. For the first time since being diagnosed, I don't feel well.

Part of me thinks my stomach pain might be the result of my discussion with my son and grandson last night. It didn't go as well as I'd hoped, although I have no idea how I thought it would go. And part of me, the part that's still sitting in bed with a laptop between my legs, thinks this may be the beginning of what Dr. Romaro told me to expect; occasional but increasingly frequent stomach pain and cramps.

As I type, I hope my concentration on my journal will distract me from the pain. To be fair, it's not too bad, yet. But, it's enough to remind me something is very wrong in my guts. I have an image of a time bomb in my pancreas that's ticking constantly and just a little faster each time I dare to listen.

Bending my knees seems to ameliorate the pain so I've decided to stay in bed this morning and work on my journal. It seems the more I type, the more I realize I want to say, and the more I fear I won't have enough time to say it all. I have a growing sense of finality to just about everything I do. I've thought about this a lot, and I'm okay with dying sooner than I'd hoped. But, I don't want to die without finishing this task. I want my children to understand the man they called dad.

Sometimes I feel like I've put an unnecessary burden on myself at exactly the wrong time. Maybe my limited time would be better spent just talking to my children and telling them what I want them to know about me. The truth is, I don't have the courage to do that.

****

On Wednesday, I flew back from Florida, leaving two weeping daughters in my wake. I'm glad they have each other. And I'm glad I stretched the truth a bit about my doctor's prognosis. By implying there are options yet to consider, I left them some hope. But eventually they'll know the truth. I just didn't have the guts to tell them everything. The truth is I just didn't have the guts to tell them the truth. And I guess that's always been a problem for me.

Thursday, I met Stephen at five thirty for a game of racquetball at a tennis center near his home in Merrick. I took the Long Island Railroad from Penn station to Merrick, then a cab to the center, and arrived just a few minutes before Stephen, who'd worked from home yesterday. His wonderful wife, Lilly was with their only child, Peter and waited for us for dinner after the game.

I dreaded the conversation with Stephen and Lilly, but I dreaded the one with Peter even more. My only grandson and I have developed a bond, a closeness that I treasure.

We've spent a lot of time together, partly because I mind him when Lilly needs to leave the house for work, but mostly because I love doing it. I look for excuses to have him to myself. I scour the newspapers in search of some Disney-on-Ice thing he hasn't seen or a Paw Patrol event at the mall. A walk on the beach, a trip to the supermarket; anything to spend time with this precious little kid. Now that he's in second grade, our time together is limited but I think he enjoys my company as much as I do his.

"I have a little bad news," is how I started the conversation with Stephen and Lilly after Peter left the dining room for his twentieth viewing of the Batman Lego movie. I'd catch up to him later.

Lilly was immediately concerned. Perhaps she sensed my discomfort. "What is it, Pop?"

The three of us were still seated at the dinner table. "My doctor saw something in my bloodwork when I went in for my last physical. At first, he wasn't concerned, nor was I. But after he repeated the tests, he ordered a whole bunch of more tests." I paused to lighten the moment. "Believe me, other than this one thing, I'm in great shape."

My attempt at levity missed its mark. No one was amused. So, I continued, "They suspected a form of cancer, so they sent me to a specialist. They put me through all sorts of tests again and it turns out I have some cancer cells in my pancreas."

Neither Stephen nor Lilly have any medical training so I thought I could bullshit them a bit. "It's early stages and we haven't even figured out a treatment plan yet, so don't get too excited. I should be around for a long time." I faked a chuckle.

Lilly spoke first. "How do you feel pop?" Her sincere concern for my comfort was touching.

"I feel great!" Which was a truthful statement yesterday. Not so much today. I added, "They still have a lot of tests they want to do, then we'll figure out what to do about it."

"How long has this been going on?" Stephen asked. His voice sounded weak. His head was in his hands.

"I started with the doctors few weeks ago. But I only got confirmation about the cancer last Friday."

"No, I mean, how long have you had this?"

"Oh. They don't know and it doesn't really matter. They say it may have begun within the year or I may have been walking around with this for many years. But it doesn't matter. What matters is what we do from here."

"Which is what?" Lilly pressed.

"Don't know yet, honey. I go back to the specialist in early December and we'll figure it out then." I lied but could tell she wasn't convinced.

Nor was my son. "Pop, you need to go to a cancer specialist. This could be really serious. You can't just rely on your general care doctor. We have to get…" I cut him off.

"Stephen, I've been to a guy from MSK that specializes in exactly what I've got. He's supposed to be the man to go to when you've got what I've got. This Dr. Romaro is good. It took me two weeks to get an appointment to see him." Again, I lied but it seemed to calm Stephen down. Just hearing the words Memorial Sloan Kettering is both alarming and reassuring at the same time. Alarming in that if you're going to MSK, you've got some nasty bugs. But reassuring because there's no place better to zap those bugs.

Then, for reasons I don't yet understand, I shared something with them. "Look, nobody's using the word 'terminal' yet." Obviously, that was not true. "But, even if this is what eventually kills me, I'm okay with it. I mean, I don't want to die, but we're all going to die at some point. And I have absolutely no regrets about the life I've had. More importantly, I'm not afraid to die. I don't fear death."

Lilly started to cry quietly.

"It's okay honey, really. When mom was sick, it was different. I feared death. But I later realized what I feared wasn't her death, it was me being left behind, alone. Death is a natural part of life. It's what makes life interesting. Think about this. If you thought you'd live a thousand years, wouldn't every day be sort of boring? It would be to me.

It's the fact that life is so short that makes us cherish the limited time we have."

Lilly got up from her chair and came around to my side of the table. She leaned over and hugged me tightly.

"We love you, Pop. We need you around for a lot more time."

I must admit, the hug felt wonderful.

It was at that moment that Peter came back into the room. "I can't get the movie to start. Hey, did you guys have dessert? What was it?" He circled the table mimicking an airplane banking hard to the right.

Stephen was quick to attempt a cover up. "We were just about to call you in for ice cream cake."

Peter leaped into my lap. "I want a piece with pink flowers."

"I like the plain white part," I said. "Let's get our pieces and eat them in the living room. There's something I want to talk to you about anyway." I tickled him as I said it.

"Oh, no Pop." Lilly said. "I don't know if that's a good idea."

"Come on mom. We won't spill any."

Lilly gave me a look of questioning disapproval. She shook her head. "I don't think he's ready for this." She looked across at Stephen for a reaction.

"Come on, Lilly." I said. "Let us boys have some fun." I gave her a look that indicated it would be okay.

Still not convinced, Lilly added, "He's only a kid, Pop. He's not going to understand." She looked at me, her eyes pleading with me to spare her son.

I turned to Peter, still wiggling on my lap. "Why don't you go into the living room and I'll get us each a piece of the ice cream cake. Mine will be all vanilla and yours will be full of those nasty pink flowers."

"Cool!" And off he went.

Stephen put his hand on mine. "Dad, he's not going to understand. Why don't we wait until you know more about your treatment plan?"

I realized, based on the half-truths I shared with my son and daughter-in-law, that they were right. Why burden Peter with this until we know more. But I do know more. And I wanted to be the one who tells Peter. We have a special relationship, one that connects us in a way he's not connected to even his parents. Peter tells me things he doesn't want his parents to know. We have a closeness that is hard to describe. The sixty years that separates us seems to also glue us together.

Maybe all grandfathers feel this way. I don't think so.

"Dad, please. Don't say anything yet. Stephen was still holding the top of my hand. It felt like he wasn't going to let me up from the table until I agreed.

"Okay, not tonight. But I want to be the one who talks to him about it. Okay?"

"Absolutely." He let go of my hand. "So, when will you know more?"

Again, I lied. "I'll know a lot more right after Thanksgiving. I see Dr. Romaro the first week in December."

VIII

In the spring of 1976 the country was preparing for its bi-centennial. There were posters all over New York hyping Operation Sail, a regatta the likes of which New York harbor had never seen before. There were to be fleets from other countries, armadas from distant yacht clubs, meticulously restored tall-ships, and what seemed to be the full force of the United States Navy. All of this was to converge on New York harbor on July fourth, two hundred years to the day, after Jefferson and his friends signed the Declaration of Independence.

A reasonable person would think that with all that boat traffic sailing under the Verrazano Bridge on the same day, the Coast Guard would have restricted all other boating from the area. On the contrary; they were encouraging people to join the party. That meant any moron with a fourteen-foot runabout and the standard six-gallon gas can, could join the party. And this particular moron was not to be left behind.

I had convinced my good friend Jimmy Flannery to ask his father if we could use his Grady White to properly honor our country's birthday. Jimmy and I had been working together at U.S. Life, a third-tier life insurance company, for the past three years. It was my first job out of college and most guys there were like me- liberal arts majors who didn't fit in at the banks or brokerage houses but who wanted to work in the Wall Street area. It was fun because there were plenty of us and I was actually learning the ins and outs of the life insurance business. I know it sounds painfully boring, but you'll see later how it was important to my future.

Anyway, Jimmy's dad foolishly agreed to let us use his boat to cruise from Freeport to New York harbor, about twenty-five miles. It was a beautiful, hot day and fortunately the Atlantic was unusually calm. We invited a couple of girls from work to join us, packed a cooler with Miller High Life bottles, and made the trip in under two hours. It took that long only because of the boating congestion going under the Verrazano Bridge. Although most of the large ships had arrived in the harbor earlier in the week, Jimmy and I weren't the only local morons to think this would be a great idea. There were thousands of small boats all headed in the same direction at roughly the same time. Everyone wanted to be near the Statue of Liberty.

The promise was there'd be a spectacular fireworks display in the evening and the center of it all was to be the Majestic green statue sitting in the harbor. So, Jimmy and I and... I can't even remember the two girl's names, took Mr. Flannery's eighteen-foot fishing boat under the bridge and anchored within spitting distance of New Jersey. We had a fantastic view of Lady Liberty and the New York skyline in the distance. All we had to do was wait six hours for darkness to arrive.

The harbor continued to fill with small boats, all there to await the fireworks. It got to the point that each boat was less than five feet from the next and we were all constantly rubbing up against each other as the incoming tide pushed us around. But when the afternoon turned to evening and the supply of Millers was dwindling, one of the girls from work announced she had to pee. Like I said, we were on a very small boat; one without a head. This presented a problem we hadn't anticipated.

"Leo, I really need to go!" The taller of the two insisted. And, as soon as she did, the other one chimed in.

"Actually," she said with an almost comical Staten Island twang, "I need to go too."

"Well, we're not leaving." Jimmy protested. "If we leave now, they'll never let us back this close. And, anyway, where would we go?"

He had two good points. Unless we went all the way back to Freeport, and missed the entire event, there was nowhere we could sail to that would have public bathrooms. And, we had positioned ourselves in the perfect spot to watch something historical. Something that only happens every two hundred years. We couldn't give that up. The girls would just have to "hold it".

But around seven-thirty, just as dusk was beginning to overtake the harbor, the girls made it clear that wasn't going to work.

"We need a bathroom! I can't believe you two Einstein's didn't think about this. Leo, I really need to go." To her credit, she was being very nice about it. And when I think back on it, we were fools for not anticipating that the beer had to go somewhere after a few hours. After all, you never really buy beer. You only rent it.

So, we were faced with three unpleasant options: go home, jump in the water to pee, or find a bigger boat and ask to use their bathroom. We opted for number three and luckily there was a forty-eight-foot Bertram anchored about a hundred yards from us. Jimmy motored over to the stately cruiser and tied up next to them. The girls used all their charm on the captain, a douche in green pants covered with tiny whales, and he lowered a ladder over the side.

They hurried up the ladder, made some quick introductions, then disappeared into the beautiful vessel to deal with nature's call. Jimmy and I were left bobbing next to the Bertram in our tiny Grady feeling like the dopes we were.

When Laverne and Shirley returned, the guy in the whale-pants offered to have us join him on his boat.

"Hey, you'll have a better view from up here," he said referring to the expansive rear deck of his boat. Still, I think the view he was concerned about was that of our dates in their bikinis. The girls were still prancing around in their tiny bathing suits even though the sun had gone down over an hour ago.

"Oh, that would be great. Thanks so much." Laverne was already making herself at home on a navy-blue cushion along the stern.

I offered, "Thanks. We have a few beers left in our cooler. I'll bring them up."

Whale-pants yelled back, "No, no. We've got plenty in the fridge. Just put a couple of fenders out so you don't scratch up my transom."

Luckily, Jimmy's dad did have two small plastic fenders aboard and we rigged them between our two vessels, then climbed the ladder and joined the party. Neither of us knew what a transom was but we seemed to have satisfied whale-pants.

"I'm Mel," he said as he extended his hand. "There's only four of us on board. Seems a shame to have you try to see the show from way down there." He was motioning down at Mr. Flannery's boat. "Anyway, we've got plenty of food and liquid refreshments aboard."

"Thanks man. I'm Jim and this is my friend Leo," Jimmy said. He probably introduced Laverne and Shirley as well, but like I said, I can't remember their real names.

"Well, welcome aboard folks. My wife and guests are below. They're looking at baby pictures. Our daughter just had a baby boy, her first."

I said, "Congrats," although I thought Mel looked too young to be a grandfather. Hey, it's none of my business.

Jimmy and I accepted beers from our host, an imported brand I'd never seen before, and settled onto the bench next to Laverne and Shirley. Mel offered the girls champagne and they fell over themselves saying yes.

To be fair, his yacht was pretty impressive. The decking was polished teak as were all the rails. The rest of the floating home was either snow-white fiberglass or navy upholstery. And, best of all, unlike Mr. Flannery's boat, it didn't smell of gasoline.

"So, where you folks from?" Mel said as he sipped his gin and tonic. It seemed to me that he'd positioned himself over the ladies so as to ensure a clear view of their bikini tops and all within.

"I'm from Oceanside, Leo lives in Valley Stream and the girls are both from Queens."

Without taking his eyes off their breasts, Mel said, "Molly and I live in Tarrytown. We sailed down last night and harbored in Jersey City. They have a wonderful marina. Probably could accommodate a boat your size although most of their slips are for forty and up."

"Fuck you, Mel," I thought to myself. But, I said, "That's nice."

To ensure he'd amply impressed the women, Mel went on to say, "I run Ford's reelection campaign in Westchester. The president and I played ball together in college." I guess he had no way of knowing in a few months Ford was going to get his ass kicked by a peanut farmer from Plaines, Georgia. Too bad for Mel and for Gerald Ford.

He was just beginning to tell us something else about himself, when three people emerged from the cabin below. One was his wife, Molly, who seemed way to normal to be married to such a pompous asshole. The other two were his unmarried daughter and her friend Annie O'Brien. I don't remember much about his daughter. She seemed pleasant enough. But Annie I remember.

She was twenty-four, just a few months older than me. She had a petite little figure and big green eyes that seemed sad. Her face was angelic, but in a tom-boyish sort of way, if that makes any sense. She wore a yellow sundress with spaghetti straps that hung loosely on her delicate shoulders. And around her neck hung a gold locket with the initial "A".

If it seems odd that I remember so little about the others on the boat that night but so much about Annie, it's because I spent the next thirty-eight years married to her. But I'm getting ahead of myself.

****

Lucky for me, Annie introduced herself and sat on the other side of the L-shaped bench. She told me she was a secretary for Peat, Marwick, Mitchell. I had no idea who those guys were. I later found out it was a big accounting firm in Manhattan and that Annie worked for one of the partners. Actually, I didn't care what she talked about. I just loved listening to her. The words danced from her lips like musical notes from a piece of sheet music.

Needless to say, Laverne, or maybe it was Shirley; I can't even remember which one was supposed to be my date; wasn't as excited to meet Annie as was I. But she was filling her mouth with champagne and little brown chips and her head with Whale-pants' stories about himself and his "very important job", so she really didn't mind me ignoring her.

Oddly, I don't remember much about the fireworks that night, but I bet I could tell you everything Annie and I talked about the entire evening. As the harbor sky filled with spectacular color over Lady Liberty, my attention was fixed on Annie's beautiful eyes and the way they reflected the fireworks exploding behind me.

I was instantly infatuated with her. This had never happened to me before and although I was uncomfortable with the feeling of helplessness, I was happy to surrender to it. She was just so beautiful. And more than that, she was intensely interested in my stories about growing up in Valley Stream, my family and even my painfully boring job. She listened intently. Those with better vocabularies than me might say empathically. All I know is, she cared about what I had to say. Up to that point, I don't think I ever dated anyone who listened the way Annie did.

At the end of the evening Mel invited us to join them for a nightcap at his dock in Jersey City. I really wanted to go but unfortunately, Jimmy had to work the next morning and had sworn to his father that he'd have the boat back before midnight. My time with Annie was about to end.

Now, I'm not a total clod, so I wasn't about to ask for her phone number in front of Laverne or Shirley. And this presented me with a dilemma. I had to see her again and I knew I'd be dreaming about her every minute until I did. So, pretending I might actually know someone there, I asked her which partner she worked for at PMM. I figured I could always call the switchboard and ask to speak with mister so-and-so's secretary. Clever, right?

Annie saw right through my ploy and smiled as she said, "It was really nice meeting you. I hope to see you all again." To be nice, she looked over at Laverne and Shirley when she said "all".

But then she looked right at me and said something I would hear ten thousand times again during my life. She whispered, "Good night, Leo."

IX

On my first day back to work after the Bi-centennial weekend, there was nothing but Annie on my mind. It had been that way the entire weekend. I couldn't get her out of my mind. And so it was, that on my lunch break, I took the E train uptown and planted myself outside the headquarters of Peat Marwick Mitchell on Park Avenue in hopes of catching a glimpse of her. In retrospect, it was a stupid idea. After all, there are about eight million people walking around New York on any given day, and about ten thousand of them work in the same sixty-story skyscraper as Annie. The chances of Annie going out to lunch, through the doors I was watching, at precisely the time I was there, well, pretty slim. As you would expect, I didn't see her.

The next day, I was far more scientific in my approach. I bought a small box of chocolates at a candy store in the World Trade Center, had it gift wrapped, and re-boarded the E train on my lunch break. I worked up the nerve to enter the PMM building, asked the receptionist on what floor I would find the senior partners, and pretended I had a package needing delivery. When the elevator doors opened on the fifty-second floor, I was confronted by polished mahogany floors that smelled of money. I realized I was way out of my league.

But as I retreated into the elevator to hasten my escape from this potential embarrassment, a lovely woman with a heavy Scottish accent approached me.

"Can I help you?" she inquired.

I stammered and held out the gift-wrapped chocolates. "I, um, I, um…"

"I assume you didn't bring those for me," she said. "Perhaps I could deliver them for you. My name is Mairi Bannon. What's yours?"

She was so sweet, my tongue loosened for a moment. "Leo Monday."

"Well Leo, to whom would you like me to deliver your package?" I think Mairi could tell I was terrified and that my presence on that floor was for other than purely business purposes. I think she was taking pity on me.

Somehow, I got out the words, "I wanted to give it to Annie, Annie O'Brien. Does she work on this floor?"

"Yes, she does. In fact, she works just across from me. But she just left for lunch. Shall I leave it for her?"

I guess she could read the disappointment on my face as I extended the package in Mairi's direction. "Thank you. I'm sorry, I'm sorry I missed her."

Then she said the most wonderful words through an accent so heavy I could barely understand.

"If you don't mind my saying, and I'm sure Annie will be cross with me for opening my mouth, but I think she was disappointed when she didn't hear from you yesterday."

I couldn't believe what I'd just heard. "You mean she actually mentioned me?"

"You're the young man she met on the boat? Am I right?"

"Yes. Yes. Yes! That's me. She mentioned meeting me?"

"She most certainly did. She told me all about it yesterday. It sounds like you had the perfect spot to watch the fireworks."

"Yes," I said drifting back to the fourth and whale-pants' boat. "It was wonderful. Could you give this to her, and could I leave my phone number?"

Mairi couldn't have been nicer. She walked me over to the receptionist's desk and offered me a piece of paper and a pen, both of which were of a quality I'd never experienced. I scribbled, "Sorry I missed you. How about a movie next weekend? Leo"

****

To my sheer delight, there was a pink message sheet on my desk when I returned. I guess Annie didn't remember I worked downtown or maybe just had no idea how long it took to ride the E train nine stops in the middle of the afternoon. Maybe she'd never rode the subway in her life? Maybe she was what Billy Joel would later call an "Uptown Girl". Based on what I saw at her office, she could be completely out of my league. I was clearly a "Downtown Guy".

But when I called her back, she couldn't have been sweeter. Although our conversation had to be short because we were both at work, she agreed to a movie on Friday night and gave me her address. She ended the call with, "Thanks for the candy. I love it."

When I got home that night, I borrowed one of my dad's coveted Texaco maps and looked up Tarrytown, a place I'd never heard of before. From Valley Stream, my hometown, Tarrytown was a world away both in distance and atmosphere. But that's where Annie lived so I needed to find a movie theater somewhere nearby and was lucky enough to find a theater and restaurant right on Main Street in Tarrytown. We didn't have Google back then, so just that little bit of research took me all night. But it was worth it.

Friday couldn't come fast enough for both of us. I called her at home every night that week but talking was a distant second to seeing her. We were both excited about our first date, so when Friday finally arrived. and I pulled up in front of her parents' home in my six-year old Pinto, I didn't try to hide my enthusiasm. I carried a small bunch of daffodils to the front door and was met by Annie's mother before even ringing the bell.

"You must be Leo," her mom said. "Please come in. I'm Daisy, Annie's mother."

Now when I tell you that Mr. and Mrs. O'Brien were nothing like my parents, I'm not exaggerating. And when I say their home was nothing like the one in which I grew up, I'm also not exaggerating. I grew up in a one story, two-bedroom ranch house. Our one bathroom was shared by all and when you sat at our kitchen table, the place we ate dinner every night, you could reach the silverware drawer and the refrigerator without getting up from the table. It was convenient but made for tight quarters.

The O'Brien house on the other hand, was, to me, palatial. It was so huge, I remember thinking you could land a plane in their living room. Annie was an only child, yet they had five bedrooms and five bathrooms. Their kitchen was huge but contained no table. All meals were taken in the formal dining room, where only a small plane could land. And throughout the house was the most luxurious burgundy carpet I'd ever walked on or even seen.

Annie appeared at the top of a long staircase and I will never forget what she was wearing. It was a black and white checkered dress that clung tightly at her waist and ended about three inches above her knees. She would wear it on several other occasions during our courtship. I loved seeing her in that dress.

"Hi, I'll be right down." Then she disappeared somewhere into the cavernous second floor.

"Come in and sit down." Daisy offered and led me onto the smartly decorated tarmac they called a living room.

She filled the void with pleasant small talk and asked me questions about my job and my family. In fairness, Daisy was, that day and always after, very kind to me. She was a very regular person; no feigned air of sophistication. She was a person who grew up during the depression in a family that had little and she never forgot her humble roots.

Her husband Don, on the other hand, who I wouldn't meet that first night, turned out to be a complete ass. And, can you believe it- Daisy and Donald?

I would later learn the head Duck was in the house that night but thought it beneath himself to greet me on our first date! I was told he said something like, "If it works out there will be plenty of time for him to get to know me."

Anyway, Annie did eventually descend the curving staircase, something else I'd never seen before, and we had a great dinner and saw Rocky at the only theater in Tarrytown. Years later, when we reflected back on our first date, Annie would remember everything we ate and talked about at dinner and I would remember how she cried at the end of the movie. To this day, I don't even recall the name of the restaurant, but I can still quote most of the dialog from Rocky by heart.

After Rocky lost a heartbreaker to Apollo, Annie and I drove around Tarrytown and she showed me where she went to school, where she learned to ride a two-wheeler, and the tree under which she had her first kiss. It sounds foolish now but back then, it was a part of the world I'd never been to. Before Annie, Daisy and Donald, I didn't know a soul from Westchester. I was a Long Island boy.

When we finally arrived back at the Duck palace, I parked in the street and walked her to the front door.

"Thank you for a wonderful first date," she whispered.

I responded with the most debonair phrase that ever dripped from my lips and, to this day, I don't know where it came from. "Can I assume the word 'First' was intentional?"

"I hope it was our first."

"Me too."

Then I leaned in to give her a good-night kiss on the cheek. She held close for a moment, then she gave me a kiss on the lips. "Good night Leo."

I never got tired of hearing those words. Over the next few decades I'd hear them every night and they were always said with the same sincerity and sweetness as the first time.

I drove home listening to Cousin Brucie on the radio and humming the theme from Rocky.

It was a wonderful night.

I was already in love.

X

On August 15, 1978, Annie and I decided to celebrate our first wedding anniversary by going out to dinner at the same place we had our first date. I still don't recall the name of the restaurant.

Some things hadn't changed much in the two years since our first date. We still shared my old Pinto. I was still working at U.S. Life, although now I was an Assistant V.P., a title I later figured out they bestowed like cheap candy just to get eager young people to stick around a little longer. And Annie was still working as an executive assistant at PMM. Oh yes, and her father was still an asshole.

Our wedding had been sensational. Annie and her mom were in their glory planning the affair and working tirelessly to stay within the budget Donald allotted. My wedding was the first wedding I'd ever attended so I had little by way of comparison, but my friends tell me it was the best wedding they'd ever been to.

It was lavish. We had a two-hour cocktail party followed by an amazing dinner, a great band, then two hours of dessert, dancing and drinking. Annie and I laughed all night. It was wonderful. I wish my parents could have been there. They would have loved Annie.

But Mom died shortly after their divorce and dad just kind of gave up shortly thereafter. Although they'd been separated for several years, my mom's death hit him hard.

He was killed in a car accident about a year before our wedding, but I think he deliberately ran his Impala into that overpass because he just didn't want to carry the pain around any longer. The death of my sisters, the ensuing divorce, then mom's death; it just overwhelmed him.

"Do you still love me?" Annie asked as we shared our second glass of Merlot.

"More than ever." I responded. "I think I'll stick around for another year.

"Do you remember what you told me on our honeymoon?"

I figured this was something important to Annie so I tried to remember anything profound I might have said while we were in Barbados. I came up blank.

"What specific pearl of wisdom are you referring to?" I was stalling while I thought back.

"Remember when we were lying in the hammock on the beach that night? Remember, we drank those apple cosmos and were both wasted?

Still nothing was coming to me.

"Come on. Don't you remember? You told me you'd love me until the moon stopped shinning. That was the most romantic thing I'd ever heard and if I remember correctly, you were amply rewarded that night for being so sweet."

"And I thought you were the one being rewarded." I teased.

Annie reached across the table and squeezed my hand. "I think we both did okay."

So, I spent the rest of the meal trying to come up with something equally romantic to dazzle her with, not that I was purely interested in the reward, but because I knew Annie loved that sort of stuff.

Our first year of marriage had been great. Then again, neither of us had a point of comparison, but we were both very happy. We got a cool little apartment over Martoni's cheese store in Astoria, an area of Queens that had yet to be discovered but suited us just fine. On the weekends, we'd ride our bikes all over the city and sometimes even out to Long Island where I still had lots of friends. We'd furnished our one-bedroom apartment mostly with hand-me-downs from my parents' house and with some new stuff from Sears. Fortunately, Annie had her mother's sense of style which helped keep me out of the color/fabric decisions. I did all the painting and even some minor repairs to the walls, skills I got from working with my dad on weekends. That made Mr. Martoni very happy to have us living over his store and occasionally resulted in a complimentary wedge of imported Swiss, Annie's favorite.

After dad died, I sold my parents' house. After paying off the two mortgages and some other debts he'd run up, there was very little left to call an inheritance. But we took that money and opened a bank account at Astoria Federal Savings. The bank rewarded us not just with interest but with a toaster-oven, an appliance we didn't know we needed until we had one. The account would become the start of our savings for a house, the one we eventually bought in Huntington, and the one in which we raised our family.

But I'm getting ahead of myself.

From our apartment, we had a short walk to the subway. Annie and I would usually leave for work at the same time each morning, not because I needed to be in the office as early as she did, but because we were in love and did just about everything together. I remember fondly the walk along Ditmars Blvd. to reach the subway. The street was lined with interesting shops that made up our neighborhood; dry cleaners, meat markets, fruit stores, bars, barber shops, and even a palm reader. There was a deli just before we would descend into the subway. That's where Annie got her second cup of coffee every weekday morning and would sip it on the train. Her first cup always came from me.

Making Annie coffee in the morning was a chore I cherished and one I did exceptionally well. She was a coffee aficionado. She loved good coffee and I loved making it for her, even though I grew up with Sanka and actually preferred its bitter taste. For our six-month anniversary, I bought her an electric coffee bean grinder, knowing that I'd be the one doing the grinding.

I brought Annie a cup of hot black coffee nearly every morning of our marriage; right up until she got sick and her esophagus could no longer tolerate the acidic liquid.

But again, I'm getting ahead of myself.

Annie loved her job at PMM. She learned something new nearly every day and would share it with me that night over dinner. Sometimes it was just the name of a city one of the partners had traveled to; cities we'd never heard of before. Places like Dubai, Bogota, and the Maldives were all new to us.

While she was doing her learning on the job, I was going to night school to work toward an MBA. On Mondays and Wednesdays, I'd take the subway up to NYU after work and sit through painfully boring lectures by professors who wanted to be there less than I did. But because my employer required I get at least a "B" in each class in order to qualify for tuition reimbursement, I had to attend every class and apply some effort. It took me three and a half years of night school, but I eventually got the coveted degree. And never less than a "B".

Annie reached across the dinner table after we'd shared a huge chunk of cheesecake and asked, "We should make some big plans for our next anniversary. We should do something really special. Where should we plan to go?"

"How about we just come back here for dinner again?"

I could see the disappointment on her face.

"I was thinking maybe, if we can afford it, we could go somewhere special. Maybe someplace we've never been before."

It pained me to disappoint Annie, and every time I failed to grasp the substance behind one of her suggestions, I know she was disappointed, not in me personally, but disappointed that we weren't on exactly the same page. This was a perfect example. She was probably hoping I would have come up with something special on my own. Now that I think of it all these years later, she was probably disappointed I didn't come up with something better for our first anniversary too.

"How about the Hamptons? Maybe we could go out there for a weekend?" She pleaded.

And so it came to be, that for our second anniversary, we spent two wonderful nights at a tiny cabin sitting atop the bluffs overlooking the Peconic Bay in Hampton Bays. My boss at U.S. Life rented the cabin for the month of August but needed to attend the wedding of his niece in Albany from the tenth to the twelfth and was happy to sublet it to us. We paid $150 for the two days, which at the time was nearly what I earned in a week, but it was worth it.

My boss allowed us to use his kayaks and Hobie Cat, a sixteen-foot catamaran sailboat. It was our first experience using a sailboat of any kind and we took to it like ducks to water. Spectacular sunshine and clear skies sparkled overhead the entire weekend. We spent hours on the Hobie Cat, returning to shore only to have lunch, then went out again. Both of us quickly learned to maneuver the sleek craft over the tranquil bay. Annie preferred to work the sails and I tended the rudder.

Late in the afternoon on our second day, we found ourselves over a mile offshore when the mild winds died and left us drifting smoothly on the clear gentle water. We decided, rather than trying to pick up a gust here and there and tacking our way back to shore, we'd relax and wait it out. We stretched our sunburned bodies on the canvas trampoline slung between the two pontoons, occasionally dipping our hands into the sea and splashing each other to cool off.

For two people who knew zero about sailing forty-eight hours ago, we were doing pretty well. We had a plastic soda bottle filled with fresh but increasingly tepid water, and not a care in the world. Staring up at the wispy clouds rifting by I thought about how happy I was. This is the way I wanted all life to be.

"Do you still love me?" I asked in little more than a whisper.

"Leo, you know how much I love you. Why are you asking me that? Is something wrong?"

"No. That's just it. Things are so perfect. I never want things to change." For once, I think I said the right thing.

"Umm, isn't this wonderful?" Annie moaned.

I leaned on my elbow and looked into her emerald eyes. "Perfect." Then I kissed her on the lips then on her forehead. That's how I told her I loved her. The kiss on the lips followed by a kiss on the forehead meant, "I love you. I love kissing you. And, I'm not just doing this to have sex! I just love kissing you."

"This is the perfect way to spend a Sunday afternoon."

"Maybe we should get a sailboat," I suggested.

"After we have a house."

Still gazing up at the sky, the infrequent clouds and the top of the mast, I said, "How much do you think a Hobie Cat would cost?"

"And where would we keep it?"

As usual, Annie's practical side trumped my dreamer side. We still lived in a one-bedroom in Queens and there was no way I was going to ask Donald Duck if we could park a sailboat in his driveway.

"Okay, so house first," I agreed. "Where should we look?" I was hoping she wouldn't say exactly what she did.

"Somewhere in Westchester. I love Westchester."

This was a subject I always knew we'd clash on. At some point our plan was to have a house and have a family. That meant, Annie would stay home and raise the kids while I went to work. And, right now, work was in lower Manhattan- a long way and two train-rides from Westchester. That would be about a ninety-minute commute each way, something I wasn't willing to take on.

But I also knew Annie always wanted to live near the place she grew up with the rolling hills and small villages she'd become accustomed to. She loved walking in the woods and biking on the rural roads that led past farms and paddocks lined with clean white fencing. I had to admit, Westchester was pretty.

My problem was that I loved the ocean. I grew up living just a few miles from Jones Beach and, ever since we stopped going to Lake George, spent most summers at the beach. I wanted our first house to be on Long Island.

As I lay there on the gently rolling bay, I thought this would be a good time to raise the issue.

"Annie, if we buy a house on Long Island, we could have a sailboat. We could spend every Sunday afternoon just like this. Wouldn't that be great?" Fortunately, it didn't occur to her that I failed to mention, if we lived in Westchester, we could also sail on the Hudson River.

"I do love this," she purred. "We'll see."

And so, it was. I planted the seed that would lead us to our home in Huntington and hundreds of weekends sailing the Long Island Sound.

The blissful days continued. But not forever.

XI

I can remember the horrible feeling of betrayal like it was yesterday. As I sat on the edge of our bed, still holding the phone in my right hand, I used my left hand to steady myself against falling. The call I'd just gotten was like a bad dream — something you always thought was a complete impossibility; something that would never happen to you. And the news hit me like an Ali punch to the guts. I couldn't catch my breath. This couldn't be happening to me.

It was November 2, 1979. Autumn had been warmer than usual, and a few golden oak leaves still clung to the huge trees surrounding our house on Warren Street. We still had boxes that had yet to be unpacked after the move from Astoria, but our four-bedroom Cape already felt like home. We were looking forward to our first Christmas in our new place.

I was excited for Annie to get home from work. I had big news. It was the day I learned I had been promoted; a real promotion with more money, vacation and responsibility. I was going to run a new department that would calculate the company's risk profile each month. That's a big deal to an insurance company which needs to know its loss exposure in order to satisfy the State of New York regulators. I know it sounds really boring but, at the time, it was very important to my career because it also meant I was put in charge of the fledgling Information Technology Department. More about that later.

Anyway, I couldn't wait for Annie to get home. I was giddy with excitement. My plan was to pick her up at the train station, tell her the great news, then take her to dinner at the Miller Inn, a place she'd always wanted to try but we could never afford. Now we could afford it.

But shortly before her train was due, she called to tell me she was going out for drinks with people at work because one of the secretaries was leaving to have a baby. She said she'd be home around ten but would call from Penn station to tell me what train she was taking. I knew for Annie to stay in the city on a Friday night, it must be something important, so I swallowed my disappointment and decided to tell her my news when she got home.

It wasn't unusual for one of us to get home before the other. I was still a semester away from finishing my MBA so two nights a week, I didn't get back to Huntington until after eleven. And Annie would occasionally stay late to finish work rather than have to go in early the next day. But it was unusual for her to stay in the city on a Friday. That was our time. We tried to keep Friday nights reserved for each other; I made sure my monthly poker games with the guys were never held on Friday and Annie usually kept Friday nights clear for our "date night" as she liked to call it.

Even so, I didn't think it odd that she decided to linger for a drink with the girls. She was close with the people at PMM. She'd been working there since college. PMM was like a second home to her, and through Annie's colorful stories about its people, I felt I knew many of them. I knew Ginny was her best friend at work, that her boss, Mr. Bideaux was more like a father to her than a boss, and that a guy named Chris from PMM's accounting company had taken Annie and Ginny out to lunch a week ago in an attempt to curry favor with the secretaries. His firm was pressing the PMM partners for a new piece of business and I guess he figured if he got in tight with the secretaries, he'd have better access to their bosses, the decision makers. It must have worked because I remember my wife telling me she was impressed with him, especially his expensive loafers that, as she put it, "had these really fancy tassels."

Because Annie said she'd be home late, I made myself a grilled cheese sandwich for dinner and had a beer at the kitchen table while watching the Knicks lose to the Bulls in double overtime. I knew I'd have to drive to the train station to pick her up in a few hours, so I limited myself to just the one beer. The game ended at 9:30 and I still hadn't heard from my wife about what train she was taking. I was getting concerned that she might have forgotten to call me.

Around 10:30 my concern turned to worry. Even if she'd forgotten to call before boarding the train, the 8:45 would have been here by now and she would have called me from the Huntington station house. If she missed the 8:45, there wasn't another train until almost eleven. Surely, she would have called by now.

When eleven o'clock came and went, I was frantic. My mind started to imagine the worst; that she had been hit by a cab, fallen on the train tracks, or been mugged on her way to Penn Station. I felt so helpless. I didn't know what to do. What do you do when someone is missing for a couple of hours?

But she wasn't missing, she was just late. Late without an explanation. She was an adult who was late a couple of hours. You don't call the police about that, right?

I called her office phone but got her voicemail. I thought about calling her mom, but they were in St. Thomas on a cruise. And I didn't want to needlessly worry her parents anyway.

I had no other numbers to call. I had no idea how to get in touch with her friends from work, not even Ginny.

I was in the bathroom brushing my teeth when I heard the phone ring. Our only phone sat on the nightstand next to Annie's side of the bed. I ran into the bedroom, climbed clumsily over the bed and grabbed the receiver, hopefully before it stopped ringing. When I answered, I was already out of breath.

"Annie, is that you?" I said trying to regain control of my hurried breathing.

"Leo, it's me." She sounded sad. Something was wrong but it was such a relief to hear her voice.

"Are you at the station? I can be there in five minutes. Don't take a cab, I can…" She cut me off.

"Leo, I'm still in the city." She said very slowly.

"Where are you?"

"Leo, I didn't want you to worry. I knew you'd be worried."

"Where are you Annie?"

"I'm at a hotel."

"What? What hotel? What are you doing at a hotel?"

"Leo, I can't really talk now. I just wanted you not to worry. I'll be home tomorrow."

My first thought was that she and her girlfriends had too good a time, a bit too much to drink and must have gotten a hotel room near the office to spend the night. I could envision a bunch of gaggling secretaries overdoing it and realizing one or more of them was too wasted to travel home. But that wasn't it.

"Where are you Annie? What hotel are you at? Who's with you?"

"Leo, I can't talk now. I'll be home tomorrow. We'll talk about it then. I have to go."

"Wait!" I shouted in desperation. "Where are you Annie? I need to know where you are."

There was a long, painful silence. Annie sounded so sad, but she didn't sound drunk. In fact, it didn't sound like Annie at all. It was a soft melancholy voice. Annie's voice was usually very alive and full of her constant energy. This voice sounded tired.

"Look Annie, I'm not mad. I'm just so glad you're safe. I was worried."

"I know." In barely a whisper.

"Just tell me where you are so I don't have to worry."

"Leo, I can't lie to you, but I don't want you to worry. I'm okay. I'll see you tomorrow. I'll explain everything then."

"Explain what? What is there to explain?"

"Leo, I'm…, I'm with a…, Leo I'm with a man."

"What?" I said incredulously.

"Leo, I have to go now."

"What are you talking about? Who's with you?"

"Look, I don't want to hurt you any more than I already have. Just know I'm safe and I'll see you tomorrow."

"What do you mean hurt me? How could you hurt me?" I don't think the term, "with a man" had sunk in yet. I was still concerned about her safety, not her fidelity.

"Leo, stop!" She sounded less melancholy and more annoyed. Perhaps annoyed that I was pushing the issue.

"Leo, I don't want to talk about this now. I can't talk about this now."

"Why can't we talk now?"

"Leo, stop it! I can't talk now. Chris will be back any minute."

That's when it dawned on me that, "with a man" meant more than I thought.

"Who the hell is Chris and what are you doing at a hotel with him?"

"Look Leo. I'm staying in the city tonight with Chris. He understands me."

There was a prolonged silence as my brain caught up with the words; words, that with every syllable were destroying the life I thought I had.

Then, "Leo, I'll see you tomorrow. I'm safe. Don't worry about me."

I began to say something but realized she'd hung up. I sat on the edge of the bed, our bed. My mouth hung open. I pictured her sitting on the edge of a bed somewhere in the city, putting down the receiver and looking up at another man. The image crushed me like an elephant sitting on my chest. I felt like I couldn't breathe.

One thing was for certain. I didn't expect to sleep much that night.

XII

The sky was an odd color, the color of lilacs. Annie's white dress was blowing in the wind as she walked toward me in a field covered with tiny yellow flowers. She was smiling. I could tell from her face that she was happy. We both were.

There was loud music playing from somewhere in the distance. I think it was Sousa marching music. But suddenly the music went silent and we both looked toward the horizon as if expecting someone to come over the ridge. No one did. Everything was very still. The breeze had disappeared completely. We looked back at each other. Just a few feet separated us.

Then a mighty roar rang out from beneath us. It sounded like metal crunching painfully against other metal. It was deafening. We both covers our ears. That's when a giant claw came out of the yellow flowers and lifted Annie and all the earth around her. It was the bucket of a huge excavating machine of some sort and it was lifting Annie high into the air. She reached out for me to save her, but we were already too far apart. I tried to scream to her, but no words came from my mouth.

Within seconds, the giant machine had scooped up everything around Annie and was lifting it all higher and higher into the purple sky. Annie screamed my name, "Leooooooo, save me!"

I stood helplessly on the ground looking up at her terrified face. Then the ground beneath me began to shake and I too was consumed by the metallic teeth of a huge earth-moving machine. At first, I thought I'd be brought up and closer to Annie, but I quickly realized we were being pulled apart by the machines. I was being taken backwards, away from Annie and she was still yelling my name.

I awoke from this nightmare only to be reminded of the real horror. I'd slept just an hour or so. The clock on my nightstand glared 6:14 A.M. I was hopelessly entangled in the flannel sheets Annie insisted we use as soon as we had the first cool night of fall. I struggled to free myself. I was sweating. My tee shirt was drenched, and the dampness felt cold against my hot skin.

It took a few seconds, but the reality of the previous night hit me like a hammer.

Annie had spent the night in the city with another man! A stranger, as far as I knew. But what did I really know? It occurred to me that I was painfully out of touch with what was really going on in my wife's world and certainly in her head.

The mental image of Annie in bed with someone else made me cover my face with my hands. I hoped when I pulled them away, this would all have been a bad dream, like the ones I'd just had. But it wasn't a dream. When I finally peaked out from my sweaty palms, I saw the phone sitting atop the nightstand. The phone that gave me the horrific news just a few hours earlier. I hated that phone.

I decided to shower once I could extract myself from the flannel trap. I needed to prepare myself for what I expected would be one of the worst days of my life, yet I had no idea what to expect. Would Annie even come home? She said she would. She said we'd talk in the morning. But what the hell was there to talk about? Did she think I'd want details of her affair? I didn't even want to think about it.

At that time in my life I'd been running a lot. Not long distances but frequently. It helped me relax and often was the only time of the day I could take for myself and feel like I was doing something for myself. I desperately wanted to go for a run that morning, but I didn't want to be away from the phone for even a minute, in case Annie called. This was years before people carried cell phones so that horrible blue princess in our bedroom was my only hope of hearing from my wife.

I showered with the bathroom door open, so I'd hear the phone if it rang. It didn't. I ate a bowl of Raisin Bran on the edge of our bed, even though I wasn't hungry, because I didn't want to miss her call. And I paced the green shag rug in our bedroom for two hours waiting for the call that never came.

About nine-thirty it started to rain lightly. From our bedroom window, I noticed Annie had left her bike in our backyard, so I ran down to save it from the rain and stowed in in the shed I'd built next to the big oak tree. The bike was already wet, so I found an old towel in the shed and did my best to dry the frame. As I did, it occurred to me that what

I was doing was a bit insane. I was worried about Annie's bike developing a little rust while she was in the arms of another man! Yet the mere act of caring for one of her possessions made me feel like I was somehow showing her I still loved her.

As I toweled the handlebars, I began to sob. Just a little at first, but as soon as I became aware of my tears, I wept with a force I'd never done before. I wasn't sure if I was crying for myself or for the loss of the perfect life I thought we had. Losing the later would be as painful as losing, well, just about anything else in my life. I realized I'd come to identify myself with the "us" of our marriage. I was Annie's husband. At some point, I'd ceased to think of myself as Leo Monday. I was now one part of a whole, a whole that may no longer exist. So, what did that make me? Had my self-worth already been abandoned to the "us" that was now threatened by some faceless man?

I buried my face in the towel and wept openly. I found myself saying things like, "What have you done? How could you do this? How could you do this to me, to us?"

I'm not sure how long I was in the shed. The only time that mattered now was the distance between now and when I heard from Annie again. But to hear from her I'd need to be near the phone, so I stowed the bike and started for the back door. That's when I heard it. A car door slamming, then the sound of a car racing away. As I entered our home from the back door, Annie was coming in the front.

Someone had dropped her off and disappeared into the rainy mist.

I saw her first. She still had on her coat and, of course, the clothes she went to work in yesterday. A paper bag dangled from her left wrist. I saw the word Delucca on one side of the brown paper.

I wasn't sure what to say. How do you begin this conversation? This confrontation?

My wife saw me standing in the kitchen. The blue jeans and M.I.T. sweatshirt I wore must have struck her as odd for some reason because the first words out of her mouth were, "Where have you been?"

"Gee, I thought that would be my question." I barely whispered.

She let her coat drop on the kitchen table. "Leo, I don't know what to say." She shook her head as if to seek something in there that might assuage my pain.

To this day, I don't know where it came from, but something told me to can my usual sarcastic self, to get her to talk in a way that might lead to me understanding her.

"Why don't we sit in the living room and talk about it?" I said a calmly as I could.

"What is there to talk about? I had an affair. There, I said it. I had an affair with a man I met two weeks ago and who I think I'm in love with." She paused briefly. "I don't know what else to say. Nothing I say will make it right or change anything."

My dry mouth hung open. "You're in love with this guy?"

Annie sat on the edge of the sofa and motioned for me to sit across from her on the maple rocking chair we inherited from my grandmother. Part of me was afraid to sit, afraid I'd hear more terrible words. But most of me had to know more. I had to know if my life, our life was over. Had someone else taken my place so easily? Can you be so easily replaced after years of marriage?

"Leo, please listen to me and try not to get crazy. Okay?"

I nodded but wasn't sure I could deliver.

She swallowed hard, then began. "Chris is the guy I told you about a few weeks ago. The guy from work who took Ginny and me out to lunch. Remember, I told you?"

I couldn't look at her.

"Leo, please try to understand. I didn't want any of this to happen. It just did." Again, a pause. "Leo, I'm going to tell you one hundred percent of the truth. I want you to know what I'm going through. I want you to understand."

I erupted, "You want me to understand!"

"Please, don't do that. I want to tell you about this. I need to tell you. Mostly because I don't completely understand it all myself. But I need you to stay calm."

I thought it odd that she'd said that twice- 'stay calm'. I'm not a guy who flies off the handle. I don't scream or yell and I certainly had never given Annie reason to think I'd ever hit her. Why the sudden concern with my temper?

"Okay. I'll stay calm." I said with a questioning tone.

"I don't know how to explain it because I don't understand it myself. I've never done anything like this. You know me." She said pleading.

"I thought I did." I replied with just a bit too much sarcasm.

"Leo, up till last week, I never looked at another guy, never even thought about it. But after our lunch with Chris, he called me for another lunch, just me this time. I didn't tell you about that one. It didn't seem like something I needed to hide from you, but as it turned out, it was. We had lunch at a place in Little Italy and took a long walk around a park down there. We sat on a park bench and talked for almost two hours. I had to find a phone booth and call Ginny to say I needed to run an errand. I hated lying to her."

She saw the look of disbelief on my face.

"Yes, I hated lying to you too. Anyway, we talked for a long time, mostly about me. No one has ever listened to me like that before. I felt like I could tell him anything, and I barely knew him. It was a wonderful feeling. He seemed to understand me. He seemed to understand the things that are important to me." She shook her head. "I don't know how to explain it. I could say things to him...things I've never even said to you."

"Like what?"

She hung her head. "Leo, please don't make me do this."

"Do what?"

"Look, for two hours last Thursday, Chris made me feel like I was the only person in the world. He genuinely cared about what was important to me. I loved that feeling."

"I don't get it. What type of things could you say to him that you can't say to me?"

She looked at me as if I knew what she had in mind. I didn't.

"Leo, let's not do this. Not now."

"Do what?" I barked. "I don't know what you're talking about. Look, Annie. I'm trying to understand what happened. I mean, this isn't you. This isn't the way the Annie Monday I know acts. It's kind of like someone else is in your body."

As soon as I said the words, I regretted them. The image of someone else in my wife's body came into focus. Someone else named Chris!

Annie looked at me without saying anything for several minutes. Somehow, I was able to keep my mouth shut. I guess I was trying to get the picture of another man straddling my wife out of my head. It wasn't easy.

I knew Annie wasn't a virgin when we met. Nor was I. But ever since we started dating, the thought of her with anyone but me never crossed my mind. It never seemed like a possibility. Maybe I was naive. Isn't fidelity something you have a right to expect, especially when you give it in return?

Finally, Annie looked up and nearly whispered, "Leo, I think we need to be apart for a while so I can figure this out. I need to think about what I want, and I can't do that with you here."

The words stuck in my throat like dry powder. "You mean a separation?"

"I just think we need time to ourselves. As I hope you know, I've never done anything like this before. I need to think. I need to work this through."

"Don't you mean we need to work this through?" I asked adding extra emphasis to the word we.

The answer caught me by surprise.

"No, I need to do this." Then she added in the saddest voice I'd ever heard, "I need to be alone for a while."

We were now standing in the kitchen. A steady rain now poured down the window. Annie leaned against one side of the counter, me against the other. No one spoke for a while as the words, "I need to be alone for a while" hung in the thick, humid air.

I was terrified. Looking back on it with a much clearer lens, I think I was most frightened by two things. First, the behavior of my wife; the woman I thought I understood completely. But maybe even more frightening was the abyss that stretched before me. I had no idea what was coming. Where would I go? And for how long? How could I not see Annie first thing in the morning, every morning, as we had for so long up until today?

Apparently, the ride home from the city had given Annie time to think this through because she seemed to have a plan for both of us.

"Leo, I think you should leave for a while. Just leave me alone for a couple of days. I need to think, and I can't do that with you here."

Well, there it was. I was being asked to leave our home.

"And I don't think we should talk for a couple of days. I know this is hitting you by surprise…"

"Oh, you think?" I interrupted sarcastically.

She pushed on with what seemed increasingly like a pre-rehearsed monolog.

"Try to listen, please. I know this was a big surprise. It was for me too. And I don't understand it at all, not yet."

Annie slid her hand along the cooktop and bit her lower lip gently as she often did when thinking.

"Leo, I'm so confused. I just know I need to be alone."

"So, where do you expect me to go and for how long?"

"I don't know," she confessed. "I just know I want to figure this out on my own. You've been watching over me for so long and so closely, sometimes I feel like I'm suffocating when you try to help me. I know you want to solve this for me, but you can't. I need to do it."

I said, "Can we just go back to the fact that you feel you can say things to this guy that you can't say to me? I need to know..." She cut me off.

"I don't want to have this discussion now. I want time to think. Now, please pack some clothes, maybe enough for the week, and leave me alone. You can take the car. I don't need it."

I didn't know what to say. This was my wife and she was treating me like I was a child. But I wanted to do whatever would lead us back to the life we had a few weeks ago. So, I grabbed a few suits, five shirts and ties, socks, shoes and underwear for a week. All but the suits fit into one of our honeymoon suitcases. The suits I left on hangers and stowed them in the back of our Pinto.

Leaving our house was the hardest thing I ever had to do- at least up to that point. And leaving Annie seemed impossible but, there I was, walking down our driveway and looking back at Annie in the doorway. I prayed she'd come running out into the misty rain and kiss me and tell me not to go. But, she didn't. She closed the front door to what had been our home, and I was left looking back at the number 1849.

When I pulled out of the driveway I had no idea where I would go. A hotel was a luxury I couldn't afford. We couldn't afford. I needed to go to work on Monday so I couldn't wander too far from home. I drove west on 25A, the primary east-west corridor of the north shore. As I did, I thought of friends I could impose on for a few days, friends who weren't married themselves.

The list was short. Most of my friends were married and I certainly couldn't go to one of Annie's friends. My only real option was my closest friend Jerry who lived in a large one-bedroom apartment in Laurelton, just over the Nassau-Queens border. Jerry was engaged but still living alone. He and I had known each other since we were eight years old. I had no doubt I'd be welcomed there.

XIII

The ride from Huntington to Laurelton usually takes about an hour, so I wanted to be sure Jerry was home before I drove all the way. About three miles from the home I'd just been thrown out of, I pulled into a diner. I needed to call Jerry and I also needed to put something in my churning stomach. The Blue Dolphin diner was an institution in Huntington and always reliable for good eggs and coffee.

I sat at the counter and ordered two eggs easy over with home fries from Sally, an overweight but very pleasant lady from the Philippines. Then I called Jerry from the pay phone on the wall near the bathrooms. No answer.

I called again after finishing my food but still no answer. It occurred to me that I'd neglected to pack any belts or cufflinks and since all my pants need a belt and most of my shirts need cufflinks, I decided to head back home. I could try Jerry again from there.

The misty rain was still coming down; just enough to require wipers but not so much that I couldn't see without them. As I turned onto our street, I thought about the first time Annie and I drove down Warren Ave. We'd spent weeks looking for houses and were getting discouraged that nothing in our price range met our expectations of what a first home should be. The first time we pulled up in front of our house, Annie said, "This is it. This house was made for us."

And I thought so too. At least I did up until about two hours ago.

This time, when I pulled up in front of our house there was a black Lincoln Continental in the driveway. I turned off my engine and sat in the Pinto trying to decide if I should go in to retrieve my things. I'm not even sure why I hesitated. After all, it was my house. I'd only been gone a couple of hours, if that. I had no idea who the black car belonged to but what did it matter? This was my house, our house.

But then I saw him. Through the front window I could see a man standing in my living room. He seemed to be admiring the pictures hanging on the wall, as if he was killing time waiting for someone. He was about thirty-five, tall with blonde hair. Even through the rain-soaked car window I could tell he was a good-looking man. His blue sport jacket covered a pale blue button-down oxford. Both looked like they were from Brooks Brothers. I hated him.

It only got worse.

He seemed to turn as if someone else had entered the room. Someone else had- my wife. Annie was in a pair of jeans and a yellow v-neck sweater. Her hair was pulled back in a ponytail. She looked beautiful, but more than that she looked young. So much younger than him.

They stood a few feet apart and seemed to be talking about something. Annie shook her head as if disagreeing, then stood there just looking at him as he spoke. The look on her face was something I don't think I'd ever seen before on Anne. She was looking at him like he was some sort of god.

I wanted to kill him with my bare hands. I leapt from the car, careful not to slam the door. I didn't want them to know I was coming. This was going to be an ambush. I may not have had size, but I did have the advantage of shock and awe and anger on my side. I think I ran to the front door.

My plan, if there ever was one, was to surprise them both, then beat the shit out of him before throwing him out the front door and onto my lawn. I was enraged to the point of feeling a little lightheaded, but I was determined to take back my woman by significant force. Annie had said he was an accountant. How tough could he be?

But when I got to the door, something happened. I can't explain it. Even today, so many years later, I don't understand what happened. Something made me stop. Something made me turn around and go back to my car. The only thing I know for sure is that it wasn't out of fear that I backed off. Something told me that if I went through that door, I would lose Annie. I can't explain what I mean by something. It was as if a higher power of some sort, knew what was best for me and physically picked me up and led me away from trouble. That's the only way I can explain it. Devine intervention? Maybe.

I climbed into my car, turned the ignition and drove three blocks to a nearby high school parking lot. There, I sat in my car, rain now hitting the roof harder than before, and began to sob. I sat there, alone in the pouring rain, for almost an hour.

Long story short- Instead of going back to the house, I drove to Roosevelt Field Mall where I bought two belts and a cheap pair of cuff links which I have to this day. I drove to Jerry's where I was welcomed with open and very understanding arms.

All I know for sure is that by not confronting the man who slept with my wife, I probably saved my marriage and maybe a long jail sentence.

What's that they say? Revenge is a dish best served cold.

I agree.

XIV

It's been three days now since I left Stephen, Lilly and Peter. I still regret not talking to my grandson about my early departure from this lovely planet, but I felt it best to respect his parent's wishes. They felt he wasn't ready for such a conversation. To be honest, I'm not sure I was either.

It snowed a bit last night. As I scan the view from my living room window, I can see a dusting of white on the trees in the park, trees that are increasingly baron. All but the hardiest leaves have fallen to the ground leaving thousands of stick-figures standing side by side, each holding up their arms as if trying to reach for the heavens. Trees can be many things, especially those that go through the four seasons with differing attire for each. Today, they look like naked stick figures gazing skyward, awaiting the arrival of their next spring.

If my doctors are correct, I suppose I've seen my last spring. I don't expect to be around in four months when all these sad stick figures start blossoming again. It saddens me to think I've seen my last spring. I always loved walking in the park in early March when the grass begins to show signs of new life, daffodils are pushing their way up, and the trees are showing a hint of light green tips. To me, it's testimony to the perpetual nature of our world. The earth has an inner clock that ticks only to its own cadence. It cares not about man's schedule. Especially mine.

This morning my stomach pain is a little better than yesterday. When I went to sleep last night, I took an Ambien. The stomach pain, which feels like I'm always very hungry, was so bad, I knew I'd never get to sleep without help. Ambien lets me sleep through the night; a few hours I can escape the torment. My doctor says it's okay.

I want to write this morning. When I sit and type, for some reason, I forget about my cancer. I forget about everything except what I'm writing about. And this morning, I want to tell you the rest of the story about Annie's affair.

As she'd requested, I stayed away from the house for several days. After seeing her standing in our home with that guy, I didn't want to go back anyway. But sleeping on Jerry's couch was painful and I could tell I was already wearing out my welcome in Laurelton. I knew that, not because of anything Jerry said or did, but because of the looks I got from Jessie, the hateful bitch he intended to marry. Side note- you never met Jessie because Jerry had the good sense to dump her three weeks before their wedding. He later married Mary Jane and lived happily ever after.

But as I got off the train in Laurelton the following Friday, I decided I'd had enough. I'd been away from my home, my bed, for six nights. In all that time, I got only one call from Annie. She called me at work on Monday, just to say she was okay and to ask where I was staying. Since then, nothing.

So, I was determined to call her when I got back to Jerry's apartment and demand to see her. How were we ever going to work on this if we never speak?

Jerry wasn't at the apartment when I got there so I changed into a pair of jeans and a mock turtleneck and dialed our home number. Annie picked up on the first ring. She chipped, "Hello?"

"Annie, it's me. I want to talk to you tonight. We need to talk." I tried not to sound desperate.

There was a short silence, then, "Leo, I want to talk to you too. I'm just not sure if I'm ready. A lot has happened this week. I'm just trying to process it all."

"Alright, good. I'll come over in about a half hour. I just need..." She cut me off.

"No. Leo, not tonight. I can't see you tonight."

"Why not?" As the two words fell from my lips, my mind conjured a very unpleasant image.

"Look, Leo. Not tonight. I have to see Chris tonight. It's important."

"Are you fucking kidding me? You have to see him?" I emphasized the word "have".

She began to explain but I cut her off.

"Annie. I'm your husband. I'm the one you need to talk this through with. I'm the one you promised to love till the day we died. Do you remember any of that or were those just bullshit words for you?"

"Leo, can't you…" Again, I cut her off.

"Those words meant something to me. They meant we stick by each other when it's fun but also when it's hard. This is one of those hard times Annie. We need to honor the commitment we made to each other. We owe that to each other. We need to work on this together. How can we do that if you keep seeing this guy?"

"Leo, I can't see you tonight. I promise, tomorrow we will talk. Come here around noon. We'll talk then."

And the line went dead. She hung up on me. I stood there in Jerry's kitchen like an idiot, holding his phone in my hand.

Was I wrong to push for us to work on this together? Was it unreasonable of me to demand she see me? I didn't think so. I think we owed each other that much.

Then, it occurred to me. The tone in Annie's voice as she answered the phone was meant for him. She thought he was calling. I'd already been replaced as the person who made her happy. Now, I was the person who was forcing her to deal with reality. I was the person pressing for a confrontation.

Realizing there was little I could do tonight to better our situation, I decided to get drunk. I scribbled a note for Jerry on a napkin and headed for the Back Door, a local bar we used to visit when we were on breaks from college. What the Back Door lacked in charm and cleanliness, it more than made up for with color and cost. Located just a few blocks from Jerry's apartment, the Back Door attracted an eclectic group of locals, commuters who couldn't bear to go home, and amateur musicians who were given a chance to do their thing on the tiny stage, at least until they got booed off.

It was also cheap. For ten bucks a guy could get comfortably drunk, especially if Mike was behind the bar. Mike, the rotund owner, would buy you a drink for every two you paid for.

So, I walked the six blocks over the city line and found a perch at the end of the bar closest to the pool table and farthest from the stage. Mike wasn't behind the bar but Marilyn, his wife was just as liberal with the buy-backs and a far more empathic listener. Tonight, at least until Jerry got there, I needed Marilyn.

"Hey, what's shaking Leo? Haven't seen you in a long time. You still married?" Marilyn got right to the point.

"Jack and ginger. Nice to see you Marilyn."

"Oh, we're in for some serious drinking tonight? Something wrong sweetie?" A professional psychiatrist would have said, "How do you feel about that?" Marilyn always opened with, "Something wrong sweetie?" But she was a lot cheaper than a shrink and I don't think they let you drink in a psychiatrist's office.

There were only a few other people in the bar, most playing pool. It was only 7:45 P.M. on a Friday night. The Back Door didn't start cranking till after ten on most Fridays. So, I sat on my stool and spilled my guts to Marilyn; the whole ugly, embarrassing story. Even in the poorly lit bar, I think she could tell I was near tears as I explained how lost I felt.

"Hey, listen honey. I'm sure it all seems pretty bleak right now. But these things sometimes work out. My first husband, Butchy, he left me twice in the first year we were married. Both times he took up with some blonde whore he used to date in high school, long before we met. And both times, he came crawling back because he realized where the sugar is. You just got to make sure you the sugar and not the vinegar. Times like this, it's easy to be full of righteousness and all that shit; that's the vinegar. Nobody likes vinegar. You just need her to realize, even though she shit in your hands, you still love her. You still the sugar."

I appreciated Marilyn's direct and to-the-point psychoanalysis. And I could see the wisdom in her carefully crafted words. I just wasn't sure I could stand to watch my wife throw away our marriage without putting up a fight.

"Another Jack and ginger please."

"You listen to old Marilyn honey. I know what I'm talking about. When it comes to baseball, or Wall Street, or most other stuff, well, I don't pretend to know shit. But when it comes to women and why they do what they do, I know a lot. I've seen a lot and I've been married to three different men. I know how it works. I know what women want."

I looked up from my second drink. "Really?" I said skeptically. "What do women want?"

Marilyn looked pleased that I'd sought her counsel. She poured herself a shot of something and threw it back like it was water. I'm pretty sure it wasn't water. She pushed her hand through her oily black hair and looked around as if someone else was trying to listen. Then she leaned across the bar, her hot breath just a few inches from my ear.

"All they want is to be the only thing." She leaned back and nodded her head. "That's it."

"What's it?" I asked, confused by the simplicity of her wisdom.

"What's your girl's name, sweetie?"

"Annie."

"Well, what Annie wants is to be the only thing you see when you get up in the morning. She's supposed to be the only thing you see when you enter a crowded room and she sure as hell wants to be the only thing you're thinking about when you get into bed at night. Women aren't satisfied with being a part of your life. They want to be the reason you want to live another day. You remember that."

"Seems pretty simple. But I think my wife is a lot more complicated than that."

Marilyn poured herself another shot of the clear liquid and put her bar rag on the bar directly in front of me before leaning in again. "Nope."

Then she turned and served beers to a few guys on the other end of the bar.

A half hour later, after I'd finished the ice in my first buy-back, Jerry walked in and hopped onto the stool next to mine. I bought him a Bud then shared the gist of Marilyn's wisdom with him.

"So, is she right?" I asked. "Can women really be that simple and needy?"

"How the fuck do I know?"

"I just thought you'd have an opinion." I realized I'd slurred the word opinion. The Jack was winning.

"I don't know man. I don't think anyone knows what women really want. But, I'll tell you this." He moved closed to me, so he didn't have to yell over the music. "Women are a lot of work. Sometimes I'd rather just beat my meat on the bedpost than deal with Jessie."

Eloquently put, but of limited help.

"Let's shoot some pool. You'll feel better." He grabbed me by the arm and led me to the red-felt table. A couple of guys in suits had just finished their game and offered to play us in doubles. Bar protocol says that you keep the table as long as you keep winning, so they really didn't have to risk losing the table. They could have kept playing each other as long as the quarters lasted. And they should have because, in my semi-intoxicated state, I was on fire. We won three straight racks.

"One more for drinks?" The taller suit asked.

"Rack 'em." I bellowed. "You can even break."

As Jerry and I leaned against the wall watching the suits drop ball after ball, it became increasingly obvious we'd been hustled. These guys were good. We didn't get our hands on a cue stick until they'd run two and a half racks of balls.

"You're an asshole," was my best friend's synopsis of my bravado. "You just cost us a round."

And he was right. I sent the nine ball off the table with my first shot and the game and table went to the suits. Fortunately, they were only drinking beer.

****

I awoke on Jerry's couch with a massive headache. The sunlight poured through the living room window mercilessly. My watch said 8:34 but it felt like I'd only slept a few hours. Turns out I had.

When Jerry emerged from the shower, he informed me we closed down the Back Door at four then walked to the Valley Stream all-night diner for cheese omelets. That explained both why I wasn't hungry and why my head felt like I'd been hit with a hammer.

"How many did you have before I got there last night?" He asked as he sprayed Right Guard under both arms.

"Two or three."

"Well, I've known you a long time Leo old boy, and I've never seen you that wasted. You were walking down the middle of Merrick Road after we left the diner. Looked like you thought the center line was a tightrope."

"I need to brush my teeth."

"You do that. I'll make coffee."

A hot shower helped a lot. When I emerged from the steamy bathroom cloaked in a Mickey Mouse towel, Jerry handed me a mug of coffee. "Get dressed. Jessie's coming over. She wants me to go look at silverware. Like I give a shit about what kind of forks we use."

"Get used to it."

A few minutes later the apartment door swung open. Jessie wasn't in the room ten seconds before I got the "Are you still here?" look.

"Hey Jess. What's up?" I offered politely. Although I hated the bitch for the way she was castrating my best friend, I didn't want to get between them. I didn't want to be the reason he killed her. I just wanted him to kill her.

Fortunately for all concerned, Jessie seemed to pretend I wasn't in the room. She bundled poor Jerry up and whisked him off to the mall so they could agonize over what pattern of flatware would help lead them to eternal marital bliss.

I planned to go to the house to see Annie, but I didn't want to show up too early. She'd said, "come at noon". So, I slipped the rubber ban off the Daily News and read about the owners of Studio 54 getting arrested for tax evasion and a billion-dollar loan from the US government to bail out Chrysler. Then there was the increasing tension between the US and Iran because the Ayatollah seemed to be siding with the student radicals and had no plans to release the American hostages anytime soon.

I didn't really care about any of the news, especially news about people five thousand miles from Huntington. All I cared about was here. If the story wasn't about Annie, I didn't want to read it. With that as my criteria, obviously, my disappointment in the newspaper was inevitable.

I killed another hour doing the crossword puzzle, then got dressed and headed for my car. I figured by the time I drove all the way back to Huntington, it would be after twelve, the time Annie said it would be okay to come. It infuriated me that I was being kept from my own home, perhaps because my wife might have just spent the night with another man.

But I wanted Annie back and if I had to endure…., well, I'd do anything to get her back.

On the drive to Huntington, I thought about what I'd say to my wife. I had no idea what she was going to tell me, so I had no idea how to prepare a response. She could go anywhere from, "I've decided I'm leaving you and I plan to marry Chris," to "I realize now that what I did was insane. Please take me back." There were probably a hundred variations that lay somewhere in between, but that didn't help me prepare for the conversation I assumed would make or break my marriage.

I think that somewhere along the Southern State Parkway I came to accept the reality that much of what was about to happen was very much out of my control. No matter how much I wanted life to be the way it was, if that's not what Annie wanted, there was little I could do to change her mind. My future was going to be determined by my wife and, perhaps, some guy I've never met.

When I pulled up in front of our house, I couldn't help noticing the peeling paint on the trim around the windows. Had I been so blind to so much for so long? Maybe Annie had been miserable with me for months and, like the window trim, I just hadn't seen it. Maybe she'd been reaching out to me and I didn't notice.

At the front door, I wasn't sure if I was supposed to knock or just go in. My instinct said knock. But Annie must have seen me from the window and opened the door as I was about to knock. I stepped over the threshold and noticed it immediately.

"What happened?" I said.

She closed the door behind me and sighed. "Oh, Leo. I've been such a fool."

Well, that was a good start, but I wanted to know about the large black and blue bruise on the right side of her neck.

"What happened to your neck? Did he do that?" I said a silent prayer the answer was yes.

It was.

"Come in. I really need to talk to you." She took my hand and led me to the kitchen table. We sat facing each other on the wooden chairs we'd picked out before we were married. I never imagined we'd have to use them for this conversation. The round oak table was empty except for a small pile of mail. She extended her hand and held mine on the table.

"Leo, I'm so, so sorry. I can't believe what's happened in the last few weeks." Then she started to sob. Just a little at first, then more and she buried her head in her hands.

"I can't believe what I've done." She said with her head still lowered. "I can't believe what I've put you through. I'm a monster. I'm a horrible person."

As much as this was exactly what I wanted to hear, it pained me to see her so distraught. I just sat there and listened. After a few minutes, Annie regained her composure, picked her head up and looked me in the eyes. "Leo, can you ever forgive me? Please say you'll forgive me."

"Annie, what happened to your neck?"

She gripped my hand tightly. The look on her face was difficult for me to see. She looked so ashamed and yet so full of pain. There were a thousand things she wanted to say to make it all go away but first she had to tell me what happened.

"I can't tell you anything until you tell me you can forgive me. I need to hear that we can be saved. Because if we can't, if you can't say that, well then, I don't care what happens. I need to know you still want me."

All I could do was look deeply into her eyes.

"Please, Leo. Please say we can be saved. Please tell me I'm still worth loving." She was pleading.

In my whole life, I've never felt so sorry for another human being. She was in so much pain, not from the surface bruises, but inside. Inside she was in agony. And it killed me to see her suffering.

"If it's what you want, yes. We can be saved." I said it in nearly a whisper.

Annie jumped from the chair and threw her arms around me. Her hug almost crushed me, but it felt wonderful.

"Oh, Leo. I love you so much. I can't believe what I've done. How could I do this?" She was pummeling me with kisses.

****

To this day, I don't think either of us really understand what happened. Annie would say she had a temporary bout of insanity; that hormones and emotion and a need for recognition conspired at precisely the moment Chris came along. She would say her head was turned by the sophisticated and worldly older man. She might even say she was momentarily in love with the idea of being in love. We never really got to the bottom of it.

We spent three months seeing a marriage counsellor, a middle-aged ex-priest who tried to make more of our problems than we both felt necessary. Dr. Foley, as he insisted we call him, looked for meaning behind every word, every thought and every dream we'd ever had. But, in the end, we both accepted Annie's frail explanation: she made a terrible mistake. And we were both able to get past it, although when I learned Chris had been in our bed, I insisted we get a new mattress.

And that should have been the end of it. If we were really going to put it behind us, if we were really going to move on, then we both should have tried to forgive and forget. Everyone fucks up, right. Everyone makes mistakes that they wish they could take back but can't.

I was able to forgive Annie because I loved her. Maybe, I was afraid of what my life would have been without her, but I think it was genuine love. Forgiving Annie was easy.

I wish I could have been so forgiving of her lover. But once I saw the bruises on her neck and back, I knew I couldn't. I'm not that good a person.

That morning, at the kitchen table, Annie told me how she'd come to the realization that she'd made a terrible mistake three days earlier. She met Chris in the city after work on the Wednesday night and explained their week of passion had been a mistake. She told him she was going back to her husband. He tried to convince her to give it more time, that he'd never met anyone like her before. He begged her not to make a final decision yet.

She agreed to see him again once more the next afternoon. In her mind, it would be the last time.   So, when he suggested lunch in the lobby of the Sherry Netherlands Hotel, she agreed. She reiterated her position over lunch and was satisfied that she'd closed the door on a horrible chapter of her life. He said he was sad but understood why she felt that way. After all, she was married, and he was not. She said he seemed sincere.

He offered to give her a ride back to her office. But instead of taking her back to work he drove to a remote street on the west side and parked the Lincoln where no one would hear her screams.

Annie said he stopped short of rape, but I've never been sure she was telling me the truth. She was badly bruised inside and out. The last haunting thing he said to her was, "You're not done with me, bitch. You don't just fuck me and walk away. You'll see me again."

He was wrong about that.

I saw to it.

XV

I didn't write yesterday. I felt lousy. I felt old. Maybe it's as Emerson said, "**It is time to be old, time to take in sail.**"

Dr. Romaro said I should expect this. Without the chemo and radiation, I should expect the stomach pain to increase significantly. I just didn't think it would happen so soon. And I can't really say its pain. It's more like constantly feeling very hungry but not wanting to eat. It's hard to explain.

Anyway, this is the road I've chosen. No chemo, no radiation. I'd rather spend my last weeks or months dealing with this discomfort than with nausea and constant diarrhea.

So, today I will write again. I feel a little better and I want to finish the story of Annie's affair with the guy I came to learn was Chris Hoffman.

Two weeks after I moved back in with Annie, she came home from work in tears. I'd picked her up at the train station and within seconds of getting into the car, she erupted.

"He keeps calling me!" She cried. "He keeps calling me at work and asking me to meet him for lunch. He even said he was going to come to the office and make a scene so I couldn't refuse."

I tried to be supportive. "He can't hurt you anymore, Annie. You don't need to worry." But I knew that wasn't true.

Through her sobs she murmured, "He said he's sorry. That he made a big mistake. That he thinks about me all the time. He's a fucking pathological liar. I hate him. I hate everything about him."

I knew she was trying to prove she no longer held any feelings for this guy. I didn't doubt that. Over the last two weeks she'd cried almost every day. She was punishing herself for what she could only describe as her "temporary insanity". Annie had no more understanding of what occurred than did I, but she took complete responsibility for all of it. Not once did she imply that I'd done anything to drive her away or cause her to doubt me. She took it all on her shoulders and the weight was becoming more than Annie could handle.

Dr. Foley had told us to expect this and tried to convince Annie she had to forgive herself just as I had. Until she forgave herself, she wouldn't be able to move on.

Now, being reminded of her indiscretion on a daily basis by Chris' phone calls and badgering, she was slipping backward. He was probably doing her more psychological damage now than he had in the car when he attacked her and left her physically bruised.

"Annie, maybe the best thing to do is just ignore him. Don't even take his calls. If he calls again, just hang up. He'll get the message."

She looked up at me. "Oh, Leo. You've been so good to me all through this. I made this mess and you've been so wonderful."

"That's what you do when you love someone. You love them unconditionally."

She gave me a questioning look, as if she didn't understand.

I explained, "Look Annie, when I married you, I promised to love you no matter what. I didn't promise to love you only if you loved me. I didn't promise to love you only if you were perpetually faithful. And I didn't promise to love you only if it's what made me happy. I promised to love you without conditions. Period. That's what true love is."

I don't know from where I conjured those words, but she seemed to understand.

"Okay, I'll try. If he calls again, I'll just hang up."

If it had only been that easy. If the son of a bitch had just left her alone, we all would have been so much better off. But he didn't leave her alone. He kept calling and two days later he showed up at Annie's office. Fortunately, she was out running an errand at the time and Ginny, her friend, told him she wouldn't be back that afternoon. When Annie did return from the errand, Ginny filled her in, and Annie freaked out.

When she got home that night, she told me she wanted to call the police. "Leo, this has got to stop. Even if I have to tell them about my affair and him beating me, this has got to stop."

"Honey, in that case this would all become very public. At this point only you and I know what happened. If you go to the police, your parents will know, everyone at work will know. You don't want that. I certainly don't want that." Looking back on it, I'm not sure if it was Annie's reputation or mine I was actually concerned with. Sure, no one wants to be known as an adulterer, but what man wants the world to know that his wife needed to look elsewhere for love? There would be shame for both of us. And, at the end of the day, I'm not sure a police report would help anyway. The beating in the car would be her word against his. And the affair, well, in 1979, after the decade of free love and all that, who would care about what two consenting adults do?

Her husband, that's who. There was no way I was going to let this guy get in the way of my marriage again. So, I decided to take the fight to him.

"I'll go talk to him," I said even before I fully understood what I intended.

"What?"

"I'll go to his office tomorrow. He's not going to cause any trouble where he works."

"And what are you going to say?"

I had to think quickly to convince my bride I knew what I was doing, which I didn't.

"I'll tell him if he doesn't leave you alone, we'll get a restraining order. I'm sure he doesn't want to deal with that. That couldn't possibly be good for his career. He doesn't want that."

I didn't even know what a restraining order actually was, but I'd heard the term used by lawyers on TV and it seemed to convince Annie there was a way to end this.

"I'll take care of it." I promised her. And I meant it. "Just give me his full name and tell me where he works. I'll make it stop."

The next morning, I called in sick. I told my boss I felt like shit (which was true) and that I'd be in a few hours late. Then I took the train to Hoboken, New Jersey and showed up at 9:30 A.M. at the offices of Baker and Baker CPAs, where Christopher Hoffman was a junior partner. The office wasn't that big, so the receptionist knew him by name.

"Oh, Mr. Hoffman's not in today," she reported. "I'm pretty sure he went skiing for the long weekend."

I'm not sure what long weekend she was referring to. Christmas was three weeks away and Thanksgiving was in the rearview mirror.

I'm not sure what I intended to do with the information, but I inquired, "Do you know where he is? I have a form that he forgot to sign for his brokerage account. If it isn't filed by Monday morning, he will be really pissed. I can have someone get it to him this weekend."

Milly, the receptionist, quickly volunteered, "Let me see if his secretary knows where he is."

She made a call while I flipped through a Fortune magazine in the reception area. It didn't take long for her to motion me back to the reception desk.

"Mr. Hoffman's secretary, Jane, says that if you leave the form with her, she'll get it to him." She still had Jane on the line.

"I can't do that. It's a confidentiality thing." I winked as I said it.

Milly relayed the new information to Jane and I saw her writing something on a pad. When she hung up, she handed me the piece of Baker & Baker letterhead. He's booked at the Sugarhaus Inn at Jay Peak until Sunday night. He's a really serious skier. I think he won some sort of medals in college."

Clearly, Milly liked to gab. "I think he's there with a couple of other guys from the Estate and Trust department. They go away a lot. Why not? They're all single. Except for Chris, but his wife doesn't like skiing, so he goes with the guys."

Annie hadn't mentioned that the man she was sleeping with was married. I doubt she knew. In fact, I'd bet my life that she wouldn't have gotten involved with a married man. But, then again, I would have bet my life that she wouldn't have cheated on me either.

I played it cool. "I didn't know Chris was married."

"Yeah, he got married over the summer. I was invited to the wedding, but my stepfather had just had a stroke and mom needed me around."

Although I didn't give a shit, I asked, "Oh, I hope he's okay now. Did he pull through?"

Fortunately, Milly had to answer a switchboard call, so I snatched the paper from her outstretched hand and was back on the train to the World Trade Center by 9:45.

On the ride back to New York I decided to use the information I'd gathered to our advantage. I just hadn't yet figured out how. One option was to let his wife of four months know he was already fucking around. That would kind of even the score. But an even score wasn't my objective. As much as I'd like to fuck up this guy's life, I wasn't sure about his overall sanity. I mean, if I told his wife about his affair with Annie, maybe he'd go nuts and take it out on Annie in some way. That was unacceptable. If Mrs. Hoffman was to find out about the affair, it couldn't come directly from me. I decided to put that option on the shelf, at least for now.

No, the better option was direct confrontation. I needed to let him know his harassment of my wife had to stop. I needed him to think that I was capable of much more retaliation than was actually the case. He needed to believe I would hurt him, that I was capable of taking a bat to his knees.

The problem is, anyone who knows me would know I'm not that kind of guy. I mean, I'd do pretty much anything to protect my wife, but the thought of hitting someone with a bat, just as an example, and hearing bone crack or seeing blood erupt from someone's head, well that's just not me. I get queezy at the thought.

No, I'm more the sort of guy that would hire someone to do it for him, or just figure out some sort of sneaky indirect way to get my point across. That brings me back to the notion of having someone else get the message to Mrs. Hoffman. Then, she'd be the one to kick the shit out of dear Chris. He'd never know that Annie or I were involved, although he'd probably have his suspicions.

All of this is what went through my head back at my desk. I kept thinking of how I might use the information gathered to my advantage. My goal was to make sure he never bothered Annie again. Period. If, along the way I could somehow inflict some sort of physical or emotional pain on this prick, that would just be a bonus.

I think it was around lunchtime that I came up with my plan. If Chris Hoffman was skiing, then I want to ski. I need to ski. I could drive up there Saturday morning and hope to find him on the slopes. I'm a capable skier and have been to Jay Peak many times so I know my way around. If I wear a ski cap and goggles, there's no way anyone would know it's me. Now, I'm free to impose my self-ordained justice. I just hadn't figured out what that would be.

But six hours in a car would give me plenty of time to work out the rest of my plan. First, I had to come up with a plausible excuse for my absence. I hated the idea of lying to Annie, but I didn't want her to know what I was up to. Actually, I had no idea yet what I was up to. But I had the sense it wasn't going to be completely legal, so no need to get my wife involved.

I decided on the following, which worked well, and I was surprised how easy lying came to me. I would say I had to work all day Saturday, something that had happened before. Then to cover the last few hours, basically, my drive home, I would say I was going straight from work to a poker game at Jerry's. That would allow me to leave the house at around 7:00 A.M., drive six hours to Jay Peak, confront my wife's ex-lover, and be home by 11:00 P.M., no questions asked. I'd just need to secret some ski clothing in my car. Even that wouldn't be a problem as Annie was unlikely to be awake when I left.

It all seemed surprisingly easy to plot. The difficulty came in the execution.

Saturday morning was crisp but not so cold that skiing would be uncomfortable, even three hundred miles to the north. Annie never awoke as I carried my ski gear from the basement to the Pinto. We didn't have our own skis or boots, so it was just my ski jumpsuit, goggles, a heavy black cap, and extra socks. I backed out the driveway convinced I was doing the right thing; sort of going off to war to project the honor of my bride. I still didn't have a complete plan for the day but knew a long drive lay ahead. I'd think on the thruway.

But my first thoughts were of Annie. When I left the house, she was lying face down, entangled in the yellow sheets her mother gave us last Christmas. She looked beautiful. Part of me wanted to go back, forget my sinister goals, and get back into bed with her. But that would only add to my anger.

In one of our sessions, our marriage counselor made it clear to me that Annie's reluctance toward physical intimacy with me was completely normal and to be expected considering what she'd been through. First, there was the self-loathing stemming from her guilt about what she'd done. Dr. Foley explained that Annie might feel unworthy as a wife for some time. I had to be patient. Then there was the attack in the car. She still hadn't told me exactly what he'd done to her, other than to say she hadn't been raped. But it was some level of physical attack and violation. He said it might take a while for her to feel safe with me again. That, in some way, I represented all men, and all men are potential rapists.

Anyway, we hadn't had sex since her affair, which was now about five weeks ago. I think I was doing a pretty good job of being patient. Whenever Annie was ready, was okay with me. This was something I didn't want to screw up.

Then there was the other side; the side Dr. Foley never touched on. In some odd way, I was intimidated. Maybe it was the idea that sex with me wouldn't measure up to what she had with Chris. After all, with him she was intoxicated by passion. Maybe that was the best sex she'd ever had. What if everything after that was a disappointment? Could I stand to see disappointment on her face as we cuddled side by side after sex?

And there was something else. A part of me felt that my space had been invaded. That another man had been where only I was supposed to venture. We were married. Didn't I have a right to exclusivity in the space between my wife's legs? I know it sounds strange but that's how I felt and I'm being honest about it. This all made me very angry, an anger I'm not sure I understood at the time. I was subconsciously angry at Annie and I was overtly angry at the prick who invaded my space, no pun intended.

It wasn't until years later, after my own affair, that I understood this anger because now it was directed at me. But…, I'm getting ahead of myself.

So, while driving north on the New York Thruway and then the Northway, I formulated what I thought was a sound and reasonable plan. It took a couple of hours, but I was pretty sure it was the appropriate level of confrontation, intimidation and bravado. But I still wasn't sure I had it in me to pull it off.

My plan was to first find him. On a mountain as huge a Jay Peak, that might take some time. But I was sure, if I planted myself at the base of each of the chairlifts, eventually he'd come by. I'd get a good look at what he was wearing so I could spot him on the slopes. I'd shadow him on the mountain for a few runs to get a sense of his skiing style. Nobody skiing down a steep hill would ever know they're being followed, stalked from behind.

When I became familiar with his turning radius, I'd pick a spot to ambush him. I'd cut him off and force him to veer off the trail and into deep snow. I'd make sure our impact, if any, wasn't so severe that I'd fall but I wanted to make sure he did. When a skier falls in deep snow, they're in a difficult position. It's impossible to extend an arm or ski pole to try getting back on your feet. The snow's too deep. All you can do is take off your skis and sheepishly make your way back to the trail. And I wasn't going to allow that.

Once he was on the ground, with me standing triumphantly over him, hopefully a few feet away, I would scream, "If you ever go near Annie again, I will come back and kill you. That's a promise." Then I would turn on my skis and ski down the rest of the hill, go straight for the parking lot and drive home a victorious gladiator.

It was a wonderful plan. As I exited the highway at the Jay Peak sign, I was filled with enthusiasm. I was confident. I was looking forward to humiliating him and then threatening him. It was perfect.

But, that's not what happened.

****

I arrived at Jay around noon, rented skis, boots and poles, then did a couple of runs on the Sundowner just to loosen up. Sundowner is an easy run that ends back at the main chairlift near the base. It was still early in the season, but the mountain had a good base and the Jay Peak personnel had done an excellent job of snowmaking and grooming. I took special note of the snow's depth just a few feet off the trail.

Then I went up to the Jaytrain lift, about half-way up the mountain. Jaytrain led to a bunch of blue runs and a few black diamonds. I was hoping my target wasn't skiing the black diamonds. It would be much more difficult for me to keep up with him on such steep slopes. I'm not that strong a skier.

Once I had the lay of the land, I skied down to the base and planted myself against a ski rack a few yards from the main chair lift. From there, I had a clear view of everyone waiting on the lift line. Sooner or later, if Mr. Hoffman was coming down to the base, he'd have to get on this line.

While I waited, it began to snow lightly. The pleasant and peaceful feeling that light snowfall, without any wind brings lulled me into a sense of calm I hadn't felt in weeks. Perhaps it was my resolve. Perhaps it was simply that I finally had a plan to execute. I don't know why but I began humming the Beatles song "Yesterday". And once it was in my head, well, it wasn't going anywhere.

The digital thermometer on the building attached to the chairlift read 29F, which is a delightful temperature for skiing, but kind of cold if you're just standing around waiting for your prey. I could already feel my back stiffening a bit.

I ate the Milky Way bar I'd stuffed into the zippered pocket on my ski jacket and prepared myself for a long wait.

After an hour, I kept seeing the same people going up the lift. If Chris Hoffman was skiing this mountain, he wasn't coming back to the base, he was taking the higher runs and using the Jaytrain lift back to the top. I needed to move up the mountain, so I took the lower lift up to the Jaytrain lift and repositioned myself there. Because only more advanced skiers would be on the runs on this part of the mountain, the lines on this lift weren't as long as below. And this chairlift only accommodated two skiers at a time.

The snow was now falling a bit harder but still, there was little wind. The new powder made for excellent conditions and if I wasn't stalking my prey I would have enjoyed getting up on the mountain for a few runs. But first things first. I'd come this far. I needed to find him.

And it didn't take long.

Fifteen minutes into my vigil, a group of kids from the ski school lined up at the lift with their instructors. They all had the same yellow ski hats. I suppose this was the instructors' way of keeping eyes on their groups. The kids were about twelve years old, kids who were just short of caring about the opposite sex.

And just behind the yellow hats I spotted him. He was wearing a red ski jacket and aviator sunglasses. His long blond hair protruded from the black ski band that covered his ears. He cued up for the line next to a shapely young lady in a white one-piece jumpsuit. I couldn't tell if they were together or if chance had placed them on the same chair. Either way, I stepped onto the line and was only four chairs behind them. My chair partner was a guy from the ski patrol who was on his way up to the summit.

The ride took seven minutes. The ski patrol guy insisted on talking the entire way to the top. He filled me in on the history of the mountain, the depth of the base and how much snow they were capable of producing every night. If I wasn't so focused, I might have been interested in his monolog. But today I had other interests. The red Jacket four chairs ahead was my focus, my prey.

As Chris and the white jump suit stepped off the lift at the summit, they swished off in the same direction. It quickly became obvious they were skiing together. They both stopped to adjust their pole straps about fifty yards from the top of the chair lift. As my chair reached the summit and I was disembarking, I could see the two of them begin a leisurely run down the left side of the slope. I followed fifty yards behind.

The fact that he wouldn't be skiing alone had never occurred to me and greatly disrupted my planning. Who was this woman? His wife? Another lover? Or maybe just someone he'd met on the mountain? It's hard to read body language when two people are sliding down a mountain at twenty miles an hour. If the same two people were sitting in a booth at a quiet restaurant, I bet I could have told you if she was his wife. You can tell by the subtle differences between new lovers and people who have been married for years. New lovers, especially the females, laugh a lot and reach out to touch their partner's hands. They flick back their hair and make more eye contact than two people who have grown accustomed to seeing each other at the breakfast table countless mornings.

But there was no way to tell today. Obviously, there was no eye contact, no physical contact, and no conversation as they continued down the mountain in the lightly falling snow. She could have been his wife, his lover, his mother or a total stranger. And this presented an unforeseen problem. If they were skiing together, how could I isolate him for my ambush?

At this point, they were more than one hundred yards ahead of me and, if I hadn't seen them together on the chair lift, I wouldn't be able to tell if they were skiing together or two people who just happened to be swishing down the slope at about the same pace. At times, he'd be on the extreme right side of the slope while she was making a turn on the left. I continued my surveillance from a safe distance.

When they reached the bottom of the run, they got in line together for the chair lift and boarded a chair together. Okay, so they were together, but who is she? And how could I isolate him for the few moments it would take for me to execute my plan? I got on the chair just two behind theirs. This time I rode alone. It gave me time to review and modify my plan to deal with the added complication.

On the slow ride up, I realized getting him alone wouldn't be difficult, especially if they continued to ski as they had. If she made a long turn to the left as he was making one to the right, I could force him off the trail. By the time she skied back to the center of the slope, expecting to see him, she'd be sixty to seventy yards down the hill. Even if she spotted him in the snow, hopefully lying prostate beneath me, she'd be helpless to do anything. You can't ski uphill. It could work. It would work, I told myself. I just needed to find the right spot on the hill for my ambush.

My next run down the slope confirmed my resolve. They continued to ski in opposite directions, passing each other near the center of the hill, then each continuing in opposite directions until the next turn. Then the pattern would be repeated. They were both very competent skiers. I could tell he was a strong skier. She was graceful and very smooth on her turns.

Once again, I followed them from a distance. This time I was more focused on finding a spot on the right side where the forest cut in close to the trail and there was plenty of snow. Eventually, I found one that would be perfect. There were plenty of small trees to get in his way as I forced him off the trail. It was just below a snow-making gun so there was deep soft snow that had not been groomed. Snow that would swallow him when he fell.

But, best of all, my chosen ambush was on a bend in the slope. If she was even just fifty yards ahead, she'd already be around the bend and not able to see where he and I would be. It was perfect. As we neared the end of the run, I decided I'd execute the plan on the next run.

I cued up on the lift line just behind them. I wanted to be on the chair directly behind theirs so I wouldn't have a lot of ground to make up once we hit the slope. Like I said, he was a strong skier. It would be a challenge for me to stay with him even if we started together. Catching him if he had a twenty second head-start would be nearly impossible for me. I'm just not that good a skier.

But then the unexpected happened; an event that would have dramatic consequences for both our lives. Just as they made the last turn to position themselves to sit on the oncoming chair, she shook her head at something he'd said and stepped off the line. She poled her way to the right and disappeared into a crowd of other skiers. The attendant who was helping people onto their chairs motioned for me to step up.

"Move up. Take this one." He said with what sounded like a Canadian accent.

And before I knew it, I was on the same chair as Chris Hoffman; sitting just to the right of the man that had seduced, fucked and physically beaten my wife! It was surreal. I sat in silence for several moments as the cable lifted our chair ever higher into the air. He was taller than I'd thought. In a sitting position, he seemed to tower over me by a full head. He had broad shoulders and a skier's tan.

The snow was falling harder now, limiting visibility from the chair. Below us I could see ambitious skiers traversing the jagged and steep terrain directly below us. They were about forty feet beneath the chair and just about all I could see through the snow. The best of them skied between the huge boulders that lined the left side of the trail below. My eyes followed them because I didn't want to look anywhere else. I couldn't stand the thought of looking at my future prey; a man I was increasingly loathing with every breath.

"I thought I had that one bagged." He said as if to the wind.

"What?" I found myself saying incredulously.

"I met this coed from Vassar this morning. The one with the tight little ass in the white jumpsuit. We've been skiing together all day. I thought I was getting somewhere. Then, as soon as I suggest dinner in my hotel, she gets cold feet and takes off."

"Wow!" Was all I could offer in response.

"Yeah. Bitch." He said with callous distain.

That was the last thing he said for a while and I offered no further conversation. I sat there, stunned. Even if I wanted to speak, there were few words to express my contempt. This guy was fucking my wife a little over a month ago. He's married. And he's pissed off that some kid from Vassar had the good sense to run from him. I wondered if there'd been any others between Annie and the white jumpsuit.

He hadn't pulled the safety bar down yet and he asked me, "You want the bar down?"

I shook my head. I really wasn't thinking about our safety. I was thinking about my plan. In less than seven minutes we'd be at the summit and I'd have to chase this piece of shit down the mountain to my ambush point. And I was beginning to question the effectiveness of my plan. I mean, this guy was far more arrogant and a little bigger than I'd expected. What if my threats meant nothing to him? What if, instead of scaring him off, my threats only infuriate him? Could this make things worse for Annie? Would he now feel challenged to pursue her with even more ambition?

I couldn't have that. I promised her I'd make the problem go away. I promised her he wouldn't bother her again. I had to make good on that pledge.

Maybe I needed to abort. Maybe my plan wasn't strong enough. Maybe it wasn't as well thought out as I'd hoped. Already, there were obstacles popping up I hadn't anticipated.

Shit, the top of the lift was just a few hundred yards away. I needed to decide if this would work; if this would be enough. I needed make good on my promise. I needed to scare this prick off. But more than that, I needed to punish him for what he'd done to Annie. And, I'll be honest, I wanted to punish him for what he'd done to me; the way I felt humiliated by what he'd done.

There was very little time left. I needed to decide quickly if I was going to go through with this or if I needed to go home with my tail between my legs and regroup. I could already see the terminus for the chair lift rapidly approaching above us.

The snow was now nearly a squall. I could barely make out the skiers below us or the rocks they zigged and zagged between.

Suddenly the chair lift stopped, and we swung back and forth but no longer moved ahead. Such an occurrence is no call for alarm. Normally, it just means they stopped the cable to accommodate a skier who needed a little extra help getting on or off the chair. Usually, you'd start moving in a few seconds.

As we hung there, forty feet in the air, snow starting to stick to my goggles, I knew I needed to decide. When the chair started to move again, I'd have only thirty seconds before we were at the top. I needed a decision. Was my plan strong enough? Would it ensure Annie's safety? Would it guarantee he'd never want to see her again? Would it satisfy my promise to Annie?

I just couldn't be sure and not being sure was not acceptable.

The chair began to move again. I looked ahead at the lift terminus, barely fifty yards above us. Then I looked down at the snow below. The skiers were gone. The terrain was now too steep with many small rocks sticking up through the snow. Nobody could ski there. The cable hummed as it carried us closer to the top. I needed to decide. Was my plan enough?

It wasn't. Or, at least I couldn't be sure and that wasn't good enough. I needed to take action; to do something definitive. I needed to save my Annie and at the same time inflict an appropriate level of punishment to satisfy my tortured ego.

The chair now moved more vertically as we came within yards of the top. We were now about thirty feet above the rocks. Something screamed in my head, "Do something!"

Chris edged forward in preparation for our departure. As he did, I slid my poles behind his back and used the chair as a fulcrum to separate him from the seat. I pushed with all my might and he slipped forward and off the end of the seat. He tried to grab the safety bar, but it was too far above. He fell silently toward the rocks. I didn't watch. My eyes were on the attendants helping the skiers two chairs ahead of me. I wanted to be sure they hadn't seen what happened. They hadn't. No one was facing my direction. And from behind, it probably just looked like he'd fallen accidently. It happens.

I never looked down to see how he landed. I never looked back to see if something had broken his fall. He went down in complete silence. I never heard him hit the ground. For a moment, I feared he might have landed on his skis and slid down the hill unscathed. After all, he was an accomplished skier. Maybe he landed on a patch of deep snow and avoided the rocks all together.

But it was far more likely that the thirty-foot fall, the equivalent of a third-story window, would cause him some distress: maybe something between serious bruises and a couple of broken bones. That would get his mind off Annie. That seemed like an appropriate level of payback; proportionate punishment, if you will. A few months limping around in a cast would cool off his raging pecker. Think about something else, asshole.

As I disembarked the chair lift, I heard someone yell, "A guy fell off the chair! He's down there." The cry came from the women on the chair behind mine. As much as I would have liked to, I didn't stick around for the drama. I quickly made the turn from the lift and skied calmly down the other side of the mountain and directly to the main lodge. I returned my rented equipment and was in my car even before the ski patrol got the call of an "injured skier under the Jaytrain lift."

I felt exhilaration. I felt triumphant. It was a wonderful feeling. I'd made good on my scared promise. My woman was safe. And I'd extracted my pound of flesh. As I drove down route 101 and away from the Jay Peak, an ambulance screamed by in the opposite direction. I smiled and said out loud, "Take that you son of a bitch." In my rearview mirror, I saw the ambulance turn at the sign for Jay Peak.

****

It wasn't until the following Tuesday morning that Mr. Bideaux, Annie's boss at PMM, mentioned to her that, "That nice young man from Baker and Baker, the one who was courting our business, had been in a skiing accident. It seems he fell off a chair lift. I'm told the fall broke his femur and he bled to death on the way to the hospital. Poor guy had just gotten married."

XVI

As I sat in my kitchen this morning, trying to decide if I should eat the Eggo waffle that was staring up at me defiantly, I thought about how much I used to enjoy food. I loved food. Now, I eat six times a day simply to avoid nausea. The food has no taste. It's just fuel; fuel to keep me alive a little longer. Hopefully long enough for me to finish my journal.

Last night, I Facetimed my grandson, Peter. We chatted about the Christmas play he's been practicing for at school and how much I was looking forward to seeing him as one of the Wise Men. He has one line in the production, "We come with gifts", for which he's been rehearsing two hours a day, three days a week. And still, he's nervous about it.

My time on my laptop with Peter's angelic face looking back at me, made me think about just how much I love that kid. Sure, every grandfather loves his first grandson in a special way, but our relationship is different. Maybe because I spent so much time with him when he was just a baby, or maybe because it was a time that I needed just to be around someone; someone who was the future. It was just after Annie left me that I began babysitting Peter five hours a day while Lilly went back to work part-time. He was only about a year old and I got to watch him transform from baby to boy over those three years. It saved me.

And I still cherish my time with Peter, now more than ever. Perhaps because I know our time together is so short, I try to impart some nugget of grandfatherly wisdom each time we chat. Sometimes, it's as simple as reminding him of the importance of looking someone in the eye as you shake their hand. Or, how to know which direction is north when walking in a forest; something my father taught me long ago.

But this morning I realized why Peter is so important to me. It's not just that I love him. It's not just that he is my flesh and blood. I think he's so important to me because I understand he's the end of a line. He will be the last person on earth who ever met Leo Monday. Long after I'm dead and long after my children have grown old and perished, Peter will be the last person left alive who ever knew me; who ever actually met me, spoke to me, physically touched me, cared for me. The sole living testimony that I ever existed.

And, when he draws his last breath as an old man, hopefully surrounded by his children and grandchildren, he will extinguish the only flicker of light that Leo Monday ever existed. No one left alive after Peter, will have ever known who I was.

That sobering thought made me very sad.

Perhaps, writing will cheer me up. I wanted to tell you a bit about my career in the insurance and technology businesses. Let me begin at the beginning.

As I said earlier, straight out of college, liberal arts degree in hand, I landed a job at a mid-size life insurance company on Maiden Lane in lower Manhattan. I went through their training program and after a few months, was moved into the underwriting department. My role was to assess the risk involved with people who wanted to buy life insurance. In other words, how likely was it that they were going to die in the next few years and U.S. Life would have to pay a claim?

I know it sounds painfully boring, and it was. After a year, I was moved into the department that did the same risk assessment but for companies that wanted to buy life insurance for their employees. Remember, this was back in the seventies, long before anyone had a computer on their desk. So, when a new company came in, I would have to manually calculate the chances that each person would die in the next twelve months.

Let's say, for example, the new customer was a mom-and-pop grocery store that wanted to provide its ten employees with a $5,000 life insurance policy in case someone died unexpectedly, leaving behind a family, an unpaid mortgage, and a car loan. Each employee would fill out a card that, among other vital information about their health, included their gender and their all-important date of birth. My job was to manually enter each piece of data onto a piece of paper that looked a lot like graph paper. By figuring out how much insurance (risk) we were taking on at each age level and for each gender, I could manually calculate a rate that we would have to charge that customer for the total amount of insurance.

And when I say manually calculate, that's what I mean. After I wrote all the information on that graph paper-like form, I had to add it all up, which meant I used the state-of-the-art technology at the time- a manual adding machine. This green monstrosity made by the National Cash Register Company (NCR) took up half my desktop and required that I pull a large handle on its right side in order to enter each number. When I was finished entering the last number, I'd pull the massive handle twice to get a total. It was a modern miracle. And remember, this was several years after we'd put a man on the moon!

If I haven't put you to sleep yet, wait, it gets worse. After completing my task and coming up with the proper rate to charge mom-and-pop, I would hand off the paperwork to the drone-like creature sitting next to me and she would redo all my work, just to be sure I got it right. And the worst part is, I had to do the same for her work. And this went on all day long, five days a week.

Fortunately, my supervisor, a nice guy from Staten Island named Felix Lewis, cut me some mind-saving slack. As long as I got my work done each day, Felix didn't care if I took a two-hour lunch. And usually, I did. Sometimes I'd pick up a game of chess in the company cafeteria. Sometimes, after grabbing a slice of pizza, I'd walk a few blocks to the South Street Seaport, sit on a park bench and watch the boat traffic slide past on the East River. Sometimes I'd even take a nap.

This monotony went on for almost a year. It was my good fortune, that on a cold morning in November, I happened to board the same elevator as Michael Chatterton. Chatterton was the head of a three-man department known as information technology. At the time, I had no idea what that meant. And, at the time, everyone thought Chatterton was nuts.

"Hey, you work for Felix, don't you?" He started what would be the most fortuitous conversation of my life. "Felix told me you beat him at chess pretty regularly down in the cafeteria. Is that right?"

"Yeah, maybe I win four out of five." I proudly reported.

Chatterton gave me an odd look from his side of the elevator. Then he blurted out, "Okay kid. What's the bigger fraction, five-sixths or seven-eighths?" I later learned it was a test he gave people to instantly determine if they were intellectually worth his time.

"Seven-eighths," I reported almost instantly.

He ran his hand through his longer-than-acceptable hair. I studied him while he seemed to be thinking to himself and staring straight ahead. He was a few inches taller than I but weighed twenty pounds less. He made no attempt to dress like other people at US Life. While most of us were aspiring to someday make it to the twenty-third floor, where all the suspendered guys worked, Michael Chatterton had no particular aspirations within the corporate world. All he wanted to do was play with the company's new toys. And those toys were a pair of IBM computers that were supposed to bring us into the light from the dark ages.

Chatterton had been hired straight out of M.I.T. to head up the company's fledgling Information Services department. This was the guy that was going to rid us of those green monoliths on our desks and use the power of computing to revolutionize how insurance companies operated. Met Life and Prudential were probably two years ahead of us on this but Gordon Carlson, our CEO was a believer and was looking to catch up fast.

"You got some time today to have a chat?" He asked without looking at me.

And that's how I was saved from the underwriting department and came to work for Michael Chatterton. The late seventies and early eighties were exciting years to be around technology. Everything was happening so quickly. Those miracle-working machines in the basement, transformed how work got done. We went from pulling a lever on an adding machine, to electronic calculators, then to desktop terminals that were connected to the big basement brains that did all the computing.

Then, in the early eighties, Mr. Jobs over at Apple, figured out a way to put a colorful computer on everyone's desk at a price that corporate America couldn't resist. The personal computer was suddenly as ubiquitous in the office as was a stapler. Selectric typewriters, the wonder-machines just a few years ago, were now obsolete. Progress rocketed through the halls of US Life and Michael Chatterton was its astronaut. He was usually, one step ahead of most of our competitors, a quality that wasn't lost on our chairman.

In the beginning, working for Michael was like trying to hold on to the back of a surfboard that just caught a killer wave. I never knew what brilliant idea he would come up with next. Sometimes, I'd come in on Monday morning only to find our tiny office completely rearranged to accommodate the wiring required for his latest toy. Michael had done the work himself over the weekend because working with computers was his favorite pastime and he had no other real interests.

His reward for the efficiency he brought to US Life was an increasingly unbridled budget to "do more". The "toys" as Michael called them, were expensive. But management was sold on Michael's vision and that meant keeping up with his relentless demand for more technology. "There will come a time," he told the board of directors, "that we'll need only ten percent of the employees we now have. Machines will do all the work." That got their attention.

And Michael seldom failed to deliver on his bravado. By 1989, the company which had increased its revenues tenfold from the start of the decade, had six hundred less employees. Profits soared. The stock price soared and so did Michael's position in the organization. Instead of being the head of a support function, he was now a strategic planner. And, although he still didn't dress the part, he was moved to the twenty-third floor to be close to the other decision-makers. No one at US Life made a major decision without first consulting the "tech guy". Everyone wanted to know what was coming next and Michael always seemed to know. Or, at least he was happy to offer a well thought out prediction.

Luckily for Michael, few others on the management committee understood technology or its potential. They deferred to Michael on all matters that weren't directly insurance matters. They even consulted Michael when, in 1984, the firm decided to restructure its pension plan. It was Michael who nearly insisted they abandon the pension plan in favor of a 401K savings plan, something virtually unknown at the time. "You can't retain the best people by offering them their father's pension plan. People want to control their own destiny. Let them save on their own. And if you want them all rowing in the same direction, give them stock."

For that single idea, Michael became something of a cult hero at US Life. The company froze its old pension and installed a 401K plan. He insisted the company's contribution be made in US Life stock, and since the stock price was soaring, everyone was happy with the decision.

And instead of a cash bonus, Michael asked for annual stock options which the company was happy to grant its visionary seer. As a result, by 1989, he was the highest paid Chief Information Officer on Wall Street, not because of his direct compensation but due to the value of his options. In a decade, the stock had moved from under ten dollars a share to one hundred forty-six. Most of Michael's options were granted in the thirties and forties. He was suddenly a very rich man.

And it was my good fortune to be along for the ride. Michael had taken me under his formidable wing. And, for some reason, technology, a field I'd heretofore ignored, came very naturally to me. It just all made sense and I was one of the few people who could follow Michael's ranting visions. As a result, he gave me increasing levels of responsibility, staffing and money. By the time my daughters were born, I was making more money than I'd ever dreamed possible, allowing Annie to comfortably stay home to be a full-time mother.

I remember someone once asking Peter Fleming, John McEnroe's doubles partner, what was the secret to his tennis success. He and McEnroe had won just about every doubles tournament they entered. Without hesitation, Fleming responded, "Just pick the right partner!" Well, that was surely the case for me. Michael Chatterton was the reason I had achieved the success I had. Without him, I never would have been turned on to the miraculous world of microchips, terabytes, and the soon-to-be world wide web.

That's why I was stunned when he came into my office on a Friday afternoon in November 1989 and said, "Leo my boy, it's time for us to leave."

"Leave what?" I asked. I thought he meant, leave for the weekend.

"It's time for us to leave US Life and start our own company. I'll run the tech and you run the business. You know I have no patience for the business side."

"What the hell are you talking about, Michael?"

He sat on the chair next to my desk and leaned in as if someone might overhear. "Look, what we do here we can do for a thousand other companies. Once our guys write the code to do a task, that same code can be used elsewhere. But it's not. It just gets wasted. I want to use what we're capable of doing for one insurance company, for many. And it's not just insurance. We can sell our applications to anyone."

"Why would anyone else need us. They have their own IT departments?"

He smacked his hands together as if I'd just figured out the puzzle. "That's exactly right! They all have their own IT departments. They all spend millions on hardware, software, and people. They do this just because they think it's the only way to do it. Well, why can't we put together the best hardware, software and people, then rent ourselves out to everyone? Hell, most of the code we write could be used in so many ways. It kills me to see it wasted."

Years later, what Michael was describing to me that day in my office, became known as outsourcing. And it made perfect sense. Why does everyone need their own computers? US Life for example had a room full of massively powerful machines that were capable of doing the work of ten insurance companies. Why not share their untapped potential?

"Why should a company that is focused on selling insurance, be distracted by anything that doesn't directly help it sell insurance? Why should a bank, for example, spend millions every year on a bunch of programmers it doesn't know how to manage and for whom it can offer no career path? They're not bankers, they're computer programmers. Why not centralize the best hardware and talent, then sell those services back to the insurance companies and banks so they don't have to be distracted from their real purpose?"

Apparently, Michael had given this a lot of thought. He was full of great ideas. And I quickly found myself as excited as he was. But the thought of leaving the security of my current job was terrifying. I had three young children and a wife who no longer brought home a paycheck. I was our sole provider and although I was making great money for a thirty-seven year-old, we hadn't yet gotten to the point where I could afford to be without a paycheck, even for a few months.

I expressed my concern to Michael who laughed. "Listen to me, Leo. I've thought about this a lot. You're not going to miss a single paycheck. No one is. What do you think would happen if you and I and say, our best thirty people were to quit tomorrow? What do you think Carlsen would do? He'd be fucked. There'd be no one left to do even the simplest tasks. Hell, I doubt anyone would even know how to get the dumb terminals to turn back on Monday morning. They need us."

I must have looked confused because Michael shook his head. That was what he did when people weren't keeping up with him. "Look, I'm not proposing that you and I quit to form our own business, then search around for our first client. That would require massive capital. No, what I'm proposing is that I talk to Gordon on Monday and tell him that I'm leaving and that I'm taking you and our best thirty people with me. That I'm going to set up shop somewhere outside the city where rents are much lower and that he's going to be my first customer. From his perspective, nothing will change. The same work will get done. The same people will be doing it. It's just that we'll be doing it as a separate company. We'll no longer be on his payroll. And because we can spread the cost of all the hardware and people out over a dozen clients, his cost will be lower than they are now. And we'll make a fortune."

My mind was immediately focused on the computers. "Hey, since we'll all be gone, what's he going to do with all that hardware he's got in the basement?"

For the first time I could remember, Michael was looking at me like I'd just out-thought him. He smiled broadly and leaned back in his chair. "Son of a bitch! He'll sell it all to us for pennies on the dollar! Brilliant, Leo."

And that's how MAC Technologies came to be. Just as Michael had predicted, Carlsen and the entire board supported his idea and were happy to be rid of the overhead associated with an Information Technology department. And they were happy to sell us the hardware they no longer needed. The only concession Michael needed to make was to agree to a five-year contract for our services, and that US Life would be our only client for at least one year. Both provisions had been anticipated by Michael who gladly agreed.

Less than a month later, just before Christmas, contracts were signed. Michael again came to my office and sat, this time with a broad grin on his face. "Leo, my boy, I'd like to officially offer you a job at MAC Technologies."

"I kind of assumed I was coming along."

"Well, I want you, no, I need you to run the place. I need to focus on the creative side. I don't want to be bothered with all the bullshit around financials and people and sales and marketing. That's for you. You be the COO, hell, you can be the CEO. I don't care. I just need to know I've got someone I can trust. And I trust you."

"Michael, you know I'll do whatever you need."

"Great. Here's my list of who I want to take with us. There's twenty-seven names on that list. I've negotiated a nice severance package for the eighteen we're not taking because they'll be nothing for them to do here after we're gone. Seems only right."

"Have you talked to anyone yet?"

"Nope, that's your job. As soon as we get back from the Christmas break, you and I will meet with the people we're taking and giving packages to the one's we're leaving behind. I need you to have that crap ready for January second. No sense it putting it off."

My head was starting to spin thinking about how much work I'd need to do in the week between Christmas and New Year, a week I'd planned to take off. "You think we can get this all done that quickly?" I asked.

"Have to. Our new contract starts on February first. I negotiated to physically stay here till we find a place of our own but that shouldn't take more than three months." Michael was excited and it was evident by his body motion. Change was his catnip and he was biting off a whole lot of change. He looked exhilarated.

He probably saw the skepticism on my face. "You can do it kid. I know you can. I've already got some space in mind. It's sixty percent less than what they're paying to keep us here. We could have it fitted out for the hardware that's coming in less than a month. It's going to be great."

"You mind if I take Christmas Eve and Christmas Day off?" I said with a hint of sarcasm.

"Both?" He said straight faced. Then he burst out laughing.

"Kid, this move is going to make us both rich. The first few months are going to be rough, but they'll be worth it. I promise."

I suppose the skepticism on my face was still obvious.

"Leo, humor me. Pick a number from one to ten."

"For what?" I asked.

"Just pick a fucking number!"

I decided to play along. "Okay, four."

"Excellent! Your new salary will be four times what you're making now."

"Seriously?"

"Absolutely."

"What would you have done if I'd said ten?"

"Doesn't matter."

"Why's that?"

"Because Leo, you're going to make a lot more than that anyway!"

And Michael was right. MAC Technologies was a huge success and I enjoyed running the business. He did all the strategic planning, I made it happen. I came to understand that when a CEO doesn't have to concern himself with strategy or vision, his life is pretty straight forward. All I needed to do was implement Michael's vision.

By the time our constraint about not having any other clients was lifting, there were seven sizable companies waiting to sign on. Three were Fortune 500 companies. My challenge was to keep up. At times, it was like trying to hang on to a bucking bronco, where Michael and his ideas were the bronco and I was the rider.

But he was absolutely right. Once the computing capacity was in place, adding seven new clients was simple and involved only minimal additional personnel and equipment. Our overhead was fixed because he'd built in such over-capacity to start. He was a strategic genius.

At the end of our first fiscal year, Michael suggested we pay all employees a fifty percent bonus. I thought this was exceedingly generous until he told me my bonus would be $600,000, bringing my total compensation for the year to a nice round one million dollars.

"That's not all kid. I believe, in order to get everyone rowing in the same direction, I believe they have to have some skin in the game. So, I want you to come up with a plan that distributes twenty-five percent of the company stock to our employees. They can't sell it, but they'll share in the business' profits according to their ownership interest. This way, everyone cares as much as we do."

He leaned forward and clasped his hands together. "Look, you know me. It's not about the money for me. Shit, I like money as much as the next guy but what I want is the ability to play. And this place lets me play. I don't want to be a pig about it and I don't need more than..." He scrunched his face as if calculating. "As long as I keep fifty percent of the profits and seventy-five percent of the voting shares, I'm satisfied."

He could see I was quickly doing the math in my head. "That's right Leo, you get the other twenty-five percent."

I was flabbergasted. Michael was giving away a small fortune and the potential for an enormous fortune if his vision was even close to correct.

"But the equity comes with a leash. You'll get twenty-five percent of the profits each year, but the stock isn't yours for ten years. You need to stay with me for ten years Leo. Can you do that?"

"I'll have the papers drawn up," I said with a huge smile.

****

Although I couldn't wait to get home and tell Annie the news, Michael had one more surprise. This one was even bigger.

"Look kid, you know I can't stand to be bored. I have to be challenged. It's my oxygen."

I nodded, unsure where this might lead.

"So, I'm taking half the company's resources and moving in a whole new direction. In nine years, the clock will strike midnight on Cinderella and all the computer code that's ever been written will be useless. It will be worse than useless. It will be dangerous."

I knew he was referring to what came to be called the Y2K problem.

"Every line of code written in the sixties, seventies and even into the eighties only allowed two digits for the year, as if we were never going to leave the twentieth century. This is true in business, academia, hell, even the government and military. Even NASA didn't see this coming, or if they did, choose not to deal with it yet. Well, in nine short years, when we hit the year 2000, we all have to deal with it."

Although computer programming wasn't my thing, I did understand that the problem wasn't fixed by just adding two more digits to all the code imbedded deep within our software. It was a lot more complicated than that.

"So, MAC Tech is going to take the lead on this and become synonymous with the solution. We are going to be the company every financial institution wants to use to save their asses. There's trillions of dollars at risk here."

The gravity of the Y2K problem wasn't lost on me. I'd read a few articles in magazines on the subject. But I couldn't understand why the solution wasn't as simple as two more digits.

"The problem," Michael explained, "Is that we don't even know where these bugs are hidden. We don't know in how many places a programmer placed a line of code that refers to a date. It's a monumental task to fix with huge consequences if you miss one line of code. And we're going to be the solution. We're going to be the best at this."

And, as he usually was, Michael was right. As the horror stories in the New York Times began to appear, people started to listen. By the end of 1992, there was wide acceptance that this would be a major problem, not just financially, but also a safety issue. Stories began to surface about elevators plunging to the ground at the stroke of midnight, planes falling from the sky, or dams bursting because some minor computer application thought it was January 1, 1900 instead of January 1, 2000. Most was pure hyperbole, but in each, there was a gain of truth. And no CEO wanted to be the guy that didn't spend enough getting ready for the problem. No one wanted to be the guy with the burst dam.

MAC Technologies did become the leader in the solution, although others quickly followed. Even so, this end of the business was wildly successful financially. By the time New Year's Eve 1999 rolled around, and the world held its breath, MAC had become a technology powerhouse. Michael had been on the cover of several technology magazines, cited as the guru of Y2K. He was so confident in the work his team had done, and as a symbol of his arrogance toward his competition, he took off for an Aspen ski vacation before Christmas and didn't return to the office until January third.

And, when he returned he'd already set a new course for the firm. With Y2K behind us, Michael needed a new challenge and he found it in the internet. He was intent on creating a search engine that would allow the average user to see the internet as his own personal encyclopedia. As the new millennium began, most companies, and nearly all individuals had yet to embrace the power of the internet. But Michael saw things years ahead of others and wanted MAC to become the door through which all information passed to the end user.

Throughout this period, the company he'd created had been hugely successful. By 2000, I was the CEO of a major technology company that employed seven hundred people in the U.S., another three hundred in Europe and had climbed to number sixteen on the Inc. 500 list of the fastest growing privately held companies. In our best years, I made nearly three million dollars and even in years when we reinvested most profits back into the business, I was paid well. Michael continued to be a generous general.

But, on a clear crisp day in September 2001, it all changed. Michael and three of his senior tech guys were attending a symposium on some arcane topic at Windows on the World on the 107th floor of the World Trade Center. After the second plane hit the south Tower, Michael called me.

"You watching this on TV, kid?"

"Yeah, Michael. We're all here in the conference room watching. What are they telling you?"

But he never answered. I never heard his voice again.

****

Without his leadership, MAC Technology wasn't the same. Although we retained most clients, the company was in turmoil because Michael died without a will and his interest in the company became the subject of several court battles amongst his four siblings. I stayed on and helped the company limp through the next few years but by 2007, I'd had enough. My friend and mentor was gone. There was no longer any joy in the work. It was, for the first time, just a job. I'd made enough money. I didn't need to work. So, despite many offers to work elsewhere, on June 15, 2007, I retired.

It was a good thing I did because I was soon faced with my next major challenge.

Annie was sick.

XVII

Last night, I wasn't sure I'd still be alive this morning. Right after I got off the phone with Veronica, and lied to her bout my most recent fictitious doctor's appointment, my head started to throb. This wasn't just a headache. This felt like the pressure in my skull was about to explode. It actually felt like there was pressure behind my eyes trying to push them out of my head. It was horrible.

Then came the nausea. I barely made it to the bathroom when I surrendered what little dinner I had in me. I retched for several minutes. Then, just as quickly as the nausea and head pain had come on, it was gone. Both disappeared within minutes of vomiting. I was exhausted and completely spent but without pain.

I climbed onto my bed and braced myself for the next round of torture. But it never came. Instead, the fatigue of the day and the vomiting pulled me into a deep sleep, one from which I wasn't sure I'd emerge. It was the first time in my life I wasn't sure I'd awake from sleep. It was a terrifying feeling, but I suppose, one for which I need to prepare myself.

So, it is with greater resolve that I sit and write this morning. Last night, I came to appreciate the lack of new mornings I have left. I can't waste any more time. I need to finish this journal and there is still so much to tell.

So, let me tell you about Nicole.

I first met Nicole Sullivan on December 10, 1990. It was a Monday. As usual, I arrived in the office before most others. As I recall, on that particular Monday, I was the first one in. We'd only been in our new offices a few weeks. In fact, some of our people were still working at the US Life office while we got things set up at MAC Technologies. But the plan was to have everyone under one roof before the summer.

Our new office was a far cry from the posh surroundings we were accustomed to at US Life. Michael found three floors of office space in the garment district of Manhattan, which suited me fine since I was commuting into Penn Station, just a few blocks away. This was a far better commute than going down to Maiden Lane, US Life's home turf. But, of course, Leo Monday's commute wasn't what drove Michael to the garment district. It was the cheap rent. Which meant he could lease far more space than we currently needed and would be able to grow without relocating.

We learned with our first move, that relocating large main-frame computers isn't easy. Computers, like the ones we'd purchased from US Life needed special care; a dust-free environment and temperatures that would make most office workers uncomfortably cold. So, Michael dedicated an entire floor to the machines. The humans occupied the tenth floor and the computers were on the eleventh, clean and cool.

As I said, on this particular Monday, I was the first human to arrive on the tenth floor. Michael had insisted I take the largest office, the one in the corner with two glass walls facing the street and one facing our employees. From my desk, I could make eye contact with just about every one of our original twenty-nine employees. Remember, this was still before email, so having people in my line of sight was helpful. I could wave my arms and they'd know I needed them. Intra-office communication was simple.

I was going through some of the prior week's mail when my secretary, Judy, walked in.

"What brings you in so early?" I asked.

"I knew you'd forget. Hello! Vegas? Remember?" Her sarcasm was painful, but by now, Judy knew me well enough to get away with it. Especially when I deserved it.

I gave her a blank stare.

"Come on, Leo. I told you three times and even reminded you on Friday. I'm going to Vegas for the rest of the week. I know the word vacation is alien to you but for the rest of us mortals, it's an important thing."

"Sorry. Yes, now I remember."

"So, I've got a temp coming in who will unsuccessfully attempt to fill my shoes for the rest of the week. Please don't damage her."

"Now that's not fair."

"Yes, it is. The last time I got you a temp, she quit after six hours. If I recall, she said you were the most arrogant ass she'd ever worked for. And then she didn't come back the next day. You know what that means? That means, when I get back from vacation, I have to basically do a week's worth of my work just to catch up to Monday! That's the work the temp is supposed to do so I really get a vacation."

"Okay, okay. I get the message. Be nice to the temp." I had to say it or deal with Judy's relentless badgering until I acquiesced. Judy had been my secretary for six years and knew me better than I knew myself. Or, so she said.

"Good. She'll be here at eight. I'll spend a couple of hours with her, showing her the ropes, basically showing her how to survive you for a week, then I'm catching a plane from JFK at three-thirty."

"Seriously, Judy. I don't think I need anyone this week. I've got a conference downtown all day Thursday and Friday and it should be quiet around here until then. Why don't you tell..."

She cut me off. "Don't start with me, Leo. You need her. More importantly, I need her. Now, her name is Nicole Sullivan. Please be nice to her. At a minimum, please don't scare her away."

"Where'd you get her?"

"Regis. They usually send good people."

I had some calls I needed to make so I said, "Okay. Introduce me before you leave."

About twenty minutes later, while I had my feet on my desk and deeply involved in a conference call with two barristers in London, I notice Judy talking with an attractive woman outside my office door. Assuming this was the temp, I motioned for them to come in and take a seat on my sofa, the one Annie insisted I buy in case I needed to sleep in my office. I covered the receiver and whispered, "Be with you in a minute. They're almost done."

But they weren't. As Brits often do, they droned on for several more minutes until I said, "Look guys, if you can come to an agreement on the contract language, fax it to me. I just need to know where you stand by tomorrow morning, New York time. Right. Cheers." Then I turned my attention, all my attention to the women on the sofa.

"Mr. Monday, this is Nicole Sullivan." Judy made the introduction a bit more formal than necessary.

I dropped my feet from the desk and rose to greet her. She stood up from the deep sofa. Her navy-blue skirt and white button-down oxford blouse complimented a shapely figure. My guess was she was about my age, thirty-eight, or maybe a little older.

As I think back on the event all these years later, I don't recall thinking she was what most men would call beautiful. She was pretty, but in a unique way. Sensual, but in a very classy way. Tiny wrinkles at the corners of her eyes only made her more interesting. Her dark brown hair was silky, shoulder length and pulled back in a pony-tail. But it was

Nicole Sullivan's smile that any man would remember. It was a smile that made you smile.

"Nice to meet you, sir." Her voice was soft but throaty. I remember thinking she sounded like the actress Kathleen Turner.

"Well, let's stop with the sir stuff. It's Leo and it's nice to meet you Nicole. Please sit." I motioned for her to rejoin Judy on the black leather sofa.

"So, you'll be here the rest of the week?"

"Yes, just till Friday."

"Great. Well, I'm sure Judy's going to show you around before she heads out." Which made me think, "Judy, why don't you give Nicole a copy of that phone list we made up for the Board meeting last month? That should give her a reference about who's who."

"Already done. I also gave her the US Life phone book in case you need her to get in touch with people there." Judy was super-efficient and enjoyed reminding me of it.

"So, where are you from?" The awkward question was for Nicole.

"I live out on Long Island. Brookville. My husband has horses so we had to leave the city a few years ago. I like it out there."

I spent a few more minutes making polite small talk, then Judy reminded me of a nine o'clock meeting I had with Michael and a headhunter downtown.

"You'd better get going. I will probably be gone by the time you get back so if there's anything you need, let me know."

"Just confirm my lunch with Atul Chavda for noon at Hatsuhana. Leave me a note."

"I already did. You're on, but I don't know how you can eat sushi. It's disgusting."

"Not if you love it like I do. Nice to meet you Nicole. I'm sure, despite whatever Judy's told you, that you'll enjoy your week here at MAC."

And it was nice to meet her. And I still think that today. But, so many people would have been better off if we'd never met. Some would still be alive.

****

My downtown meeting with Michael and the headhunter ran a little late so I grabbed a cab back to the office alone. Michael was going elsewhere. All the way up Eighth Avenue I was thinking about how much I was looking forward to my sushi lunch meeting. Not because of Atul, a senior guy from US Life, but because I really love sushi and I was hungry.

So, when I returned to my desk and found a note from Judy saying he'd called and cancelled while I was downtown, I was very disappointed. I was about to head down to the building's cafeteria for a consolation-prize ham sandwich when Nicole knocked on my door.

"If it's okay, I was going to grab some lunch for a few minutes." She said.

"Sure. I'm heading out too. Just let someone out there know to cover the phones."

She lingered at the door a moment, hands behind her back. "How's the cafeteria here?"

"It probably won't kill you but it's not the Ritz."

Then I added, "Hey, do you like sushi?"

"To tell you the truth, I've never tried it."

"Well, I've been stood up by my lunch date but still have a reservation at the best sushi place in Manhattan, so would you like to try? My treat. It's just a few blocks away." I was hoping she'd say yes.

"Sure, thanks. I'll try anything once."

By the way, that's probably the most provocative four-word phrase any woman can speak.

So, we walked the three blocks to Hatsuhana and got a table along the window. We sat facing each other with shoppers strolling by on the other side of the frosty glass.

I ordered a mixture of sushi, sashimi and teka maki rolls, hoping that some of it might be to Nicole's liking.

"So, tell me about yourself." I asked. "You said you're married. Any children?"

"No, Roger has one daughter from his first marriage and we see her a lot. But no, none of our own." Her lips drew in tightly as if she regretted something.

"So, you and Roger live all alone out in Brookville? Aren't the homes pretty big there?" I asked while dipping a piece of pink tuna in soy sauce.

"Yeah. We live on almost ten acres. The horses take up a lot of space and need room to run."

"Do you ride?"

"A little, but the horses are Roger's. He plays polo."

Polo was something I knew absolutely nothing about. I mean, I knew it was a sport played on horseback and you use a stick to hit a ball, but that's about it. But Nicole explained how most good polo players need to keep several horses and actually used several during a match. Apparently, running up and down a long field carrying some entitled rich guy on your back while he swings a long stick and keeps whacking you on the legs, is tiring, and probably annoying for the horses.

Then Nicole changed the subject. It was obvious, she didn't want to talk polo.

"So, Leo..." She said my name slowly as if to be sure it was okay to call me by my first name. "Tell me about yourself. Are you married?"

I'm not sure why, but I felt it necessary to respond, "Yes, very much so."

Then I went on to tell her about Annie and our three kids.

"How did you and your wife meet?"

I told her the story about the Operation Sail adventure fourteen years before. Nicole thought it was very romantic, especially how I later tried to woo Annie at her office.

"So, was it love at first sight?"

"It was for me. I knew immediately Annie was the woman I wanted to spend the rest of my life with. I'm not sure if she felt the same way at first, but I grew on her."

"Tell me about your children."

"Stephen's the oldest. He was five in January. Veronica and Paula are his little sisters and he teases them constantly. But, They're all wonderful and, thankfully healthy." I think I talked about the kids for another twenty minutes. Then I realized, since Nicole didn't have children of her own, maybe she'd rather not have someone's else's happiness thrown in her face. So, this time, I changed the subject.

"Tell me more about you. What does Nicole Sullivan do when you're not temping at MAC Technologies?" I really did want to know.

She sat back and dropped her chop sticks on the table. "That was delicious. I guess I have one more food type I now love."

"I told you. So, tell me about yourself."

"Well, I usually temp a few months a year, when Roger is busiest with polo. From November to March, he's away a lot, traveling with the polo circuit. So, I like to experience new things. I mean, I'm not going to Florida to watch him play polo. I register with a temporary agency and ask to be put on one to two week assignments. That gives me a chance to see several different companies and meet a bunch of new people. I like it. It works for me."

I was curious. "Do you ever come upon a company that wants you to stay full time?"

"Yes, but I have no interest in full-time work."

"But wouldn't the pay be much better if you worked directly for the company instead of going through an agency?"

"It would. But I'm not working for the money. I just like meeting new people all the time. It keeps life interesting."

"So, you don't need to work?" I wasn't sure if I was now prying but I wanted to know all about this woman. The more she spoke, the more I was intrigued.

"No. Not really. I'm one of those very lucky people who had wealthy parents. They left me, how should I put it, financially comfortable."

"Are they gone now?"

"Yeah, they passed about five years ago, right before I met Roger. Actually, dad died in '85 and mom died the following year. I swear it was from a broken heart. She was so in love with my father, she was lost without him."

"That's tough." I was tempted to tell her about the similar fate that had befallen my parents but was afraid any conversation about my parents would lead to the origin of their pain- the death of my sisters. I didn't want to go there. I never did. So, I said, "Mine are gone too."

We sat in silence a few minutes, perhaps each reflecting on memories of our lost lineage. The waitress came and asked if we wanted dessert and since I wasn't ready to end our time together, I ordered green tea ice cream for both of us. Another first for Nicole.

Later that afternoon, as I sat through a boring presentation by a guy from CISCO, I couldn't help thinking about the way Nicole looked sitting across the table at lunch. There was something about her, something that kept bringing me back to that tiny table at Hatsuhana. Maybe it was the way the afternoon sun was lighting up her face. Maybe it was just the sound of her slightly raspy, but very sexy voice. Or maybe it was her intoxicating smile.

It was an innocent lunch. A boss taking a new employee out for lunch. Happens every day. So why did I feel like I'd done something wrong? I didn't flirt with her. And I certainly don't think she was flirting with me. It was just lunch. Two nice people enjoying good food. Two married people sharing stories about their lives over raw fish. Completely innocent.

So why did I feel like I couldn't tell Annie about it?

XVIII

The ride on the Long Island Railroad from Huntington to New York usually takes about an hour. But this morning, with a dreary cold rain falling outside, my daily commute seemed to be taking forever. It was Nicole's second day of work and I found myself looking forward to seeing her. I even wore my favorite yellow tie- the one I bought in Hong Kong when Michael and I were there in August. I save that tie for special occasions. Why did I think this was one?

I'm not going to tell you that I couldn't get her out of my mind. The truth is, once I got home last night, all I could think about was giving the three kids a bath and reading them stories from their go-to book of fables. It was a typical night at the Monday house. I made a point of getting home before seven whenever possible. And although I missed dinner with the kids, I got to spend an hour with them, usually on the floor of our family room. Then I'd get them to bed while Annie straightened up the kitchen and put away all the toys the kids and I had left scattered on the family-room floor. Once the lights went out upstairs, I'd come down for some reheated dinner and Annie would sit with me, sometimes with a glass of Merlot in hand.

I loved my life. I loved everything about it. I had a wife that adored me, three healthy kids, a beautiful home and a job that not only paid well, but that I truly enjoyed going to each morning. Few men my age were as lucky. And I knew it.

So, why was I daydreaming about a woman I only met the day before? A married woman. I had no idea. What I did know was that I hadn't felt like this since the day I met Annie. Why was this married woman having this effect on me?

As I disembarked the train at Penn Station and shuffled up the stairs with thousands of other commuters, I saw a woman selling small bouquets of roses. I wanted to buy a bunch and surprise Nicole. Sort of a thank you for having lunch with me. Fortunately, I realized how ridiculous that would seem. Or was I just conscious of what others in the office would think. I don't know which it was but I walked past the woman and got to work empty handed.

As I said, I'm usually one of the first people in the office and that day was no exception. I hung my wet trench coat and went straight to the kitchenette to start the Mister Coffee. I needed to read through two reports before a nine o'clock meeting so I brought my mug to my office and immersed myself in stats about IBM 3033's.

I found myself continually looking up to see if Nicole had arrived. Why was I doing this? I didn't understand it at the time. I'm still not sure I understand my sophomoric behavior. But, there I was, a thirty-eight year old married man, the CEO of a small company, acting like a lovesick teenager. Upon, reflection, I should have been embarrassed. But I wasn't.

I'd finished the reports and was writing some notes in the margins when I heard her voice at my door. "Good morning Leo."

I pretended to be deep in thought and raised one finger as if to indicated, "I'll be with you in one second."

Then, "Oh, good morning. Came back for another day, huh?" I tried to be cool.

"You're stuck with me all week." She smiled that million-dollar smile, then went straight to her desk.

I said a few words to her on my way out for my nine o'clock meeting, gave her three letters to type, and didn't see her again until after lunch. By then she was helping some of the other secretaries with their work and didn't even notice my return to the office. As I sat at my desk, I again found myself preoccupied with Nicole's every movement. It's hard to explain, but I loved watching her work. I liked the way she kept pushing a strand of errant hair away from her face as she typed. I liked the way she answered the phone. I liked the way she walked and the way she sipped her afternoon tea.

I glanced out the window just to get my eyes off her for a few minutes. It was starting to snow, our first snow of the season. I was thinking why a man with as much as I had, would think about another woman. I certainly wasn't unhappy at home. Why was I behaving this way?

My intercom buzzed.

"Leo, your wife is on line one."

Those words quickly brought me back to reality. I exhaled deeply before picking up.

"Hey love. What's up?"

"Sorry to bother you. I just wanted to see if there's any way you could get home a little early tonight. Stephen's got a little fever and I want to bring him in to Dr. Brussman to make sure he doesn't have strep again. Can you watch the girls? I can get an appointment at six-thirty."

"Sure. I'll get the 5:02. Does he have a sore throat?"

"No, but his temperature this morning was almost 102."

"Okay, I'll see you around six-fifteen."

"Thanks love. How's your day going?"

I glanced in the direction of Nicole and noticed she seemed to be watching me. As soon as our eyes met, she looked away.

"Good. I'll see you tonight."

"Who answered your phone? That wasn't Judy."

"Oh, no. Um, Judy's on vacation. She got me a temp for the week. Nice lady." I realized I'd used the term 'lady' to imply Nicole was elderly. I felt like a fool.

"What's she like?"

"Who?"

"Your temp. What's her name for when I call again?"

"Oh, um, Nicole, I think."

"You think? Don't you even know her name? Leo, you have to start taking more of a personal interest in the people around you."

"You think so?"

"Yes, I do. Okay, I'll see you later. Have a great day, love. Bye, bye."

I hung up the receiver and bit my lip. Why did I feel dirty? I now realize it was because that was the first time I'd ever tried to deceive Annie. In our fifteen years of marriage, I'd never lied to her. Until now. Maybe what scared me was how easy it was.

****

Well, I don't remember whether or not Stephen had strep. I don't remember what I wore or what was going on in the office on Wednesday morning. I don't recall the weather or where I ate lunch.

What I do remember very clearly is what happened when I returned from lunch. Nicole asked if she could talk to me, privately.

"Sure," I said. "Just give me a minute to return a few calls."

Once I'd gotten back to the two people who'd called when I was at lunch, I waved at Nicole through the glass wall, for her to come in. When she did, she shut the door behind her.

"How was your lunch?" She said nervously.

"That's what you wanted to talk about?"

"No, sorry."

"It's okay. What's up?"

"I don't know how to say this so I'm just going to say it." She paused.

"Say what? Are you okay?" I was genuinely concerned. She looked upset.

"Okay. Here goes. Ever since we had lunch on Monday, I can't stop thinking about our lunch. No, I mean, I can't stop thinking about…, you. I can't stop thinking about you."

I didn't know how to respond. I was frozen. No one had ever been so honest with me. In fact, no one had ever told me they couldn't stop thinking about me. No one, including my wife.

Fortunately, Nicole must have thought about this a lot because she continued before I could speak.

"Look, I know I sound crazy. And please don't misunderstand. I don't mean this in a sexual way. I just can't stop thinking about how nice it was to spend a few hours with you on Monday. Just to have someone to talk to so openly. I mean, I have a few female friends that I can talk to but I don't have any friends that are men. It was just so nice to connect with a man."

It occurred to me that similarly, I didn't have a single female friend. Maybe that's what felt so nice about our lunch. Maybe that's why I can't get her out of my head. Nicole was probably the first woman I enjoyed spending time with, invested in serious conversation with, that I wasn't trying to bag. I mean, when I was young and dating, anytime I'd meet a woman, I was always assessing them as a potential conquest; always thinking about them in a sexual context. And then later, after I was married, it was all different. Once married, I never thought about women I met as potential sexual partners. I already had one of those and the rules, as I understood them, said you could only get to have one. Right?

Nicole seemed to be uncomfortable so I told her to have a seat on the sofa. I came from behind my desk and stood, leaning on my desk, just a few feet from her. I said, "I think I get it. To be completely honest, I really enjoyed our lunch also. And, maybe you're right. I don't have any female friends that I spend any time with either. Maybe that's it. Maybe we both just experienced something new- an afternoon with a person of the opposite sex that was enjoyable but not because it was in any way sexual."

"Maybe." She offered but didn't seem convinced. She was staring at the glass coffee table that stood between us. "Maybe. But I think there's more to it."

I wanted to know more. "What do you mean, more to it?"

She rubbed her eyes with the palms of her hands. "I'm not sure. I just think there's more to it for me. I mean," she looked up at me, "I mean, I've never felt this way before. Not even with Roger."

Now I was a little uncomfortable. Flattered, but uncomfortable. This was not the kind of conversation I'm good at. Maybe that explains why I had no female friends.

"Look, Leo, if you want this to be my last day, I'd understand."

"No, no. Why would I want that?" I surely didn't. She seemed to genuinely be in pain and I hated to see that. Maybe that's why I said, "Look, Nicole, to be honest, I've been thinking a lot about our lunch too."

She looked up from her hands. "Really?" She said hopefully.

Well, I'd gone this far. Might as well go all the way. Might as well be completely honest.

"Yeah. And, to be honest, it's not the raw fish I've been thinking about." I swallowed hard.

"I've been thinking a lot about the way you looked sitting in that window. The sun was shining on your left side and lit up your face, just perfectly. I've been thinking about how beautiful you looked."

There. I said it. I felt like I had nothing to lose. Little did I know.

XIX

There are times in life when you're sure about what you're doing. Walking your child to class on the first day of kindergarten is one of those times. There's no question that is exactly where you're supposed to be and that is exactly what you're supposed to be doing. You know it instinctively. And even if there was something else demanding your attention, work, for example; you know you're doing the right thing by taking the day off and comforting your child on a stressful day. Few people would need to think about it.

Well, I was doing the exact opposite that night in early December 1990. I was sitting at a bar, waiting for Nicole to arrive. As I nursed my Vodka/tonic, I thought about how wrong this felt. I'd called Nicole from the conference I'd been attending earlier that afternoon, and asked if she'd like to join me for a drink before heading home. I even said it that way; "Would you like to join me for a drink before you head home?" That sounded innocent enough. That implied, she was definitely heading home and that this was just a brief stop on the way. Right?

So why did I feel so sleazy? Why did I feel like everyone at Harry's was watching me, judging me? There were probably thirty people sitting and standing along the u-shaped mahogany bar that encircled Harry's and it seemed they were all looking at me.

But I knew exactly why. It was because, instead of sitting next to me and sipping a glass of white wine, Annie was at home, giving the three kids a bath. And, because I'd draped my trench coat over the seat next to mine, reserving it for Nicole, I felt like a piece of shit. For the first time in my married life, I was meeting another woman for a drink; something I would not be able to tell my wife.

So, why was I doing it? To this day, I have no idea. Maybe it was just the excitement of being with someone who'd reached out to me. Someone who'd told me she couldn't stop thinking about me. That's heady stuff and perhaps my head was turned by something so simple.

After all, although the last few years in my professional life had been challenging and exciting, life at home was becoming a predictable routine of all the chores necessary to raise a family. In fact, life at home was all about family. Every minute of every hour I wasn't at work, was devoted to the children. Stephen was running all over the house and the girls were crawling close behind, leaving a trail of plastic toys, Golden books and baby-dolls in their wake. By the time I got home at night, stories, baths and PJs was all we had time for. And I was happy to give them 100% of my attention.

Then, after they were asleep, Annie would sit across the kitchen table from me as I devoured the leftovers and told her about my day. She'd use the evening to catch up on laundry and maybe a little TV, then we'd collapse into bed around ten so we'd be ready to do it all again in the morning. I was out the door by six A.M. There was little time for each other. Annie never called me during the day to say she couldn't stop thinking of me. She was far too busy being a great mother.

So, maybe that was it. Maybe I just wanted to be important again; important to a woman. And I certainly couldn't tell Annie that. I certainly couldn't tell her that another woman thought I was interesting, maybe even sexy.

Nicole said she'd meet me for a drink and could be down here by five-thirty. I guess I really hadn't thought it through. I didn't know what to expect. I just knew I wanted to see her. I'd been out of the office at a seminar all day and kept thinking about her. The seminar extended into Friday so, because that was due to be Nicole's last day, I wouldn't get to see her again. And the thought of never seeing her again bothered me. She'd created a thirst in me I didn't know was there.

"Hey stranger. This is a busy place." The voice came from behind me. It was Nicole. She had already taken off her coat revealing a lavender v-neck sweater that looked softer than a cloud.

"Did you save me this seat?"

"I had to fight off a hundred people who wanted it."

She caught the bartender's attention and ordered a "Beefeater martini straight up." Then she sat next to me.

The crowd at the bar and throughout Harry's was loud which meant I had to lean in close to her to speak. Her perfume was intoxicating.

"Did you take a cab down?" I asked.

"Yes. It's way too cold to wait for the bus."

We continued to exchange small talk by yelling towards each other. The cacophony in the crowded room made it difficult to hear each other without shouting but I enjoyed being so close to her. Each time I'd speak I would lean in, way in, my lips almost touching her ear. I could smell her and she smelled wonderful. And sometimes she would put her hand gently on my arm to pull me in closer. It also gave me a birds-eye view of the folds of soft skin peeking out from the center of her sweater.

Then, when she would lean in to speak to me, I could feel her breath on my ear and once, her cheek pressed gently against mine.

As much as I was enjoying the closeness, I offered, "Should we get a table and have some dinner? It will be a lot quieter in the restaurant."

She nodded and we took what was left of our first round of drinks with us to a table.

I don't remember much of the dialog over dinner. I suppose we both talked about our families, although Nicole didn't have much to tell. She seemed to be lonely due to her husband's frequent traveling to follow the polo circuit. He'd spend weeks on the road or in Europe competing in polo matches while she either did volunteer work or occasional temporary employment in the city. They'd been married long enough to understand the passion that once existed had been replaced by a practical cohabitation.

And, it was all on Nicole's dime. Roger's polo ponies and his extravagant lifestyle was supported by Nicole's trust fund; the one her mother left her year's earlier.

"Don't get me wrong. I'm not an idiot." She confided. "I knew going in, that one of the reasons Roger married me was for the money. I hoped it was only one of the lessor reasons. Lately, I'm not so sure."

I have to admit, I felt sorry for her. It must be horrible to think your spouse was with you for any reason but love. But, not being a guy that came from money, I never had to worry about such things. I tried to assure her by saying, "You know, sometimes men don't completely understand what they feel. Your husband may have married you for all the right reasons, but now that you've introduced him to a pretty nice life, well, no one wants to go backwards. I guess what I'm trying to say is maybe you've spoiled him."

She finished her first martini with a long final gulp, then said, "No. I don't think that's it. But let's change the subject. It feels funny talking about Roger when I'm sitting here with you."

So, we chatted about what was going on at the office and we each had another drink with dinner. The first time I checked my watch it was almost nine. The night had flown by. I loved talking to Nicole. I could have done it all night. But we both had to get back to the lives that were ours.

Knowing that the next time I returned to my office, she'd be gone, troubled me. I wanted to see her again. I wanted to somehow keep her in my life. But that wasn't going to happen. Nicole had already accepted a two-week temp job at a staffing company out on Long Island, starting Monday. It seemed like this would be the last time I'd ever see her.

So, when we left Harry's I suggested we share a cab up to Penn Station. At least we'd have a few more minutes together. As we entered the cab, I noticed a woman standing near the entrance to Harry's who looked familiar. For a moment, I tried to place the face. She glanced in my direction but didn't seem to recognize me. It occurred to me that if she had recognized me, I'd have to quickly come up with a plausible reason for being with another woman. What if she was someone who knew Annie? Someone from Huntington? What if?

It made me realize the dangerous game I was playing. If someone recognized me, even if I wasn't aware of being observed, they could innocently mention to Annie they'd seen me having dinner at Harry's. Since I'd told my wife I was staying late at the seminar to have a drink with some software developers, I'd be caught in a lie. What the hell was I doing? And for what? To stroke my ego?

"Penny for your thoughts." Nicole whispered across the backseat of the cab.

I had obviously seemed to be lost in thought and she was bringing me back to the taxi.

"Sorry, I was just thinking I saw someone I knew."

"And you're concerned because it would be uncomfortable to have to explain...", she paused, "explain me?"

"Yes. To be honest, yes. Boy, you're good at reading people." It was as if she'd read my mind.

"I'm sorry. I hope I'm not the cause of any problem for you."

"No, No. It's fine." I lied. "Can't I have dinner with someone who works for me?" I said it as if I was trying to convince myself. I hadn't, so I was happy when Nicole changed the subject.

"So, do you have a lot of Christmas shopping to do?"

"Not really. My wife either takes care of all of it for the kids or gives me a very specific list of things she can't find at the mall. Then I search for it in the city. I really only need to shop for my wife's gift."

"What will you get her this year?"

The question caught me by surprise, not because I hadn't given it much thought yet, which I hadn't, but because talking about Annie to Nicole didn't seem right. Or maybe what didn't seem right was that the reciprocal didn't work. I couldn't talk about Nicole to Annie.

"I suppose a piece of jewelry."

"Well, if you need help, call me. I love shopping for jewelry, especially when I'm spending someone else's money. I'm very good at that." She giggled.

Was she telling me she wanted me to call her again? Or was it just a sincere way to thank me for dinner? I'm very bad at reading women. Either way, I found myself saying, "Thanks. I may have to do that. Make sure you leave your number on my desk before you disappear tomorrow."

Our cab bounced over a sizable pothole on Eighth Avenue as we crossed 23rd Street. I knew our time together was growing short. We'd be at Penn Station in a few minutes and I didn't want the night to end. But I also didn't want to be seen walking through the busy train terminal with Nicole. More to the point, I didn't want to be seen saying good-bye to her. I'd decided a quick kiss on the cheek would be an appropriate way to end the evening and it would be better if I did that in the taxi then in a crowded terminal where countless people who commuted to Huntington would be walking by.

Emboldened by the wine, I said, "Nicole, I had a great time tonight. I really enjoyed our short time at the office and chatting with you tonight was wonderful. You're an excellent listener." It occurred to me that was one of the qualities I loved most about my wife- the fact that she was a great listener. So, why wasn't I talking to her? Why was I in the back seat of a cab with another woman?

"I had a great time too, Leo. I'm very glad I got to know you." Then she leaned across the seat and kissed me on the cheek. It was an innocent enough kiss but it was her body language that spoke to me. She put her hand on my cheek as she kissed me and held the closeness for several seconds, as if she too didn't want the night to end.

But when the cab pulled to a sudden stop, I knew the clock had struck midnight. Nicole jumped out the left side door before I could say good-bye.

"I need to run for my train," she called back to me as she disappeared into the crowd.

* * * * * * * * * * * * * * * *

I'd be lying if I said I wasn't thinking about her the entire time I sat through lectures at the convention on Friday. I even thought about calling the office just to hear her voice. And when my last class was over at 4:40 PM, I raced uptown in hopes of seeing her before she left for the day- her last day at MAC Technologies. But traffic was miserable and she was gone by the time I got back to the office.

The entire weekend, I couldn't get her out of my mind. Even as I helped dress the girls for a two-year-old's birthday party, my thoughts were of Nicole and how she looked at the dinner table two nights earlier. As Veronica and Paula squealed with delight when a clown twisted balloons into magical shapes, I wondered what Nicole was doing that moment. I wondered if she was thinking about me.

It turns out, she was.

XX

Here's one I'm not particularly proud of. It's been a long time since I've thought about this. But as long as I'm coming clean about my life's transgressions, you might as well hear this one too.

It was the summer of 1987. Annie and I had walked down the street to our good friends, Herman and Phoebe Nolan who were having a party in their basement to celebrate Herman's promotion at work. The Nolans had great parties and would be happy to throw one for just about any occasion. Herman had built a beautiful bar in one corner of his basement and left enough open space for two or three couples to dance without bumping into the washing machine in the other. Since no one else had a basement bar, we would usually gather at the Nolan's. Their children were already away at college so a little late-night noise wasn't a problem for them as it would have been for the rest of us.

This particular evening, much like many others, we were all drinking Manhattans, Herman's favorite poison. I remember we were playing Pictionary and dancing to a Billy Joel song but couldn't tell you which one. Phoebe was something of an artist with a Magic Marker so she and Herman had a huge advantage when it was their turn to use the easel and draw whatever came up on those colorful little cards. What I do remember is that all of us had more to drink than we should have and by two A.M. there were only seven of us left in the steamy basement. Besides our hosts, Herman and Phoebe, Annie and I were left at the narrow wooden bar with Alice and Nick Mulligan and one part of a great couple- Cindy Moss. I say one part because her husband Jack was a Commander in the Coast Guard and stationed elsewhere for a four-month tour. Jack wasn't due back to Huntington for another month. So, we sort of adopted Cindy on her own when he was away. When Jack was around he was the life of the party but Cindy was fun too.

We were having an extra loud discussion about whether or not Ronald Reagan could be reelected in '88, even though the constitution didn't allow for a third term. Herman was of the opinion that it would be impossible because he was too old. Nick was sure the Democrats had no one else to offer in his place. He insisted it would be a landslide in favor of the incumbent if elderly Reagan. The debate raged on through two more rounds of Manhattans. It would have gone on till dawn except that Annie noticed Cindy had her head down on the bar and was snoring.

"Why don't you politicians take her across the street?" Annie slurred a bit but clearly motioning in the direction of Cindy.

The Moss's lived directly across the street from Herman and Phoebe. It was a small Cape Cod they rented instead of buying because the Coast Guard never told Jack how long he'd be in any one place. It was tidy enough but stood out from the rest of the street because of its lack of shrubbery.

There were no plantings between the small patch of lawn and the brick house. I guess since they didn't want to put down roots, Cindy and Jack never got around to planting anything else with roots.

So, Nick and I helped Cindy stand then ascend the stairs where the fresh air seemed to have the wrong effect. Instead of reviving the young lady, it must have reacted with the oxygen in her blood to accelerate the alcohol's effect. Whatever happened, when we hit the street with Cindy she went completely limp and we needed to support her, one of us under each arm.

Now, you never met Cindy Moss so, let me tell you about her. She was about thirty at the time, a bit younger than us. She had a pleasant face but it was her body that caught the attention of men. She had a beautiful figure, one not yet ravaged by the trauma of childbirth or the rigors of motherhood.

The other noticeable thing about Cindy was the way she dressed. Some would say provocative. Others might go all the way to trampy. Whatever the adjective, she knew how to accentuate the curves nature gave her. And if you asked the other wives, they would say Cindy was a little too flirtatious, especially around their husbands.

As we lugged Cindy across the street in the fading moonlight, I asked Nick, "Do you think she left the house unlocked?"

"I hope so. I don't see any pockets on this dress to keep a key."

He was right. The blue polka dot dress that hung loosely around Cindy had no pockets. And when we arrived at the front door, sure enough, it was unlocked.

"Where should we leave her?" Nick asked.

I was a little concerned that we should leave her at all. She was unconscious. I didn't know a lot about how to deal with people this drunk. Is it safe to just leave them to sleep it off? Suppose she vomits and drowns in her own vomit? For a moment I considered calling 911 just to ask what we should do. But then Cindy stirred.

"Where we going?" she asked playfully.

Nick responded, "You're home honey. You need to sleep it off. You'll feel better in the morning." Although neither of us believed that was really the case.

Cindy was now resisting our support and stepped forward to stand on her own, something she did for just a moment. Then she leaned against the wall and whispered, "Could you guys just help me to my room? I need to sleep."

We assisted her down the short hall to her bedroom. As soon as we entered the room she lurched forward and fell onto the bed face down. Her dress had flown upward revealing a pair of tiny black panties concealing a fabulous ass.

"Do you think we should just leave her face down like that?" I asked Nick.

"Yeah. She'll be okay. She just needs to sleep it off. She was really pounding those Manhattans down."

"You sure it's okay if she's face down? What if she gets sick?"

"She'll be fine."

I noticed as we stood there discussing Cindy's well-being, we were both staring at her ass. I myself, had never seen such tiny black panties on a woman before. And, as I said, they barely contained an amazingly perfect butt.

"That's some ass!" Nick offered.

"Alice would cut your balls off if she saw you drooling like that."

Now before I tell you what happened next, you need to remember, we were both very drunk ourselves. Nick was a big guy but he'd had at least as many drinks as I and dragging Cindy across the street was probably about the only physical activity we could have undertaken that night. Also, remember we were married men who, except for an occasional peek at a Playboy magazine, weren't privy to views like this very often.

The back of Cindy's slender and well-tanned legs ran all the way up to her panties revealing a tiny bit of very white, untanned skin at the edge.

Nick and I looked at each other. Then we looked back at Cindy's ass. Then back at each other.

"We have to look!" Nick whispered.

I knew exactly what he meant but I said, "What? Look at what?"

"Leo my boy, you are never going to get another chance to see that ass. She'll never know."

"Are you crazy?

"No, I'm just really horny. Booze does that to me."

"All the more reason for us to get the hell out of here."

"No. Just a peek. Come on Leo." He pleaded.

"This is Jack's wife, Nick. For Christ's sake!"

"She'll never wake up and no one will ever know."

I wanted to protest further but the sight of Cindy's beautiful ass sticking up like that on the bed..., well, what can I say? I was as curious as Nick.

"Well, I'm not doing it." Was as close as I could get to the moral high ground.

"No problem brother. I'm on it."

"Try not to get any drool on her ass," I joked.

Nick knelt on the bed next to Cindy's limp but incredibly sexy body. He put one hand on each side of the black undergarment and gently pulled the silky fabric down half-way to her knees, revealing a milky white butt as perfectly contoured as I'd imagined.

"Wow! That's some ass." Nick stammered.

"It's nearly perfect," I responded.

"What do you mean, nearly? It is perfect. It's a great ass. I will hold this image in my head for a long time Leo. A long time."

"Okay. Push them back up. You can't leave her like this."

That's when Nick gave me that look. The look that said, "One more thing."

Before I knew what he was doing, he reached across Cindy and grabbed the Magic Marker from my shirt pocket. It was still there from the Pictionary game.

"What the fuck, Nick?"

"Oh, relax. I'm not going to hurt her."

Nick took the cap from the marker with his teeth and printed the word "GREAT" on Cindy's left butt cheek. Then he handed me the black marker.

"Finish the job Leo."

I thought for a moment. I needed the perfect word. But no word was more perfect, more simple than "ASS".

I then put the marker in my mouth and pulled up Cindy's panties, completely concealing our artwork.

I often wondered how long it was before Cindy caught sight of our work in a mirror. She never mentioned it. Ever. Nor did Jack.

XXI

My visit with Dr. Romaro this morning totally pissed me off. The man who, just a few weeks earlier, seemed to give me two ways to die, was now taking one of them off the table. When he learned I hadn't scheduled the chemo-radiation treatments, what I considered the lesser of his two options, he was furious. It was as if I'd insulted him by not taking the path he might have chosen. I thought if anyone would understand that I didn't want to die that way; puking every hour, losing my hair, my strength and my dignity, it would be him. After all, he'd seen so many of his patients go through that horrible ordeal, and for what? To prolong the inevitable?

So far, the discomfort, for lack of a better word, of having a terminal illness, has been bearable. Yes, there have been days when the headaches and stomach pain have been distracting, maybe even temporarily debilitating, but I'd rather deal with this and give up an extra couple of months on the back end; months that would have been a continually blurring nightmare of nausea, only to end in hospice, cared for by people I've never met.

Maybe that's part of it. Maybe, because I have no wife to be at my side, someone to hold my hand as I draw my last diminished breath, maybe that's why I'm afraid to die Dr. Romaro's way. And, although I'm certain both Veronica and Paula would insist on caring for me, that's precisely why I must die my way. I couldn't bear the thought of my beautiful little girls watching me atrophy. I wouldn't put them through that. I'd rather they be angry with me for deceiving them.

So, even though I'm pissed off at my doctor, it's a beautiful day. Central Park was blessed with a fresh two inches of snow last night. The view from my kitchen window is inspiring. The streets are already cleared, or in most cases, just an annoying slop of brown mush, but the park, its fields and its trees remain pristine. And so, inspired by nature's beauty, I will continue to tell you the story of another of nature's beauties. It's a good morning to type.

After our dinner at Harry's, I didn't see or hear from Nicole, but by the following Wednesday, thoughts of her were beginning to become a distraction for me. I couldn't get her out of my head. Every time I looked at the work cubicle once again occupied by its regular inhabitant, Judy, I thought of Nicole. I would imagine her face as it glowed in the candlelight and the intoxicating smell of her perfume when she kissed me goodnight in the cab.

And then there was the piece of my stationery on which she'd written her phone number. The piece of paper I'd been moving from one side of my desk to the other, and then back again. The piece of paper I'd thrown in the trash on Monday, only to retrieve it like a schoolboy Tuesday morning. It got to the point where I just liked looking at it. Perhaps it was the fact she'd offered it to me at all. Perhaps, I was letting my daydreams about what might have been get the best of me. Or, perhaps I just liked seeing her petite and flawless handwriting.

Whatever it was, it was beginning to control my every thought. And so, by Friday afternoon, I knew I had to do something about it. I pulled the piece of paper from under the onyx ashtray on the corner of my desk. For no less than fifteen minutes I debated with myself. Do I rip it into irretrievable shreds or do I call her? I clearly understood one action was right and one was very wrong. One was the behavior I pledged to Annie the day we got married, the other- a betrayal of that pledge. If I chose the latter, I knew I'd feel and think less of myself. If I chose the former, I'd feel morally validated. But would I always wonder?

With the paper in hand, I got up to close my office door. Then I returned to my desk and stared for several minutes at the black phone sitting to my left. I fingered the paper which was now fairly ragged from my constant abuse. In my mind's eye, I saw Annie standing in our kitchen preparing that night's dinner. Then I saw Nicole's face pressed against mine in the back of the taxi.

I dialed 1-516-721-8365, and waited. As the phone rang, I glanced through the glass wall that separated me from the rest of the company. I felt ashamed of what I was doing.

"Hello. You've reached the home of Roger and Nicole Sullivan. We're not home but if you leave a message we'll call you back. Please leave your message after the beep. BEEEEEP." It was a man's voice.

Of course! What an idiot. She said she was working somewhere out on Long Island this week because her husband was away. Of course, she wouldn't be home on a Friday afternoon. She was at work. I felt foolish. Yet, I felt compelled to leave a message. I can't explain why. Just like I can't explain most of my behavior with Nicole.

"Um, this is a message for Nicole Sullivan. This is Leo Monday calling from MAC Technologies. You, uh, worked here last week and I think we may need to fill a spot again so, if you're interested, please give us, ...uh, me, a call. My direct line is 212-967-6657. Thanks."

I was talking to an answering machine and I was as nervous as a teenager asking out his first date. It was ridiculous.

But as I was about to leave the office that night, my phone rang. Judy had already left for the day so I answered, "Leo Monday."

The voice on the other end was immediately recognizable. Her soft but raspy tone was like music to me.

"Hey Leo. I hear you're looking for me."

"Hi Nicole. It's nice to hear your voice." I really meant it.

"Yours too. I've been thinking about you a lot."

The schoolboy in me was thrilled. She was thinking about me!

"Yeah, me too. That's why I called." I wasn't sure where I was going with this conversation so I just pressed ahead as thoughts came into my head. "I was hoping we could have dinner again."

There was a long silence on the line. Then, "Dinner?" The question confused me.

Was she making a clarification between lunch or dinner? Was she reading my mind? Or was she implying dinner was just a cover for a more intimate evening? I had no idea, so I pushed ahead.

"Yes, I'd like to take you to a place in Little Italy I think you'd like. They make outrageous desserts. I think you'd like it and it's a great place to just sit and talk because it has a nice quiet bar."

Again, a prolonged and nerve-racking silence.

"That would be nice but I'm working out in Melville this week and next so I'm not in the city."

I was about to suggest a restaurant near Melville, but she offered, "What are you doing this weekend? It's supposed to be pretty warm and sunny on Saturday. I was planning to take a walk on the beach in the afternoon. Want to join me?"

I didn't hesitate for an instant. "Yes. Where do you walk?"

"Meet me at field Five at Robert Moses State Park. I'll be down by the water. I'll see you there around noon?"

"I'll be there."

"I'm glad you called, Leo. I'll see you Saturday."

And then she was gone.

****

On Saturday morning, I needed to take Stephen to a birthday party at McDonalds. Annie and the girls were going to a local nursery school to kick the tires. Annie felt the girls should start a half-day program commencing in January and today was their open house. It was a cooperative school, which meant in addition to the painful tuition, Annie would be required to work at the school, as a teacher's assistant, one day a week. She seemed enthused about it.

But I'd be cutting it close with Stephen's birthday party. It started at nine and was due to run till ten-thirty. I needed to drop him back at the house but Annie and the girls wouldn't be back till eleven, so my departure for the beach couldn't take place until I could hand off Stephen. The drive from Huntington to Robert Moses State Park on the south shore of Long Island, would take about an hour.

I'd already lied to my wife. I told Annie I needed to go into the city to pick up some papers I needed to sign. Just in case she would suggest I take Stephen with me, I enhanced the lie by saying, "I then need to take them to our lawyer's office and review them. It will only take about an hour." I knew Annie understood Stephen could never sit still in my lawyer's office for an hour, so it was a good excuse to go alone. Besides, he usually napped in the afternoon.

Lying to Annie was surprisingly easy but made me feel like a piece of shit. I mean, what the hell was I doing? I loved my wife. I loved everything about my life; my kids, my job, our home. Why was I meeting another woman to take a walk on the beach in December?

The truth is- I had no idea what I was doing or why I was doing it. Happily married men don't need to cheat, right? And this wasn't even really cheating, was it? I mean, I was going to take a walk with Nicole, not go to a motel. We were going to talk, maybe even about Annie and the kids. So why did I feel so miserable about it?

Looking back on it with the benefit of many years gone by- I think I know why. I felt miserable because I knew I was doing something very wrong, something that would hurt Annie terribly if she ever found out. But, to this day, what I don't understand is why I would risk hurting Annie. Why take the chance that she could find out? That part of my relationship with Nicole is still a mystery to me.

Having fulfilled my familial Saturday morning duties, I jumped in the car and drove down the Sunken Meadow Parkway to the place I'd promised to meet Nicole. It was a beautiful day, especially warm for early December and not a cloud in the sky. As I passed over the majestic suspension bridge that connects Long Island to the barrier islands to its south, I had a spectacular view of the beach, the rolling dunes, and Atlantic Ocean. As usually happens when I spy something beautiful, my first thought was, "Annie would love this." Realizing the irony in the thought, I turned my attention to the round-a-bout at the base of the bridge. As instructed, I went left toward parking field five.

The digital clock on my dashboard told me I was about five minutes late. As I pulled into the massive parking field, I saw not a single car. Unusual for a nice Saturday, but then again, it was December.

I parked in the front row and waited a few minutes to see if Nicole arrived. I listened to two disc jockeys rant about how awful the Giants were last week, then turned off the car and decided to walk down to the water. That's where she said she'd be. But I was growing increasingly convinced Nicole wasn't coming- that she'd thought better of this folly and decided to act like an adult.

It's a long walk down to the ocean. I needed to traverse several dunes of sand and beach grass before I could even see the ocean. But when I did, I saw her sitting at the water's edge, staring out toward the horizon. She wore a blue hooded sweat shirt with Boston Red Sox emblazoned on the back. Even from behind and at some distance, I could tell it was Nicole. Her dark brown hair was blowing in the gentle breeze.

"Boston, huh?" I said when I was just a few feet from her.

She was startled and turned with a jerk. "Oh. You scared me. I was a million miles away. Somewhere out there." She pointed to the horizon.

"Where did you park? I didn't see any other cars."

"I parked at field four and walked on the beach."

"I thought you said to meet at field five."

"I did. But I parked at four and walked just in case somebody happened to see us. I figured that could be embarrassing to explain." Then she added, "For both of us."

She rose from the sand and put her arms around my neck. Pulling me in close, she kissed me on the lips. It was the softest kiss I'd ever experienced. That's the only way to describe it. Her lips were the softest I'd ever kissed. She held the kiss for several seconds, then pulled back and said, "I've wanted to do that all week."

We took a long walk to the east as the sun warmed our faces. We talked about her temp job in Melville, her husband's current trip to Spain, and Stephen's birthday party at McDonalds. We talked about a hundred things of little consequence and on the return walk, she asked, "Leo, can I ask you a question?"

"Sure."

"You're here with me when you should be home with your family. I don't feel good about that. It feels like I'm becoming a problem in your life."

I waited a few seconds, then said, "That's not a question."

She stopped walking and held my hand as she turned to face me.

"I need to know if you think this is going somewhere. I mean, this is crazy that we're here together. What are we doing?"

"I'm kind of glad to hear you don't understand it either." I said with some relief. "I just know I look forward to hearing your voice on the phone, to seeing you. I've thought about our kiss in the taxi all week. I can't get you out of my mind. I'm infatuated with you." There. I said it out loud. I waited for what seemed like an eternity, for a response. I didn't know what to expect.

Then she stopped walking again and said, "Maybe we just need to take it slow and see what happens. But, the truth is, I don't think anyone has ever had this effect on me before. I can't sleep. I'm always thinking about you- about what it would be like to be in your arms." She looked down at the sand, as if ashamed of her words.

I took her chin with my finger and forced her to look at me. When our eyes met, I was transfixed by a strange sensation. As I looked into her beautiful eyes, I felt like I was looking at someone I'd known all my life, someone with whom I was completely comfortable and in whom I had complete confidence. Someone I would entrust my life to. I had no words to express how I felt. I didn't understand it myself. But now that I had her chin on my finger and our eyes were having some sort of wild sex, the only thing that seemed right was to kiss her.

We walked another couple of miles along the shore before she said, "I don't want this day to end, but I know it has to.

You've got to go home and I've got to pick up Roger at JFK in an hour." She twisted her mouth as she was thinking. "Do you think we could do this again?"

On my drive home that afternoon, I was lost in thought. Frankly, I'm lucky I wasn't called on to make any sudden evasive maneuvers because I was only in my car in body. My head was miles away- still kissing a beautiful woman on the beach. A woman who wasn't my wife.

What the fuck was I doing?

****

My plutonic but sensual relationship with Nicole Sullivan continued like that for several weeks. We met for lunch in the city the week before Christmas and I gave her a Steuben polar bear. I figured it was something she could put on her desk to remind her of me without arousing any suspicion from her husband. After all, a polar bear is pretty innocent, right?

She gave me a hand-written letter in which she tried to explain how she felt about me, us, and what we were doing. I was touched. I re-read it twelve times back at my desk, then put it through the shredder.

After the kids had opened their gifts on Christmas morning, and while Annie was preparing them for our drive to Westchester, I called Nicole at her home. Fortunately, she answered and was able to speak for a moment while her husband showered. We were like two school kids but it was wonderful to hear her voice. I wanted her to know I was thinking about her. Even though we lived only a few miles apart, it felt like an ocean separated us. Our very different lives would only cross when we prearranged a crossing, and those were hard to come by.

Twice more, in early January we met for lunch in the city. Nicole was temping for a company at Rockefeller Center and we had lunch at the restaurant that overlooks the ice rink. Nicole confided that she'd never been on ice skates in her life. I threatened to take her for a lesson after lunch.

I felt comfortable in the city. On the remote chance anyone were to observe us and report to Annie that I was having lunch with a beautiful woman, my mentally- rehearsed response was that it was someone I needed to entertain professionally. After all, I did that all the time. We were cautious not to hold hands at the table or show any signs of affection, an emotion that was raging below the table. But outwardly, we were just two people having a business lunch at a business lunch sort of place- in broad daylight.

But Nicole was growing increasingly uncomfortable with our overt meetings. She was concerned more for me than for herself. While sharing a bottle of white wine and watching skaters go around the ice, she confided, "Leo, this is crazy."

"What's crazy? That I'm in love with a woman I met but a few weeks ago or that you can't skate?" I hadn't intended to declare my feelings in such a flippant way. It just came out. Maybe it was the wine.

"You think you love me?" She whispered across the table.

I made sure our eyes met before responding, "Yes. Definitely, yes."

She looked into my eyes. I could see that I'd caught her unprepared for this conversation.

"I don't know what to say."

"I think you just said it." Apparently, Nicole wasn't ready to respond with, "I love you too."

I wanted to take the pressure off her so I said, "But that's okay. There's no reason in the world why you should feel the same way. I don't understand my own feelings so I can't expect you to..." She cut me off.

"I do love you, Leo. I think I've loved you since the first day I met you. But I too don't understand it."

We were interrupted by the waitress who wanted to know if we'd be ordering dessert. We both over-reacted as if we'd been caught stealing the silverware. "No, no..., no. No dessert, thank you. I think we both said it in unison.

"Leo, you know this makes no sense at all. I mean, you're married and you love your wife. It's not like you're in a bad relationship and looking for something you don't have at home. You're happy, very happy. And I don't want to screw that up."

She was right. I wasn't there because I was trying to escape a bad situation at home. I loved my wife and my family. I wouldn't let anything come between us. So why was sitting there, drinking wine on a Tuesday afternoon with Nicole?

I walked her back to the lobby of her building, 10 Rockefeller Plaza, and resisted the overwhelming urge to kiss her good bye. Instead we agreed our feelings were getting ahead of us and we should cool it for a while. She suggested we not talk for a week. Maybe one of us would come to our senses and end this before something terrible happened.

We had half of it right.

XXII

For ten painful days, I resisted the temptation to call Nicole. But during that early part of January 1991, I was constantly distracted by thoughts of her. So much so that Michael noticed and pulled me aside in his office one day.

"Everything okay kid?" He was genuinely concerned.

I was caught off guard by the question. "What do you mean?"

"I mean, you've had your head up your ass since I got back from Vail. Everything okay at home? This isn't like you."

I didn't think my distraction had been noticed by others. After all, only I was aware of the incredible daydreams and fantasies I'd conjured. No one else knew what I was thinking as I sat at my desk pretending to be reading a trade journal, but instead imagining Nicole and I in bed. And the longer we went without talking, the more I fantasized about her in a sexual way. I think it was because the longer we didn't speak, the more likely it seemed we never would. And if we would never see each other again, it was now somehow safe for me to daydream about her sexually, since it seemed like it would never actually happen. An impossible dream is a safe one. No one gets hurt. Right?

But I needed to give Michael something. He was too smart to bullshit.

"Let's just say, yeah. I have an issue at home. But it's between Annie and me. I'll make sure I deal with it at home. Don't worry about me. It's nothing big, just something that hasn't come up before. It'll work out."

We'd only been in business about a year and Michael and I shared most of the decision-making at MAC Tech, so his concern in his partner was justified. If I screwed up something big, the business would suffer. Michael had a two-week road trip to California coming up to drum up new west coast business. For the first time, he was leaving me to run the day-to-day operations. And, although he'd be just a phone call away, his physical presence in the office would be missed by our employees. I was a distant second to his god-like persona among our tech people.

"Okay. If you need anything, just let me know." Then he added, "Shit, I've got no experience with marriage but I'm guessing it can be a pain in the ass sometimes. Just hang in there. You're a smart guy. You'll figure out the right thing."

I wish I had the same faith in myself. I was genuinely confused about the "right thing". The last few days had been particularly rough. My thirty-ninth birthday was approaching and Annie was going out of her way to prepare something special for the two of us- a weekend out at Montauk without the kids. Donald and Daisy would take the kids for two nights and we'd have a second honeymoon out at Gurney's Inn on the bluffs above the Atlantic. Annie was attending to every detail, right down to ordering us a couple's spa treatment the day we arrived.

So here I am, listening to her plans for a romantic weekend over dinner each night, all the while I'm having these incredible fantasies about another woman. Clearly, the cognitive dissonance was overwhelming. I couldn't be two people. I couldn't give Annie all of me and still pine for another. It made no sense.

Yet, I loved Annie. And I loved Nicole. Is it possible to love two people at the same time? It seemed that way. After all, a parent is capable of loving two children equally. One doesn't suffer a loss because of the parent's affection for the other. Love isn't measured in quantity. Someone can give completely of themselves to another and still have more love to give someone else. It's not a zero-sum game.

"So, you're good to cover while I'm away?" Michael was checking.

"Yeah, all good. Don't worry about me."

But I wasn't really sure.

Anyway, Michael left for California and I was left to run the shop and deal privately with my mental infidelity. Nicole and I were maintaining our radio silence and if I could keep my mind off her, I'd be fine. There was a lot to focus on that week at work. We had two new servers being installed and Gordon, the CEO at US Life was coming over for the first time this Friday, just to see our shop. I had plenty to keep me busy. Maybe attending to the mundane would keep my mind off the sublime. Maybe, if I didn't hear from her for another week, I'd begin to accept the notion that she might have moved on. Maybe, she would be the adult and put an end to our folly.

Unfortunately, that was not the case.

A few hours after Michael's plane took off, Judy yelled into my door, "Leo, you have a meeting with Steve Lapp at four and a call on line two. She says she's your neighbor, a Mrs. Moses?"

I checked my watch to make sure I had time for the call before the meeting, then picked up the phone. "Leo Monday."

"Are you always so formal?" It was her.

"Who's Mrs. Moses? Where'd you get that from?"

"Robert Moses? We met at Robert Moses State Park? Hello? Any of this ringing a bell? Our walk on the beach?"

"Who is this? I teased.

"Now you're just screwing with me."

"Sorry. You caught me off guard. It's so nice to hear your voice." And it was.

"Yours too. I'm not doing well with this self-imposed exile. It's been a rough ten days. I really miss seeing you."

"Ditto."

"How about meeting me at lunchtime tomorrow?"

"I thought you were working out on the island."

"I am, but I'll take the afternoon off. Can you meet me at the bar in the Marriott Hotel in Uniondale? How about one o'clock?"

I didn't see that coming. "Are you sure about this?" I foolishly inquired.

"Very sure."

"Okay then. I'll see you at one."

"Leo, in case I haven't made myself clear- clear your calendar for tomorrow afternoon."

****

I'd like to say I wrestled with the morality of what I was about to do. I'd like to say I debated the ethics of my impending infidelity. I'd like to say I was tortured by the betrayal of my marital pledges or the sins I was anticipating. I'd like to say any of that. But I'd be lying.

The fact is, I drove to the Marriott Hotel that day and never looked in my rearview mirror. Somehow, it seemed like the logical next step. Somehow, it seemed like I needed to do this. I wasn't driven by some primordial urge or need for validation. My relationship with Annie was completely satisfactory. I loved her. She loved me and we had a healthy sex life- as healthy as two young parents of three kids can be. I had nothing to prove and I certainly wasn't doing this to subliminally punish my wife for withholding intimacy.

No, I was driving to the rendezvous with Nicole simply because I was in love with Nicole. She asked me to do this and I wanted to make her happy. It sounded like she was thinking about this as much as I was. We were on the same page. So, it just seemed like something that would make two people very happy. Maybe.

When I arrived at the Marriott, a huge complex directly adjacent to the arena that was home to the Islanders Hockey team, I worried briefly that I'd be observed. But the fact that the Marriott hosted dozens of corporate conferences every day gave me a level of comfort. I could be there for lots of reasons. So, as I walked into the expansive lobby, dressed in a suit and tie, I fit right in with many other men walking throughout the complex. If I was observed by a friend of Annie's who happened to be having lunch at the hotel's lobby-restaurant, and they reported my presence to my wife, I had the perfect alibi: I was attending an all-day conference on this, that or the other thing.

I spotted Nicole sitting at the bar. She looked sensational. She had on a tight-fitting pair of jeans and a white v-neck sweater. She was focused on the near empty glass in front of her on the bar.

"What are you drinking stranger?" I asked as I neared.

She turned with a jerk. "Oh, shit. You scared me."

"It's just me."

A hello kiss was out of the question in such a public forum, so she said, "Pull up a stool and take a load off."

"How many of those have you had?" I inquired pointing to her glass.

"Two's my afternoon limit." She said. "This is my third. Today's special. Have one."

I motioned for the bartender to give me one of whatever lethal concoction she was drinking. From the little bit of ice remaining in her glass, I couldn't tell.

When my drink arrived, I was surprised to learn she'd been drinking water.

"I've been thinking about you all morning. I've got a problem, Leo."

"What's that?"

"Well, there's no way you're going to be as sensational in bed as I've been imagining, so I'm expecting to be disappointed." She smiled.

"Thanks for the added pressure."

"Finish your water and let's go find out. We've got room 423." She dangled a key over my glass.

I'm not sure why I said it but I heard myself saying, "Are you sure about this, Nicole?"

"Come on." She rose from her bar stool and put the key in my hand. "Meet me up there in three minutes." Then she flashed a second key and walked toward the elevators. The doors opened and swallowed her as they closed.

I sat at the bar sipping my water for a few more minutes. I actually considered leaving. There was a tiny part of me that was trying to save the philandering bastard I'd become. It tried to make me think about Annie and what she might have been doing at the moment; the girls would be napping, so probably doing laundry.

But the morally bankrupt part of me prevailed and quickly rid my mind of anything but Nicole's butt in those skin-tight jeans and how it rocked as she walked toward the elevator. I left a twenty on the bar, smiled to myself at how ridiculous that was, and took the next elevator to the fourth floor.

Now, I assume that someday, probably someday soon, my daughters and son will read this, so I'm going to resist recalling every steamy detail of our afternoon. But, I'll share this with you; it was amazing. We made love tenderly for nearly two hours. Nicole was a more gentle and passive lover than I had expected, and I loved her even more for it. And, to my credit, I tried everything I knew to make her happy. In my mind, it was her day.

About four o'clock I got up to use the bathroom and when I returned, Nicole was sitting up in bed, wearing only my button-down oxford and watching a rerun of the film "Ghost". We sat in bed watching the second half of the fabled movie and eating Raisinets from the mini bar. When the movie ended, Nicole tried to hide the tears streaming down her cheek. We made love again. To this day, I can't hear Unchained Melody without thinking of that hotel room and the passion we shared for an afternoon.

But as wonderful as the afternoon had been, it had to come to an end. I was the first to leave the room. We kissed passionately for several minutes at the door. So passionately, that I was almost drawn back into the room. But I needed to get home for an event a Stephen's school, so I said, "I have to go. But understand I'm only going because I have to". Then I added, "I love you."

"Ditto", she replied, just as in the movie.

****

When I got home that night, I quickly changed out of my suit, showered, wolfed down a piece of cold pizza, then drove to Flower Hill Elementary School where Stephen's class was holding some sort of sports night for students and their fathers. I don't remember much about the event, but I do remember all the fathers were talking about the massive invasion of Iraq that George Bush the first had unleashed that afternoon. The war that became known as Desert Storm, was enormously one-sided, with laser-guided missiles equipped with cameras and launched from US warships fifty miles away hitting their targets with incredible accuracy.

I smiled when one of the fathers confessed he'd been watching the CNN coverage all day at work. "Best weekday afternoon I've had in a long time."

"Not as good as mine." I assured him, then walked away to find my son.

Oddly, I felt no remorse for what I'd done. Making love to another woman just seemed like the natural thing to do. I loved her. I wanted her to feel that. I loved her. I wanted her to feel worshiped. I know it makes me sound like a terrible person, but I was genuinely in love with two women at the same time. I didn't run to the arms of one because I was unhappy with the other. I loved them both.

Don't judge me unless you've been in the same situation and were strong enough to behave differently. I wasn't.

****

Every logical pore in my body told me I couldn't continue to see Nicole unless I was prepared for some tragic ending. Either I'd lose Annie, I'd lose Nicole, I'd lose Nicole and Annie, or I'd just lose so much of my self-respect that I'd see myself as unworthy of either. There were no other long-term resolutions, or at least, that's what I thought.

As it turns out, there was another resolution that I hadn't considered.

Over the next few months, Nicole and I continued to see each other but with less frequency than we had in January. Maybe every second or third week, one of us would call the other to suggest lunch or a walk in the park or at the beach. Seriously, this wasn't about sex. We both loved just being with the other and most of the time that meant sitting across from one another at a lunch table with no more outward intimacy than any two other business acquaintances.

I had a separate phone line installed in my office so Nicole's calls wouldn't go through Judy's desk. I told Judy it was for family and close friends only and I didn't want her bothered every time one of my daughters needed to tell me about something she'd done in nursery school. And I did give the number to Annie of course, but the line was really for Nicole. It allowed us to "be together" when we couldn't. Sometimes as we spoke, I would imagine we were sitting in bed at the Marriott again, just talking.

Besides our phone calls, Nicole and I probably got together a dozen times that year- always for an innocent lunch, dinner or walk. Neither of us asked for more. And maintaining our relationship on that level probably gave us both a false sense of safety.

But as the summer turned to fall, I could sense there was something wrong in Nicole's life- something that had nothing to do with me. It wasn't anything she said. Rather, it was a look of sadness I would occasionally catch when she wasn't watching me watching her. And although much of our conversation would often be about my family, I noticed she wasn't mentioning Roger as often. I knew he traveled a lot and was sometimes away for weeks at a time, still, she no longer seemed to include stories of him or his polo in our conversations.

I finally asked her about it one day in September as we walked through Central Park on a spectacularly clear cool day. I'd taken the afternoon off so we could walk for hours. Remember, this was before the days of ubiquitous cell phones, so when I was out of the office for a few hours- I was isolated from work.

While we walked, she explained that they'd slowly drifted apart. Probably due to his frequent absences, they seemed to spend less and less time living together.

"I've just been so lonely." She said. "And I haven't wanted to say anything to you because I didn't want you to feel…" Her voice trailed off.

"You didn't want me to feel what, Nicole?"

"I didn't want you to feel responsible. I know you. You would instantly think this was because of our relationship. And that's not the case at all. This has nothing to do with you."

I put my arm around her. "Hey, you've got to talk to me about this stuff. When you're hurting, I want to be able to help. That's what friends do." I immediately felt foolish using the word friends.

She let me off the hook. "I know what you mean, Leo. So many times I wanted to talk to you about it, but I didn't want to call because I knew you'd stop whatever you were doing and want to be with me. I don't want to become a burden. You're not responsible for my happiness."

"Nicole, I love you. I want to…" She cut me off.

"No Leo. You have your life and I have mine. I will not interfere with yours and I don't want you to feel responsible for me."

It turns out that the Sullivan's marriage was going south long before I met Nicole. Over the next few months, she confided that shortly after she married Roger she began to suspect he was seeing a woman in Florida. It didn't take her long to confirm her suspicions. But, outwardly, when they were together, Roger was the model husband. When he was in town, he'd insist they go to dinner to celebrate even the most minor occasions; the anniversary of their first date, their first kiss, even the anniversary of the first movie they saw together. Outwardly, he was a romantic and directed his affection to Nicole.

But, when he was away, he was away. Most of the time, he insisted that Nicole not travel with him. It was only recently, she'd discovered he shared an apartment in Palm Beach with the other woman.

Nicole said she'd made the decision to leave him some time ago but was desperately afraid of being alone. She had money. That wasn't it. She just didn't know how to be alone. The irony was, she'd spent most of her marriage alone.

"I haven't wanted to burden you with this. I knew when you found out I was lonely, you'd try to solve that for me. You'd insist on seeing me more just for my benefit. I didn't want to become an obligation. And the other thing is..." She motioned for us to sit on a park bench.

"The other thing is, I was afraid. I was afraid that when you found out I was afraid to be alone, you'd get spooked."

"What do you mean spooked?"

"I was afraid you'd think I wanted more from you. That I wanted you to myself. And that's just not the case. I know how much you love your wife and kids. I never want to come between you and your family. I never want you to leave your family. You love that life so much and I know it's what makes you happy."

Actually, it was good we were having this conversation because it cleared the air about one very important truth- I would never leave Annie because of Nicole.

XXIII

Veronica called me this morning and invited me to Florida for Christmas. I'd been assuming they were coming to New York for the holiday week, just as they'd done every year since Annie died. This would be the first time in my life I wasn't in New York for Christmas. For a moment, it saddened me. Then, as I thought further, I burst into laughter.

Why should I care about this being the first time I'm not in New York for Christmas? It's also my last Christmas ever and probably the last time I'll ever see all my kids. Now that's something to be upset about!

But it did cause me to think about a box I had in storage. When Annie died, I vowed never to put up another Christmas tree. It would just depress me. But I couldn't bear to part with all the tree ornaments we'd accumulated as a family over the years, so I boxed them and put them in the basement. When I moved here to the city, I was tempted to just throw the box out without having the courage to even open it. But I put it in the small storage cage each tenant had in the basement and there it's been till now.

So, after I agreed to travel to Veronica's house for Christmas, I went down to the cage and retrieved the battered Sony TV box that had been the keeper of our family's treasured ornaments for so many years. I struggled to carry it into the elevator. Over the past few weeks I've lost about half my arm strength. Cancer sucks. I used to be able to carry that box up the basements stairs in our home without breaking a sweat. Now, it was like trying to move a piano.

I plopped it down on the elevator floor and stared at the sorry image looking back at me from the reflective wall. I'd guess I was down to less than 150 pounds, from the 195 I usually carried around before the cancer. But it wasn't just the weight loss that shook me. I was as white as a ghost. Death was knocking and it wasn't going to let me take my time answering the door.

Fortunately, as the elevator doors were closing, a nice kid from down the hall jumped in holding his Springer Spaniel puppy under his arm.

"Hey Mr. Monday. What's up?"

"Morning Ben. How's the house training going?"

"She's doing pretty well most of the time. But we still have accidents."

Ben offered to carry the Sony box into my apartment if I would hold Mia for him; a trade I gladly made.

I spent two hours sorting the tissue-wrapped ornaments into four piles: One for each of the kids and one to throw out. I tried to remember which ornaments held particular favor with each of the kids and where we'd accumulated them. Some brought back wonderful memories that made me sad. I miss Annie so much and especially at Christmas, her favorite time of the year. So many of the ornaments had been purchased on our family vacations. Each year, as we decorated the tree, Annie would hold one up and ask, "Remember when we bought this?"

By the time I had a dozen ornaments in each of the kid's piles, I realized I'd done enough. While I'm sure they'll appreciate having a memory of their childhood Christmas's, they each need to develop their own traditions and memories. I'm sure Stephen and Lilly already have their own ornaments; ones that hold special meaning to only them. Paula and Veronica will too.

So, I'd decided I'd put myself through enough pain and began to package the remaining trinkets in the Sony box for disposal. The way I saw it, I was saving my kids the aggravation of doing it after I'm gone. That's when I spotted the golfer- a tiny glass ornament we'd been putting on our tree since 1994. No one but I ever paid much attention to it, but year after year, I would quietly unwrap the fragile golfer and hang him somewhere toward the back of the tree. He was significant to only me. He had been a gift from Nicole. And hanging him on the tree was a way for me to remember her. It's a cherished memory.

But, my most cherished memory of the Christmas season goes back much further than the Christmas mornings with my three children, or my first Christmas night with my wife. It goes back to when I was five years old.

It was a few days before Christmas. We were waiting for my dad to come home from work. The house had been decorated days before and my mom was enjoying a few moments of peace sitting in a huge red velvet chair in front of the tree. She was listening to Perry Como's Christmas album and the living room lights were turned down low except for the lights on the tree.

I climbed onto her lap and snuggled beside her. The oversized chair swallowed us both. We sat there for several minutes in silence (except for Perry) just watching the twinkling tree. It was the safest I have ever felt and when, as an adult, I find myself in threatening situations, I always go back to that night. To this day, every time I hear Oh Holy Night, the image of that night comes to mind.

So, now that my chores are done, and I've taken a short late-morning nap to regain some strength, let me tell you more about Nicole.

Our relationship continued for five years. You must understand, when I use the word relationship, I don't mean to tarnish it. For five years, Nicole and I loved each other. But it wasn't an affair in the classic sense. In fact, in all the time we were in love, we'd only had sex six times, over a five-year affair. The rest of our rendezvous consisted of plutonic lunches and walks in Central Park or at the beach. We could go weeks without talking, then one of us would pick up the phone just to say, "I miss seeing you." And sometimes that would result in a lunch but more often, the words had to suffice. We both understood that we each had obligations that didn't leave us much time for love. I was extraordinarily busy helping Michael build the business and helping Annie raise three kids. Nicole got very busy and traveled a lot with a charity she'd agreed to chair.

So, when we did get together, we tried to make it count. On days I could escape family obligations for a few hours, I liked to meet Nicole at the beach. Sometimes we'd walk for miles and sometimes we'd just lay on an oversized beach towel and watch the clouds roll by. I loved those days most. There was no pressure. We had no agenda. We just got together, relaxed, and talked for hours.

And, like I said, we usually talked about my family. I remember once, during a time Annie and I were planning a family trip to Ocean City, Nicole offered several suggestions based on her knowledge of the area. It was as if she was helping us plan our vacation, even though of course she wouldn't be joining us. But that's the kind of conversations we had. Nicole probably knew more about my children than anyone other than Annie and me.

I think the only times we didn't spend hours discussing my kids, was the few times we spent in bed. I usually left those up to Nicole to plan. She would call me to ask if I could be free for a night several weeks in advance. That was code for, "I need to spend a night with you." And, if she had enough time to plan, she'd usually put together a very special evening. The best night ever was just before Christmas 1994.

We wanted to make sure we'd have time together before Christmas and before Roger returned from his trip to South America. In late November, Nicole called me to see if I could spend an entire night with her about a week before Christmas. She booked a suite at the Plaza and I made dinner reservations at Henry IV, a cool little restaurant within walking distance of the Plaza. What made the night so special was that we agreed not to buy each other Christmas gifts but instead, we agreed to write each other love letters that we would read to each other that night.

After a fabulous dinner and a bottle of a good Reisling, we walked back to the Plaza with light snow falling. When we got up to the room, I noticed we had a small balcony overlooking Central Park South. Our suite was on the fifteenth floor with a beautiful view of the park and we shared a few good kisses out on the balcony then made small snowballs with what had accumulated on the balcony railing and had a friendly snowball fight.

Then we both showered, separately, and changed into the luxurious terry robes with the Plaza's famous monogram. Wearing nothing but the soft robes and sipping from our second bottle of Reisling, we sat in bed and read each other our letters. Nicole had her head on my lap as I read her my letter. I don't remember exactly what I wrote but I do remember I spoke about how much history we had and how much I loved her. I spoke of how I felt so completely comfortable when we were together. I told her I believed she was the "Love of my life". What I meant was that I believed if I'd met Nicole before I'd met Annie, we'd be the ones spending our lives together. Nicole cried.

Then I put my head on her lap and she read me hers. In it she told me all the reasons she loved me. I was embarrassed to be so flattered. She told me how much she loved me. She mentioned some of the wonderful days we'd spent together and why they were so special to her. I was getting a little teary myself but cracked up when she ended the letter with the following sentence: "You now know how much I love you so, if in the future, anything ever happens and you find yourself single again..., you better fucking call me!"

We laughed uncontrollably for several minutes. Then we wrestled ourselves out of the robes and made love until we fell asleep in each other's arms. It was the most romantic night of my life.

In the morning, I ordered room service for Nicole, but I went for a run in the park. A half inch of clean snow covered the streets and sidewalks, but the lawns hadn't been cold enough to support the beautiful white crystals. I did about two miles then returned to the room to find Nicole sitting up in bed, drinking coffee and watching the Today Show. Matt and Katie were interviewing Garth Brooks who was humping his Christmas special.

I needed to get to the office, so I showered, dressed and drank the orange juice Nicole left for me. I sat on the edge of the bed and reminded her I loved her but that I had to get to work. She teased me by lowering the sheet that was covering her bare breasts. "Sure you don't want to come back to bed for an hour?"

"You're killing me, Nicole."

"I'm just teasing. I know you have to go. Please promise me you'll have a great Christmas."

"I already have. That was the most wonderful night of my life. I love you." I kissed her on the forehead. Then I turned and gently closed the hotel room door behind me without looking back. If I had, I'm not sure I would have left.

That winter, all the kids had Strep throats and Annie got the flu. Daisy came to stay with us for a week to help out, but I also needed to pitch in. Any chance I had to get away from the office, I spent at home trying to help. Then Nicole spent six weeks in Europe following Roger and the ponies. As a result, I didn't see Nicole again until May of 1995. Our first rendezvous was a walk on the beach on a beautiful spring day. I remember meeting her walking toward me from the other parking field, a cautionary habit she insisted we maintain. I was carrying a few pieces of plastic liter I'd come across while walking.

"Are those for me?" She feigned excitement.

"Yes. I've been carrying them around looking for you since Christmas!"

We embraced. I dropped the liter. We kissed and the time we were separated dissolved away.

On a cool day in June we met for lunch downtown. Nicole showed up with a brown bag and we ate its contents on the Staten Island ferry. It was the first time either of us had ever been on the ferry.

1995 was the summer I took a month off to drive around the southwest in a camper with Annie and the kids. It was a fabulous vacation and a terrific learning experience for the kids but, as much as I loved being with my family, I missed Nicole. There were many times I thought to myself, "I wish Nicole could see this."

So, while we waited in the Las Vegas airport for our return flight, I called Nicole and asked her to meet me for a walk on the beach the day after we got home. She enthusiastically agreed to meet me on Monday morning, which was Labor Day. I knew we had an end-of-summer backyard party to attend that night, but I could make myself available for a few hours in the morning.

"The usual spot?"

"Of course. Make sure you bring me some liter." She teased.

"I'll see you at 10:30. I love you."

* * * * * * * * * * * *

Monday morning, I awoke earlier than usual. It might have been due to jetlag but I'm pretty sure it was pure anticipation. That feeling is how I knew my relationship with Nicole was something special. We were just going to walk on the beach, after an absence of almost three months. There was no sex involved. We just wanted to see each other and be together. We were in love. This wasn't some lustful urge of a forty-three year-old having a mid-life crisis. I loved her.

I helped Annie unpack the suitcases we'd abandon in the living room the night before, and made the kids pancakes with the few supplies our housekeeper left in our fridge. Then I took Stephen with me and did a full food shopping to restock our empty pantry. All this was accomplished by 9:00 A.M. I told Annie I needed to go to the office to start catching up after my prolonged absence and she understood. Annie always understood.

It was unusually warm for Labor Day, so I put on a pair of shorts, a golf shirt and old Topsiders.

"That's how you're going to work?" She asked.

"It's just going to be me and a couple of mainframe operators. I don't need to be dressed."

"Okay sweetie. Drive carefully. I love you." Then she disappeared up the stairs carrying a load of laundry.

I'd been doing this so long- my rendezvous with Nicole- that I no longer felt guilt about it. I know it sounds strange, but it just felt like I was leaving to spend time in my other life. I loved two women and wanted them both in my life. Does that make me a monster? Probably not but it did make me a miserable husband, I'll give you that.

I drove down the Sunken Meadow Parkway and over the causeway bridges with the anticipation of a five-year old on Christmas morning. I parked at Field Five and took the large beach towel I kept in my trunk. I walked down to the water, then back toward Field Four, where Nicole always parked. Because it was the last big weekend of the unofficial summer, the beach was filled with people, most down along the shore.

I knew I was a little early, so I took it upon myself to rid the beach of a few plastic cups, empty beer bottles, an old fishing knife, and a wad of tangled fishing line I found while walking through the dunes. Steel-drum trash cans were still plentiful since officially the beach doesn't close until after Labor Day. This made my beach-sweeping easier. At least I had a place to throw the trash I picked up.

I walked about three-quarters of the way to Field Four and planted myself on the towel about twenty yards from the shoreline. Most beachgoers wanted to be down by the ocean, so I was pretty much alone back that far on the sand. I was closer to the dunes than I was to the shoreline and it was nice and quiet back there. I took my shirt off and used it as a pillow. Then I laid down to catch a few rays while I waited for Nicole. The sun was warm and there was little breeze. It was a delightful Monday morning and I think I fell asleep for a few minutes.

When I awoke, I checked my watch: 10:35. Nicole should arrive any minute. She was usually very prompt. I laid there watching an occasional cloud drift by and daydreaming about my last night with Nicole. It had been almost nine months since our night at the plaza and I'd be lying if I said I wasn't looking forward to arranging something similar very soon. I'd been dreaming about the soft skin on Nicole's back and the way she stretched her arms over her head when lying in bed and teasing me to join her. God, she was sexy.

The next time I checked my watch it was just after eleven o'clock. I sat up and looked around to be sure Nicole wasn't walking along the shore looking for me. It was unusual for her to be late. I stood up and scanned the beach. Maybe she came while I was asleep and sat down somewhere nearby. Nope, nowhere in sight. Satisfied that we hadn't missed each other, I told myself there must be traffic holding her up.

But when she wasn't there by eleven-thirty I started to worry about her. And when she hadn't shown by noon, I was beginning to think the worst. That is, that she'd been in a car accident on the way to see me. Aside from the fact she could be hurt, there was the issue of explaining to her husband why she'd been driving to the beach. An accident, even a minor one, on the way to a clandestine rendezvous, could only mean trouble. And, if she was injured in a traffic accident and the police needed to call someone, who would they call? Her husband? I didn't even know if he was in the country. How could he help? Who would be there for Nicole? Who could make medical decisions for her?

I realized my imagination was getting away from me. There were a dozen other possible explanations for her ninety-minute tardiness. Or maybe, I misunderstood. Maybe she didn't say ten-thirty at all. Maybe it was twelve-thirty, or two-thirty? Or maybe she didn't even mean Monday.

I decided to wait another hour but at one o'clock she still hadn't shown. And I needed to be home by three. My emotions swung from worry, in case she'd been in an accident, to frustration, in case one of us had gotten the instructions wrong. Remember again, this was long before everyone carried cell phones. We couldn't communicate and that lack of information was disconcerting. At one-thirty, I picked up my towel, took one more long look around the beach, and headed back to my car.

I drove home convinced she'd been involved in some sort of car trouble. Even minor trouble like a dead battery could be reason for her absence. The only thing I could do was get home and try calling her. Then I began to think maybe she'd changed her mind. After all, we hadn't seen each other in three months. Maybe she rethought the wisdom of a daytime rendezvous on a crowded Labor Day beach. Or, maybe she'd become cautious about getting caught. Maybe Roger wanted her to do something with him today. There were so many possibilities.

I got home just before three, after stopping briefly at a gas station pay phone. My call to Nicole's home went unanswered. I didn't leave a message on her machine. Now I was genuinely concerned she'd been in a car accident.

But there was nothing I could do if I couldn't reach her by phone, so I had to try to put it out of my mind.

Annie reminded me we needed to leave for our neighbor's bar-b-que by four, so I jumped in the shower, shaved and put on a pair of khakis and a blue tee shirt. Then I helped dress the kids, grabbed a bottle of red wine from our rack, and headed for the car. I was buckling Veronica into her car seat when I noticed a black sedan pull into our driveway and stop just behind my minivan. Annie had just pulled the house door closed and was walking toward the driveway. I was still preoccupied with Veronica's straps, but I heard her say, "Can I help you gentlemen?"

I looked up and saw two men in suits walking up my driveway.

At first, I thought they were lost and seeking directions. Then I saw the taller one hold up a badge. "We're looking for Leo Monday, mam."

I poked my head out of the back seat of the minivan and said, "I'm Leo Monday. What can I do for you?" As they got closer, I could see the badge looked like those carried by the police, so I added, "Officer?"

"I'm Detective Stuart Marx and this is Detective Aaron DeJesus. Have you got a few minutes to answer a couple of questions?" The shorter one asked.

"What's this about?" Annie wanted to know.

"If you could give us just a few minutes Mr. Monday, we'd like to ask you a few questions. I promise we probably only need five minutes."

"Questions about what? I wanted to know before I delayed our trip to the bar-b-que.

The tall one looked at the short one, then said, "It's about Nicole Sullivan."

The sound of Nicole's name mentioned in my driveway, in front of my wife and children, seemed inconceivable. I was immediately convinced she'd been in an accident and wanted to ask if she was okay, but Annie was standing next to me. So, instead I said, "What about Nicole?"

"Who's Nicole?" Annie wanted to know.

"She's someone who used to work for us." I answered quickly. Then I turned back to the taller detective and asked, "Is she okay?"

"Can we talk someplace, privately?" Detective Marx asked.

This was a conversation I didn't want to have in front of Annie, so I turned to her and said, "Why don't you take the kids over to the Dunn's and I'll take my car in a few minutes and meet you? I don't want to make the kids wait in the car." I pointed at our three children who were already securely fastened into their car seats.

Her motherly instincts overcame her curiosity and she relented, "Okay, but don't be too long."

Then she turned to the detectives and added, "Try not to keep him too long. We're already a little late."

Once Annie had backed the minivan down the driveway and disappeared down the street, I leaned against my car, crossed my arms and asked, "So, what can I do for you guys?"

Detective Marx was all business. "Well, you can start by telling us where you were this morning."

That caught me by surprise. I was prepared to hear that Nicole had been in an accident and had asked the police to notify me. At least, if she was able to tell them to get in touch with me, she must be okay. So, why did they care about where I was?

"First tell me if she's okay. Has she been in an accident?"

"If you don't mind, Mr. Monday, we'll ask the questions."

Now I was a little pissed off. Why couldn't they just assure me Nicole was alright?

"Well, what's your question?" I said with a bit too much attitude.

The shorter guy, DeJesus, took this one. "Where were you this morning between about nine and noon?"

I figured this would never get back to Annie, so I just told them the truth. Well, some of the truth. "I took a ride down to the beach and took a walk. It was a beautiful morning."

"Were you alone?"

"Yes. My wife and kids stayed home. We just got back from a family vacation the night..."

DeJesus cut me off. "Can anyone vouch for where you were?"

"Yeah, my wife knows where I was."

"What beach did you say you went to?

"I drove down to Robert Moses State Park."

"Did you see anybody there that could verify you were there?"

"No. I didn't see anyone I knew. I just took a long walk then laid down and caught a few rays. Then I came home around one-thirty."

Marx looked at DeJesus who was taking notes.

"Is this your car? It's an Impala, right?" The short one asked. "Is this the car you drove to the beach today?"

"What has any of this got to do with Nicole Sullivan?" I was growing impatient.

"Did you meet Mrs. Sullivan at the beach this morning?"

That one caught me by surprise too.

"No, I haven't seen Nicole in a few months. I think it was sometime in June. We had lunch together in Manhattan. Like I said, my family and I have been out west, on vacation for almost a month." I thought that truthful answer would suffice. I was wrong.

"Mr. Monday, what's the nature of your relationship with Mrs. Sullivan?" I didn't like where this was going at all and I was glad Annie agreed to take the kids to the bar-b-que.

"Just friends. She used to work at my company a few years back."

"What company is that, sir?" The short one wanted details for his notes.

"MAC Technologies."

"And what is your role there?"

"I'm CEO. But you still haven't told me if she's alright."

The tall one took a step closer and leaned against my car with his right hand. "Mr. Monday, Mrs. Sullivan was killed this morning. Her body was found at Robert Moses State Park."

My shock was apparent to both detectives. "Oh my god!" My knees went week and I felt like I couldn't catch my breath. I was fortunate to be against my car or I might have collapsed. But I hadn't yet heard the worst.

"What happened?" I stammered.

"We were hoping you could tell us."

"How could I possibly know?" I was still shaking my head in disbelief.

"Mr. Monday, someone matching your description was seen in the area where we found her body. That person then got into a blue Sedan that matches yours. And here's the funny thing; the witness got a good look at the license: MJG 138." That was my plate number!

I was still reeling from the shock of hearing Nicole was dead. I still didn't believe it could be true. I thought about her beautiful face and exquisitely soft lips. How could she be dead?

"Mr. Monday, that's your car."

I was brought back to the moment. "Yeah, I told you I was at the beach today. What's that got to do with the accident?"

"What accident?"

"I thought you just said Nicole was killed in an accident."

"No. I said she was killed. What made you think it was an accident?"

"I just assumed."

"Why would you assume it was an accident?"

I decided it was time to give them a little more clarity. "I was supposed to meet Nicole, Mrs. Sullivan, at the beach today. We were going to take a walk together. She didn't show up, so I assumed she'd been in an accident. A car accident."

Detective Marx looked at me skeptically. "What else do you want to tell me Mr. Monday?"

"That's all I can tell you. We agreed to meet at the beach at ten-thirty and she didn't show up. I waited a couple of hours, then came home. What happened to Nicole? Tell me." I demanded.

"Well, she did drive to the beach. We found her car in parking lot four. But we found her body a few hundred yards to the east, in the dunes. She was stabbed to death. Can you tell us anything about that, Mr. Monday?"

"Oh my god!" Was all I could say. The image of Nicole lying in the sand made me sick. Literally sick.

"I think I'm going to be sick." I said to the cops.

"Better here than in my car." The tall one said. Then after I'd vomited on my driveway, he added, "You're under arrest, Mr. Monday for the murder of Nicole Sullivan."

"What?" I said with a mouth full of bile.

"You have the right to remain silent. Anything you say can and will be used against you in a court of law. You have the right to an attorney. If you cannot afford an attorney, one will be provided for you. Do you understand your rights?"

"What? I don't need an attorney. I haven't done anything!"

"Funny thing is, that's what everyone says." DeJesus thought he had a sense of humor.

The next thing I knew, I was sitting in the back of the black sedan with Detective Marx at my side and my hands cuffed together.

XXIV

Labor Day 1995 was the worst day of my life- at least, at that point it was. Nicole was dead. I was sitting in an empty room at the county court in Islip, because after being booked and processed at the local police station, the detectives had to drive me to Islip because Huntington's second precinct didn't have anyone working the holiday shift. And the worst was yet to come. I needed to get in touch with Annie.

Poor Annie. In a few minutes, she was about to learn her husband had been arrested for murder and that he's been carrying on an affair with another woman for over five years. I hated the idea of hurting her, but I guess it was a little late for that regret.

My lawyer was due in a few minutes. Until he got here, I figured I'd better just shut up. Even though I had nothing to do with Nicole's death, I've seen enough TV to know even innocent people can get fucked by what they say. After I spoke to him, I wanted to talk to Annie. I had to do that myself. I didn't want her getting any of this second-hand. I owed her that.

As I sat, waiting for Larry Mentz, my lawyer, who, by the way- wasn't happy about being called away from a family reunion out in Southampton, I couldn't help thinking all this was punishment for things I'd done but gotten away with. Images of my sisters flailing in the lake and of Chris Hoffman falling from the chairlift started to haunt me. I'd gotten away with murder before. Maybe it would be fitting and just irony if I was convicted for the one I didn't do.

Having no idea how long I'd be there, I began to make lists in my head. Lists of things I was supposed to do the next day at work. Lists of people who would find out I was an adulterer. Lists of assets I could draw on to pay Larry. The lists quickly became overwhelming.

Around seven-thirty Larry Mentz was shown into the room. Unlike what you see on TV, he didn't come in a three-piece suit and place a briefcase on the table. Larry was dressed in jeans and a Bethpage Black golf shirt. He had to ask to borrow a pad and pen.

When the door was closed and we were alone, he asked, "What the fuck, Leo?"

Larry and I went way back. I met him when I first started working. He was a junior lawyer at US Life but later became head counsel. I convinced Michael to retain him for MAC when Larry left to start his own litigation company. He was on MAC's board of directors and I was concerned, because of his board position he may not be able to defend me.

Annie and I attended a lot of social functions with Larry and his lovely wife, Sarah. He and Sarah ran a charity that helped inner-city kids find scholarships. They'd done a lot of good work. I'd bet over a hundred kids owed their college degree to Larry and Sarah. They were good souls.

But I wasn't, and that's why Larry was here.

"Larry, I need to get in touch with Annie. She doesn't know where I am."

"Okay, we'll get to that. First, I need you to tell me what you've said to the detectives that arrested you. Don't leave out a single detail."

So, I tried to recount the short driveway conversation with Marx and DeJesus as best I could. That didn't take long.

"That's it?" He asked.

"Yeah, pretty much. The whole conversation took less than five minutes. As soon as they told me Nicole was murdered, I think I passed out for a few seconds. The next thing I knew I was on my knees puking on my driveway. Then they cuffed me and read me the Miranda thing, put me in the car and here I am. They took fingerprints and took my wallet, watch and belt."

"Did they question you when you got here?"

"No."

"Did you talk to anyone else since you've been here?"

"No. No one."

"Alright, good." He said very calmly.

"Larry, are you able to handle this? I mean because you're on our board?"

"No. Of course not. I'm not going to defend you. I don't do criminal law. I just want to get you out of here. Then we'll talk to a good criminal guy I know."

The word criminal made me cringe. Although I've known for many years that I am a criminal, no one else did. Now that the label was going to finally be affixed, it felt horrible.

Larry leaned back on his wooden chair and began. "Leo, let me tell you what the detectives told me before I came in. They told me Nicole Sullivan was murdered today. She was stabbed with a knife six times in the back and throat. They've recovered the weapon they claim was used in the murder. They seem certain she was killed at the beach, not somewhere else, then dumped at the beach. They told me you've acknowledged she was scheduled to meet you at Robert Moses State Park today and that you claim you never saw her because she didn't show up at your prearranged rendezvous."

Larry could tell I was upset at his description of how Nicole had been murdered. Stabbed six times in the back and throat! How horrible.

"They told me someone heard a scream from the dunes then saw someone matching your description throwing something into a nearby garbage can. The police recovered the alleged murder weapon from that garbage can. It was covered with blood. They didn't say who it was that observed you, but they did say the same good Samaritan saw you running to your car and called the police with your license plate and a description of your car."

"They told me you admitted no one can validate your story of a lonely walk on the beach around the same time Nicole Sullivan was being murdered, but that you admit being there. Is that correct?"

"Yeah. There was no one else there. I mean there were thousands of people on the beach, but I didn't see anyone I knew. No one that could say they saw me walking."

"Well, someone did."

"How can this be? Larry, you know me. I didn't kill that poor woman. How can someone say they saw me do it?"

"No one said they saw you kill her. They said they saw someone that looks like you throw something into a garbage can from which the alleged murder weapon was later recovered by the police. And they said they saw someone that looks like you running to a car that matches your car and license plate."

"I just don't understand."

"Well, let's back up and go over it, piece by piece, shall we?"

"Can I call Annie first?"

"Probably not. Let's deal with this first. I need to see if I get you in front of a judge to consider bail. It's a holiday, so I'm not even sure that's possible."

"You mean I may need to stay here?" I said incredulously.

"Leo, you've been charged with murder. Unless I can pull a rabbit out of my ass, yes, you're probably here at least until we can get in front of a judge."

"But I need to talk to Annie."

Larry suddenly got stern. "Here's what I need, Leo. I need you to tell me anything else you can remember about this morning. And I need you to tell me about Nicole Sullivan. Who is she? How do you know her and why were you meeting her at the beach today? That's what I need!"

Because he'd raised his voice, I was reminded this wasn't just two buddies having a conversation. This was a criminal and his lawyer. I needed to do whatever Larry suggested. I knew that much.

"Okay. I get it." I said contritely. I hung my head in shame and began… "Nicole was a temp at MAC back in 1990. We started an affair back then and have continued it, off and on, for five years. Annie knows nothing about it, nor does Nicole's husband. I haven't seen her since June, so we decided to take a walk on the beach this morning to catch up. That's pretty much it."

"What do you mean by the term 'off and on for five years'? Were there fights along the way. Break-ups?"

"No. Nothing like that. When I say off and on, I mean, because we were both married and had busy lives, we'd sometimes go months without seeing one another."

"And when you say seeing one another, you mean a rendezvous at a hotel, or did you ever go to each other's homes?"

"No, you're getting the wrong idea."

"I'm getting the wrong idea? Leo, I don't think you understand how bad this looks. You're married. She was married. And you two have been going at it for over five years. What am I missing that's given me the wrong idea?" The sarcasm was thick.

"It wasn't like that Larry. We were in love. Really. Although we spoke on the phone a lot, most of our time together was spent in a restaurant or walking on a beach or in the park. Like I said, I haven't seen her since June. That was a lunch. We haven't slept together since last December. In five years, we never had an argument, not even a cross word. I really loved her, Larry." My voice trailed off.

"I believe you." He said with compassion.

"Thanks. I can't believe she's gone. It hurts so much."

I think Larry was finally taking pity on me. I'd lost the woman I loved a few hours ago and was about to terribly hurt the other woman I loved. The pain was overwhelming and for the first time in my life, I think I could understand how someone could take their own life- just to end the pain.

"Is there anything about today you can remember that might help? Did you stop anywhere? Did you talk to anyone? What did you do when you walked on the beach? Did you sit anywhere? Help me here."

I tried to retrace my day in my head. The drive from Huntington, where I parked, where I walked, how long I laid on my towel. None of it seemed to help.

"I think I might have briefly fallen asleep while I was lying down, but to tell you the truth, I can't be sure. I know I was daydreaming with my eyes closed but I'm not sure if I ever fell asleep."

"Okay. What time were you supposed to meet Nicole?"

"Ten-thirty."

"Where did you agree to meet?"

"We had a routine. I would park at field five and walk west. She would park at field four and walk through the dunes to the east. We usually met down by the water about half-way between four and five."

"How often have you done this? Meeting on the beach?"

I had to think about that. "Over the last five years, maybe a dozen times."

"Was there anyone else who knew about your routine?"

"No. As far as I know, no one knew about our relationship."

"Was there anything predictable about what you two did? I mean, did you always walk? Did you ever sit on the beach, bring chairs, have something to eat?"

"No. Not really. We never brought chairs. Most times we'd take a walk, pick up trash along the shore, lie on a beach towel. One time, Nicole brought a bag of Raisinets. One time we did a crossword puzzle."

I think it was at that point Larry realized what I meant when I said, "It wasn't like that." I guess to someone else, our relationship, our affair, sounded pretty boring. Probably a little strange.

I suppose when most people hear the word affair, they think of sex. By that standard, yes, our relationship was boring. But I loved her. And as Larry continued to ask me questions, I prayed I would wake up from this nightmare. I hoped it was just a terribly bad dream.

"Did anything ever happen at the beach that might have pissed off someone else? Maybe you sat too close to someone? Maybe someone observed you and was judgmental about your behavior? I don't know."

"Larry, nothing comes to mind. We tried to stay to ourselves."

"Okay kid, here's what I'm going to do. I'll see if there's any chance we can get in front of a judge tonight for a bail hearing. I very much doubt it, but I'll try. If I can't, you're here for the night and we'll try again first thing in the morning. In the meantime, I'll get in touch with Bob Colgan, the defense lawyer I mentioned earlier. With your permission, I'll tell him what we've got and see if he's available to take your case. He's not cheap but he's the best

I know at what he does, and I know he's tried capital cases before."

I nodded.

"Then I'll call Annie."

"What will you say?"

"I'll tell her that you've been arrested, that you've obviously been mistaken for someone else who killed a woman at the beach this morning. I'll tell her that we spoke, that you're okay and that I hope to have you out of here by tomorrow afternoon. I'll tell her not to worry."

"Okay, good. I'm the one who has to tell her about the affair."

"You're damn right. But I'm guessing that the police have already been to your house, searched your car, your garage, and your closets for blood, hair, or anything that could tie you to the murder scene. I'm sure by now, your wife knows where you are and why you're here."

"Shit!" The thought of the police going through my house while my wife and three kids stood by and watched, infuriated me. This was their mistake. Why do they get to ruin my life and frighten my family? What a fucking nightmare!

"One more thing, Leo. Don't talk to anyone about anything. Don't answer even the simplest question. Until I get Bob in here, you talk only to me. Understood?"

"Got it."

"Okay. After I leave, they'll probably move you to a temporary holding cell for the night. It's going to suck. But you can deal with it. And, it's just for one night."

I nodded. Larry gave me a pat on the shoulder and left the room with the notes he'd taken.

****

Larry Mentz was right about one thing. A night in a holding cell sucks. Fortunately, I was alone most of the night in the twelve by twenty-foot concrete room. A stainless-steel toilet sat in the corner with a roll of toilet paper sitting on the floor next to it. Along three walls, wooden benches were solidly attached to the floor. The fourth wall was all bars and the door.

I was able to fall asleep on the bench farthest from the toilet but was haunted by nightmares. First, I dreamed I saw Nicole thrashing in the water next to my sister Lucy. They were both clinging to a bright red canoe and screaming my name. The sky was black, and rain was hitting the three of us so hard we could barely see. It was horrible and woke me immediately, unfortunately, after only fifteen minutes of restless sleep. Then I dreamed I was in the cradle of a huge earthmover. It was the same dream I had the night Annie stayed in the city, only this time Annie was in the steel bucket with me and crying. I tried to comfort her but when she turned to look at me, blood was streaming from her neck. Again, I quickly awoke in a sweat.

Then after a total of thirty minutes of nightmarish sleep, I got a cell mate and things got a lot worse. Levon Bermuda had been arrested for drunken behavior and disorderly conduct. Apparently, he got in a fight in a bar and gave the responding cops a rough time. He was pretty beaten up and still quite drunk, but was happy to tell me his side of the story in agonizing detail. Levon also insisted on sitting very close to me on the bench, problematic because he'd pissed himself earlier in the evening, and was beginning to stink. He was as black as a human being could be but had glimmering white teeth that were in surprisingly good condition considering the bruises on his face.

So, after Levon's arrival, at about three A.M., there was no more sleep and I started to anticipate the next twenty-four hours of my life. I dreaded facing Annie, and tried to come up with a script that would lessen the pain for her. How could I tell her I'd been in love with someone else? How could I say it had been going on for five years? That I'd been lying to her for five years? And would she even believe me when I explained most of my relationship with Nicole had been dinners, lunches and walks? Probably not, after all, I was a liar.

I concluded there was no way I could make this any easier for Annie. The best I could do was tell her the complete truth and hope she could forgive me. But even if she forgave me, could she ever really get past it? Would it always be something I'd have to answer for? Would my infidelity be a constant wedge in our relationship, and would Annie always wonder when I'd do it again?

Of course, I had no way to know the answer to any of these questions. If Larry was able to get me out of this hell, then I'd have to face Annie. By the end of today, I could be thrown out of my home. I may have to look for a place to stay. The sun hadn't yet come up on this day and I already knew it was going to surpass yesterday as the worst of my life.

I laid on my end of the bench, staring up at the pealing ceiling. Levon was snoring loudly in the other corner of the cell. I needed to think. My life, which, this time yesterday, was fantastic, was about to turn into a dripping bag of shit. Nicole was dead. Annie was probably lying in our bed crying, trying to think about how she was going to raise three kids on her own, and who she could turn to for legal advice. Hopefully, she didn't think I killed Nicole. But, given the set of facts she'd been given last night, she probably didn't know what to think. She may have even been doubting she knew me at all. After all, if I could hide a five-year affair from her, I was probably capable of hiding other aspects of my nefarious life.

I think that was what bothered me most- the idea that Annie could possibly think I was capable of killing someone. And, just as that thought came to me, I realized the irony. After all, she'd been living with a killer, sleeping next to a murderer, entrusting her children to someone who'd killed two thirteen-year-old girls. Why wouldn't she think me capable of murdering again?

What a fucking nightmare I'd gotten myself into. And poor Nicole. Who would want to kill her? She was such a kind person. How could someone take her life? And what a horrible way to die- stabbed in the neck and back! No one who knew her could possibly do that.

Around seven in the morning, a little light started creeping into the cell from a window down the hall. A new day was beginning. A day that would drag me into hell. I never dreaded a day the way I did that one. I tried to imagine what Annie was doing- probably showering so she'd be ready to deal with the kids when they woke. What would she tell them when they asked why I wasn't at breakfast? The kids were old enough, they'd want an explanation. They knew I wasn't due back at work until Wednesday, the day school resumed. She'd have to tell them something.

Around eight, an attendant brought in a tray of surprisingly decent food. Despite my dire predicament, I was hungry and ate voraciously while Levon continued to snore. Then the same guy came back to say someone was here to see me. I was led back to the interrogation room from the night before where Larry Mentz and a tall guy with a grey ponytail were waiting.

"Happy to see you made it through the night." Larry joked, but I didn't think it was funny.

"Leo, this is Bob Colgan."

I extended my hand, but the man didn't even get up from his chair. Instead, he just pointed at the third seat at the wooden table.

Larry felt the chill in the room and offered, "Leo, Bob's the guy I told you about last night. He's the best I know. He's the guy you want defending you if it comes to that."

I studied the man in whose hands my future might depend. He looked to be in his mid-sixties. The long grey hair didn't jive with the three thousand dollar Brioni suit and crisp white button-down, but I trusted Larry, so Colgan was my man. I took a seat and said, "So, you're the guy I need but probably can't afford, huh?"

"If you couldn't afford me, I'd still be in bed. My fee is twelve hundred an hour plus expenses. If we go to trial, we'll discuss a fixed fee. For now, let's take it one step at a time."

I looked over to Larry, who nodded.

"Okay, where do we start?"

"We start with bail. From what Larry's told me, you should make bail. You have no priors, a stable place in the community, a wife and kids. The judge will know you're not going anywhere. The only question is, will he view you as a threat to others if you're out? I've got you a hearing at eleven-thirty, but I don't know who the judge is. A lot depends on who we draw."

"Well, what do we do between now and ten-thirty? I asked.

Larry chimed in. "I brought you some cloths for court." He pointed at a paper bag on the floor.

"When I got to your house, the cops were just finishing up. They went through your closet, basement and garage. Of course, they came up with nothing, but they did make a mess."

"How was Annie? How is she taking this?" I needed to know.

Larry rubbed his eyes. "She's very confused, Leo. Obviously, she's looking for answers. But she's okay. I told her, one way or the other, she'd be able to see you today. Either you get bail and go home, or she comes to see you later."

I looked at Colgan. "Anything I can do to improve my chances of going home today?"

Without looking up from his notepad, he responded, "Yeah, appear innocent."

We spent the next hour reviewing the facts I'd given Larry the night before. I was happy just to be out of the cell and far from Levon. A little repetition wouldn't kill me. And Colgan asked each question a little differently. He wasn't assuming my innocence. I had to prove to him I hadn't killed Nicole. But I had no proof. There was no one who could attest to my whereabouts yesterday until I got home from the beach.

"So, tell me this," my new defense lawyer wanted to know, "How is it that someone says they saw you dropping the alleged murder weapon in a trash can, then running to your car?"

"I have no idea. Like I've said, I was at the beach yesterday. I did take a walk and then return to my car. I certainly never ran, and I certainly didn't try to stash a knife in..." It hit me like a Louisville Slugger.

"What is it?" Colgan asked.

"Holy shit!" I responded as the recollection of the previous day's trash collection hit me. "I did throw a knife in the garbage can. I did."

"You want to explain that?" Larry said with a hint of skepticism.

I closed my eyes and tried to remember the morning and what junk I'd picked up as I walked the shoreline. I remembered a beer bottle, a plastic cup, some fishing line and..., and an old fishing knife.

"That's it!" I yelled. "I did throw a knife in the trash can at the west end of the beach. I'd picked up some trash, a beer bottle, a few plastic cups, a wad of fishing line and a fishing knife. They were all along the shore as I walked."

"Why did you pick up other people's garbage?" Colgan asked.

"Because they didn't. I always pick up liter on the beach. It makes me feel like I'm doing something worthwhile."

"So, someone saw you throw a knife and a bunch of garbage in the trash can, thinks it's suspicious, so he follows you to your car, gets your plate number and calls the police." Larry was putting the pieces together.

"So, that's the knife the police recovered. They don't have the murder weapon. They have an old fishing knife that washed up on the beach." Colgan added with a smile. "Someone's going to look awfully silly."

"Leo, do you remember where you picked up the knife?" Larry asked.

I thought about it but couldn't recall for sure. "I think it was the last thing I picked up before heading for the garbage can. I can't be sure, but I don't think it was down by the water. I think it was somewhere back near the garbage can."

"Why do you ask, Larry?" Colgan wanted to know.

"Well, if you're going to bring this up at the bail hearing, and it's going to embarrass someone, we should have as many facts as possible. We should know what sort of knife it was, what it looked like, etc."

"Good point. Leo, can you describe the knife you found?"

"To me, it was trash. I really didn't pay much attention. I'm pretty sure it was a fishing knife."

"Do you remember anything about it?"

"No. Sorry. I guess my head was just in a different place. Who pays attention to liter?"

"Okay, no problem, Leo. I think we're in good shape." Then Bob Colgan turned to Larry and laid out his strategy. "It seems to me, we have a clear case of a well-intentioned good Samaritan mistaking Leo, a devoted father and husband, for someone who was disposing a suspicious knife. All he was doing was disposing of some liter he collected on the beach. He's a fucking Boy Scout. Sure, his fingerprints will be all over that knife, but it doesn't matter. It's not the murder weapon. It's just an old fishing knife."

I was still skeptical. "Okay, so what are you saying?"

"Larry responded, "I think when the ADA hears this, he's going to drop you as a suspect. We won't have to push for bail. There won't even be a charge."

Colgan chimed in. "Well, let me play devil's advocate for a minute. I'll be the ADA," he said with a long pause. "All I hear," emphasizing the word 'I', "is a possible explanation for why Mr. Monday was seen with the murder weapon and running from the scene. It just sounds like an excuse to me. This is not a slam dunk. But if they have nothing else tying Leo to the crime, I can't see any basis for a charge. At least not yet."

"What do you mean, not yet?" I wanted to know.

"What I mean is, as long as they have nothing else."

"Like what?"

"Like they find some of the victim's blood on anything they pulled from your car or home."

"Well, that's not going to happen." I assured them.

"Glad to hear that, Leo." Colgan looked at me sternly.

"So, assuming they have nothing else, do you think they completely drop the charge?" Larry asked Colgan.

"If there's nothing else, I think we can make a compelling case for a dismissal. We should have Leo back home for lunch."

The thought of not having to spend another minute in that cell was more than appealing. But, not being in the cell meant having to go home and face Annie. I think I dreaded that more than going back to Levon and his odious snoring.

We were going over the explanation of the knife in the trash when there was a soft knock on the door. A shapely young redhead walked in holding a tattered briefcase. She wore a navy- blue suit that clung to her in all the right places. She was very attractive and seemed to recognize Bob Colgan as soon as she walked in.

"So nice to see you, Rita." Colgan said. Then he got up from his chair for the first time and embraced the young woman. He turned to Larry Mentz and explained, "Larry, this is Rita Lucas. She's Harold Lucas' daughter and probably the next district attorney for Suffolk County."

"You're at least ten years ahead of yourself, Bob, but you usually are."

"You're being modest Rita."

I motioned with my hands to indicate I'd like to join the conversation or at least, understand who this was. Larry picked up on my concern.

"Leo Monday, meet Rita Lucas, Suffolk County's most pleasant Assistant District Attorney. Rita, this is Leo, a good friend of mine and currently the temporary guest of our county."

The attractive redhead put her briefcase on the table and proclaimed, "Bob, I'm not here for a social visit. I've been assigned to the eleven-thirty bail hearing."

"You? You're the ADA on this? How'd you get so lucky, Rita?" Colgan asked.

"New kid always has to work the holidays. I've been here all weekend."

Then she turned and looked directly at me. "Mr. Monday, can we go over a few things before we head into court for the arraignment?"

Colgan responded for me. "Come on Rita. You know I'm not going to let you talk to my client. And don't get too excited about this one. In fact, you may want to put some distance between yourself and this case of mistaken identity."

The shapely redhead took a seat across from the two attorneys and next to me. "What's that supposed to mean, Bob?"

"It means your witness, the guy that observed Mr. Monday disposing of some trash he picked up on the beach, is mistaken. You don't have the murder weapon. You've got an old fishing knife Leo found in the sand while he was walking the shoreline." Colgan took off his wire-rimmed glasses, ran his left hand through his long grey hair, then added, "Look Rita. You should be looking out for you on this one. Don't stick your neck out for Spada."

Dom Spada, Suffolk County's District Attorney was known for grandstanding on capital cases. He made a name for himself prosecuting drug gangs and going after doctors who were playing fast and loose with opioid prescriptions. He liked to see his face on the cover of Newsday, the local paper, at least once a month. Spada, as he was known, was elected DA the previous year and had already pissed off a bunch of his assistants because of his arrogance. But the public, who were tired of seeing their suburban communities terrorized by the drug gangs, loved him. He was quickly becoming something of a hero to the taxpayers who wanted their neighborhoods back.

"Are you saying the knife PD pulled out of the garbage, isn't the murder weapon?"

"Yep. That's what I'm saying."

"So, how do you explain why he was there? Why was he observed less than a hundred yards from the dunes where Mrs. Sullivan, someone he worked with, was killed? I'm sorry. There's a little too much coincidence here for me. I think I'll reserve judgement until the labs come back on the knife."

"Careful what you wish for, Rita. Your lab results are going to show that's not the knife. And, as for Mr. Monday's presence at the beach, he's already explained he and Mrs. Sullivan had arranged a morning rendezvous. They had a personal relationship that goes way back. My client had no reason to see the poor lady harmed. They were friends but he hasn't seen her in months."

"Well, I hope that's all true Mr. Monday. For your sake, I hope it's true." Then she turned to Colgan. "But you know as well I Bob, there was probable cause here. I mean with the eye-witness and all."

"Can I see the witness' statement? So far, we've only been told of his existence, but not who he is or exactly what he reported. You understand my concern, Rita?"

The shapely redhead who seemed to hold my fate in her hands shifted in her seat. "It was an anonymous report."

"What? Say that again." Colgan said mockingly. "You're telling me my client has been detained based on an anonymous witness? Is that what you're saying?"

"Yes Bob. The second precinct received a call at…" She checked her notes. "The call came in at 10:25 A.M. The witness reported hearing a woman screaming, then gave a description of a white male matching your client's appearance throwing something in a nearby trash can and running to a blue sedan. He even got the plate numbers, MJG 138. Is that your car, Mr. Monday?"

"Don't answer that Leo." Colgan shot back.

"A simple question." Rita answered.

"Look Rita," Colgan said with a slightly patronized tone, "Mr. Monday has already volunteered that he drove his car to the beach yesterday and was waiting for Mrs. Sullivan near where you say she was killed. He's also told us he makes a habit of clearing the beach of any trash he comes across on his walks and did find a fishing knife that he dropped in the trash. He certainly didn't have to tell you all that, but he did. He's a Boy Scout, not a killer."

"Maybe."

"No maybe about it. He's not your killer and that fishing knife is not your murder weapon. So, before you look foolish, I suggest you think about how hard you want to push this."

There was another knock at the door. This time, the ADA barked, "Come in."

An overweight man walked in. Based on his attire, he appeared to be some sort of messenger for the court. He had a uniform but, unlike everyone else in the building with a uniform, he wasn't wearing a weapon.

"This is for you Miss Lucas," he said as he extended an envelope in the ADA's direction.

"Thanks Billy. Is Judge Apgar ready for us?"

"Yeah. I think she's running on time. I'll check and let you know."

"Thanks again Billy."

Colgan turned to Rita Lucas after the court clerk left the room. "Apgar's sitting this morning?"

"Who's Apgar?" I wanted to know.

It was Larry Mentz who filled me in.

"Sarah Apgar is a cranky old lady, to be kind. She's stayed on the bench way longer than she should have. I think she was elected in the seventies."

Colgan cut in. "This could be good. I know Judge Apgar can be a pain in the ass when it comes to procedure, but she can spot a bullshit case a mile away. No, this is good. If all you have, Rita, is an anonymous witness saying he saw my client throwing trash away a thousand yards from your murder scene, I'm happy to have Apgar on the bench."

As my attorney began to reiterate all the reasons I couldn't be the killer and sang my praises as a pillar of the community, Rita Lucas opened the envelope the clerk left behind. She read its single yellow page contents. When Colgan was finished with his lecture, she handed him the yellow piece of paper and sat in silence, awaiting his response.

I could tell by Colgan's face that it wasn't good news. He cleared his throat and looked at me. He chose his words carefully.

"This is the County's lab report. Of course, we'll want to do our own. But, it says, along with your fingerprints, traces of the victim's blood were found on the knife they claim you threw in the garbage."

XXV

Because my fingerprints tied me to the murder weapon, we spent several agonizing minutes in front of Judge Sarah Apgar. The diminutive and elderly judge seemed to give me the benefit of the doubt when it came to my habit of sweeping the beach for liter. She was also skeptical about the anonymous witness report. And, despite my relationship with the victim, she saw no reason to believe the ADA's contention that I had reason to kill Nicole. But the fact that the murder weapon somehow held both Nicole's blood and my fingerprints, was too much for the aged jurist. I was charged with capital murder and Colgan's request for bail was denied.

This meant I'd be the guest of Suffolk County's detention center for the foreseeable future. As Judge Apgar checked her calendar for the earliest possible date for my trial, it occurred to me I was in for a miserable experience. Having never been in a jail before, my only reference point was my evening with Levon and what I've seen on TV, neither of which gave me any comfort. I guess I'd always assumed that innocent people don't go to jail. Those in jail, probably deserved to be there. And while my lawyer and the judge discussed availability, and I heard the words December and January thrown around, I thought about what the next few months held for me.

The first thing I thought about was my family. How would they get by without me? How could Annie handle the three kids without my help?

Then I wondered if I would even have a family to worry about. Once Annie knew all the facts about my affair with Nicole, would she even consider me part of the family anymore? And, if she knew I'd been lying to her for over five years, would she even believe me when I told her I didn't kill Nicole? I wouldn't if I were her.

Then I thought about my job. What would Michael think? How would this affect the business' reputation? Would I even have a job when this was over? I mean, I assumed, at some point this would all be over; that the truth would come out and everyone would realize I had nothing to do with Nicole's murder. But maybe that wasn't going to happen. Maybe this bizarre nightmare was going to continue. How long would Michael stand by me? More importantly, would he stand by me at all?

So, as Judge Apgar and Bob Colgan tried to agree on the time and place of my potential crucifixion, I began to realize this was real. I wasn't going home anytime soon. Like it or not, fair or not, I would have to deal with this major intrusion into my life. I also realized, like it or not, I brought this on myself. My relationship with Nicole Sullivan, my affair, was why I was in this mess. I had no one to blame but me.

True, this was obviously a case of mistaken identity, but if not for my philandering, I wouldn't have been at the beach yesterday morning. I wouldn't have put myself in a position to be mistaken for a killer. My fault. All my fault.

And worse, if not for our rendezvous, Nicole would still be alive. If not for me, she wouldn't have been at the beach yesterday. So, in a way, I am responsible for her death. I didn't kill her, but I am the reason she's dead. Thinking back on it, I think that thought weighed on me more than the prospect of a few months in jail. For the fourth time in my life, I was responsible for the death of a human being.

After about twenty minutes, it was determined the next time I would need to be in front of Judge Apgar would be early December. That meant, without bail, I'd be in prison for months.

"Judge", I shouted, "Can I say something?"

My lawyer looked at me as if to say he didn't approve, but the judge allowed me to speak.

"Certainly, Mr. Monday. What would you like to say to the court? Just keep in mind that whatever you say can be used against you by the court."

I hadn't thought this through, but I plowed ahead.

"Judge, I haven't killed anybody. I'm sure you hear that from lots of people, but in my case, it is the truth. I'm not a killer. I may be a terrible husband, but I cared deeply for Nicole. I could never think about hurting her. I'd have no reason to hurt her. Isn't that important? Shouldn't there be a motive?"

"Mr. Monday, this is just an arraignment hearing. And you're correct, it will be incumbent on the prosecution to prove beyond a reasonable doubt that you are guilty of this hedonist crime. Motive will be a component of their case. But for now, I have to rule on the information before me. And with the information the ADA has presented, your fingerprints and the victim's blood on the same weapon, I have no choice but to schedule a trial."

It sounded like she believed I hadn't killed Nicole, but needed an explanation for the knife. So did I.

"But your honor, I have a family. I need to provide for them. I have three young children. It's not fair to keep me from them just because someone's made a mistake."

"What mistake is that Mr. Monday?"

I wasn't sure if she was referring to my mistake- having an affair with another woman. Maybe she was judging me. But, I said, "Someone has to have made a mistake about the knife. My fingerprints can't possibly be on the knife used to kill Nicole. I found that knife in the sand."

Judge Apgar leaned back on her chair. "Mr. Monday, it is possible that you innocently found the murder weapon, and thinking it was just a piece of trash, threw it in the barrel. Frankly, I find it hard to believe whoever did murder Mrs. Sullivan would dispose of the murder weapon so close to the scene. And I think the ADA should also be thinking about that. And if that were your only connection to this crime, I would be inclined to release you on a sizable bond.

But, your prior association with the victim and the fact that you acknowledge a planned rendezvous yesterday morning, is too much for me to overlook. For that reason, I have no choice but to deny bail and remand you to the Sheriff's custody pending any new information your attorney or the ADA present."

She banged her gavel and calmly said, "Next case."

I turned to Colgan and gave him a desperate look. "There's got to be something…" But he cut me off and motioned for me to move to the left where a bailiff was waiting for me with an opened set of handcuffs.

****

I spent the next three hours in a cell, waiting for a transport bus to take me, and several other criminals to Riverhead. The Suffolk County detention center in Riverhead was to be my home until my trial would begin in December. The thought of spending months in jail terrified me. I've seen enough movies to understand privileged white guys like me don't do well in prison.

But before that hell was to begin, I had three hours with Larry to sort out my life. There's a lot to think about when you're facing months, maybe years in jail. Practical issues like making sure the mortgage gets paid and the family car gets taken in for an oil change; things that, up until now, I had been responsible for while Annie focused on the kids.

I asked Larry to contact several people, starting with Michael Chatterton. I needed him to explain my situation to others, so they didn't rely on the inevitable gossip that was sure to come from this. Larry was a wise man and suggested he talk to a friend of his at Newsday, to make sure they covered the story fairly and maybe even create an editorial campaign to push the DA to focus on finding the real killer.

I was astounded to learn I wouldn't be allowed to contact Annie until after I got to Riverhead. Even then, it was unclear if I would have access to a telephone the first few days. The thought of poor Annie not knowing what was happening tortured me, but I knew Larry would go straight from the courthouse back to Huntington. He promised to completely fill her in on the day's events and, to explain my history with Nicole in the best possible light- if there was one.

It became obvious to me that I wasn't going to be the one to tell Annie what had happened. She'd hear from others before I'd get to see her in person or even speak with her on the phone. So, before she heard rumors or read a torrid account of my exploits in tomorrow's paper, I wanted Larry to sit with her and explain what I had and hadn't done. I also wanted him to assure her I was okay.

Then it occurred to me, she might not give a shit if I'm okay. After all, I'd betrayed her. I'd been caught in an affair with a married woman. An affair I'd been carrying on for over five years. Why should Annie care that I'm okay?

I guessed that by now, Annie had asked her mother to come and help with the kids. In some ways, I felt a little better knowing she wouldn't be completely alone through this. But, knowing how she felt about me, Daisy would probably already be counseling my wife to hire the best divorce lawyer on Long Island.

There was so much to think about as I prepared to begin my life behind bars, and so little time to make plans. Larry Mentz was fantastic, and I will never forget how much he did for me in those very dark days. He promised to take care of everything, even the things I hadn't yet thought about. He told me he'd listed himself as well as Bob Colgan, as my attorneys. This would allow him unlimited access to me while in prison. He told me he'd bring me a notebook and pen so I could start keeping track of the tasks I needed him to take care of for me. There would also be lists for Michael.

Then, at about three in the afternoon, I was taken to a white school bus and driven to Riverhead. There were only two other inmates on the bus; a short black kid who sang the entire trip, and an emaciated white guy whose arms and neck were covered with tattoos. I assumed, based on his behavior, that he was some sort of drug addict. He was shivering and sweating on the otherwise comfortable ride, and said not a word.

When we arrived at the Suffolk County detention center, the three of us were "processed". This meant each of us would be finger-printed again, showered, and given our prison garb; an orange jumpsuit, socks, sneakers, a Fruit of the Loom tee shirt and a pair of boxer shorts. Fortunately, the clothing was all new, the tee shirt was still in a plastic bag which was quickly removed. I'm not sure what nefarious deeds an inmate could do with a plastic bag, but they were taking no chances.

Then I was handed two blankets, two sheets and a pillow and told to follow a guard who actually introduced himself as Benny. Benny showed me to my cell and gave me a six-page handout which covered all the dos and don'ts of the facility.

I was relieved to find my cell had only one bed. I later learned, because I'd been accused of a capital offense, I'd be kept to myself since I could be a danger to others.

"Read the brochure. It covers just about most of what you need to know." Benny said as I walked into my new home. "And just don't give the guards any shit. Believe me, you'll regret that big time. I'm guessing you'll stay in line and you'll be fine." And then he slammed the bars shut and I was alone. Frighteningly alone.

Like a kid just arriving for his first day of camp, I made up my bed and sat and read the rules of the house. I learned that meals in the cafeteria were served three times a day; 7:30 A.M., noon and 6:00 P.M., and don't try to get any food at any other time. Although my cell had one overhead light that I controlled, all lights went out at 10:30 P.M. I was responsible for the cleanliness of my pedestal sink and toilet and there were penalties for not complying that would be imposed on visiting hours, exercise time and yard time. My cell contained a small metal table and one chair.

My brochure explained I was not to mark-up either in any way.

All in all, these were rules I'd have no problem with, although I might have felt differently if I believed I'd be there for years.

I learned later, that the facility that now called me its guest was a minimum-security prison; meaning, I was incarcerated with one hundred fifty-two other men, mostly first-timers, who had been accused of lesser crimes than I. Apparently, Bob Colgan's influence with Judge Apgar got me this special treatment. Ordinarily, someone accused of murder would have been housed in a different building here in Riverhead, one that was more like what you see in the movies. But neither Colgan nor the judge believed I really killed Nicole, and they took pity on me. For example, I thought I'd have to follow the script from the movies- you know, walk up to the biggest, meanest-looking black guy and punch him in the face just to show I wasn't afraid of these guys. Thankfully, that wasn't the case. As it turns out, the biggest, meanest-looking black guy in my section was an actuary from Melville who had too many unpaid traffic tickets. Horatio, as I came to know him, was only with us a few days.

I was not so lucky. Larry Mentz came to see me on day two, and gave me two pieces of terrible news. First, as it turns out, Judge Apgar had a conflict with the trial date she'd originally set and had to move my trial back to January 12th. That meant, I'd be in jail at least four months including

Thanksgiving and Christmas. It also meant the chances of hanging on to my job at MAC were pretty slim. Michael couldn't run the day to day on his own for that long. He'd have to move someone up to do my job. But the other bad news was even worse.

"I had a long conversation with Annie, Leo. As you would expect, she's really hurting." Larry told me with his hands clasped between his knees. He tried not to make direct eye contact with me as he explained further.

"She's asked her mother to come and stay with her for a while. She's very upset. If there's any good news, it's that she doesn't believe you killed anyone. But the affair, well, that's the thing."

"I understand," I said. "I just need to talk to her myself. When can she visit me? Maybe I can try to explain. I mean, the affair had nothing to do with her. It was all me."

Larry gave me a stern look. "No matter how much you say that, Annie will see it as her failure as well as yours. You know that."

"Well, at least I can give her some reassurance that I have never stopped loving her. Maybe that would help. I also need to talk to her about money. She has no idea about our finances. I've always been the one to pay bills. I don't know if she even knows what bank we use. I need to help her keep that stuff straight for the next few months.

Larry, I need to talk to her before her mother starts putting ideas in her head. Daisy will use this to drive a wedge between us. She'll tell Annie to distance herself from me just to save social face. You don't know her."

"The problem, Leo," he said with a palpable sadness in his voice, "Is that Annie doesn't want to come here. I've already told her. She could have come with me today and she turned me down."

That hurt. That hurt more than any kick in the balls or punch in the face I've ever taken. It hurt more than the betrayal I felt when Annie had her affair.

"She said that? She said she doesn't want to talk to me?"

"Well, at least not today. I'll tell her how much you want to see her. Maybe that will make a difference. Maybe I can convince her to come on Friday. That's when I'll be back. I've got a board meeting tomorrow in Manhattan I need to attend. So, I'll see you Friday. Colgan's coming too. He wants to start working on your defense."

Larry was a good friend. At that point, he was the person I most depended upon. I needed him to be my voice with the world outside. I gave him a list of bank accounts, insurance policies, investments and bills that needed to be paid, and asked him to go over it with Annie. He took the three-page list from my hand and said, "Leo, you know I'll do whatever you need."

Then I handed him another hand-written letter and list, eight pages in all. "This one is for Michael Chatterton. There's so much going on at MAC the next few weeks. He's going to need this."

Larry rose from his chair in the visitor room. He looked tired. More than that, he looked genuinely concerned about me. "Alright Leo. I'll take care of everything. You just keep your head down in here and use the next two days to think about anything Colgan can use in your defense. There's a lot of work to do and believe it or not, four months isn't a lot of time to prepare a murder case.

So, I spent every minute of the next two days going over in my head how this all happened. And no matter how I looked at it, it saddened me to think my selfish relationship with Nicole is what ultimately cost her her life. There was no denying it. If I hadn't gotten involved with her in the first place, if I'd never asked her to have lunch with me that first day of work, she'd be alive today. And, I wouldn't be in jail.

The thought of Nicole, lying somewhere in a coffin, sent chills through me. She was only forty-seven. She had so much life ahead of her. The more I thought about it, the more depressed I grew. And the more I grew depressed, the less I was able to focus on the task Larry assigned me. I needed to think. It was all he asked me to do. Yet, the more I thought, the more I thought about poor Nicole.

Because there wasn't much to think about. If the ADA could prove it was Nicole's blood on the knife, and if they could also prove those were my fingerprints on the same knife, it would certainly appear I was her killer. But, if the knife I picked up on the beach was in fact, proven to be the murder weapon, then the clear explanation for why my prints were on it was simply, I had the coincidental misfortune of coming across the murder weapon before anyone else did. Thinking it was just an old fishing knife, a piece of trash, I threw it out. There was no other possible explanation.

Or so I thought.

XXVI

It's been a few days since I've written in this journal. The combination of my stomach discomfort, increasingly pervasive headaches and six inches of snow outside have kept me secluded in my apartment for a few days. Not that I have anywhere to go anyway. But, I used the time to write each of my children a good-bye letter.

After I'm gone, I hope this journal will give them some insight into who I was and the events in my life that they knew little or nothing about. Perhaps by understanding my history they will come to appreciate how much happens behind the scenes in the life of a parent. Maybe it will make them each better people and parents. Maybe they will appreciate their father was just an ordinary man, a reasonable man who wasn't perfect.

But the letters are personal. In the letters, I explained to each of them, just how much I loved them. I tried to get them to understand how much joy their lives brought to Annie and me. I want them to carry on the love their parents felt for one another. If I accomplished nothing else, I wanted them to know my death was what I wanted because of how much I love them. Perhaps it will be easiest for Stephen, a parent himself, to appreciate how important it was for me to spare them the pain of caring for me in my last days. He saw what I went through with Annie. They all know how emotionally crippling it was for me to see her atrophy before my eyes. And they understand how agonizing it was for me to watch my wife suffer, to listen to her beg God to take her.

Although I tried to focus on the positive, my letters each contained my petition for their forgiveness. What they will someday read in this journal will show them a side of their father they've never known. Perhaps it is my final act of contrition. I hope they can see it that way.

I ended each letter with the words, "I love you. Keep me in your hearts and I will never be far away."

I also wrote a letter to my grandson, Peter. I'm hoping Stephen will find the right time to read it to him. His letter completely focused on the future. Peter was just a baby when Annie died so he has no memory of her. That's a shame. He would have adored her. I included some photos of he and Annie that I took shortly after his birth. Perhaps he will keep those happy images in his mind when he is older and reflects on past generations. His letter I ended with, "Always be brave and kind and do what you know is right."

I put each letter in separate envelopes and gave them to my lawyer, who visited me this morning. Frank Martorano, an estate and trust attorney Larry Mentz recommended years ago, was kind enough to pay me a rare house-call so we could finalize my will and some trusts I set up after Annie passed. The singular upside to knowing you're going to die soon is being able to plan for your demise. More to the point, to be able to plan for what happens to your stuff after your demise. In my case, it's relatively simple. I'm dividing it up five ways; one share to each of my three children, one share for my grandson, and one share to a charitable trust Frank set up for me. My three kids will act as the trustees of the trust and make all the decisions about what charities get the money. I hope managing a charitable trust will help make them thoughtful stewards of the funds.

I was surprised to learn I am worth close to twenty million dollars. Between my MAC Technology stock, my apartment, a few mutual funds at Vanguard, and a life insurance policy, I'm worth more than I thought. If I'd known that, I might have bought better wine along the way.

Frank set up a few trusts to lessen the inheritance and capital gains taxes the kids will have to pay. There were dozens of forms I needed to sign, but in the end, I felt good about having things so well organized for my heirs. It's too bad everyone doesn't get the opportunity to do this type of planning.

After all the forms were signed, witnessed and slid back into Frank's briefcase, he clicked the clasp and moved it to the end of the table.

"Leo, we should also talk about the next six months. If you don't want the kids to be burdened with your end-of-life experience, and I know you don't, you'll need someone else to help. You'll need hospice care."

"I've thought about that Frank." Although I had no intentions of being around for six months, I knew I had to plan for the end.

"I suggest, when it's the appropriate time, you consider having live-in care. You've got two extra bedrooms here. You might as well stay in your own home and be as comfortable as possible."

Frank had no idea how uncomfortable I was already. For our meeting today, I dressed in my best Brooks Brothers slacks, shirt and sport jacket. So, he had no way of knowing it was the first time I'd been out of pajamas in four days. He had no way of knowing about the chronic vomiting and headaches that had become part of my life. He had no way of knowing how close to my end I was.

"You're right, Frank. I do want to stay in my home."

"Ask your doctor. He'll be able to give you the names of some good services."

"Oh, yeah. I already talked to Romaro. He suggested an agency that provides private duty nurses who can do eight-hour shifts with the late shift being a sleepover. They can do meds, I.V.s, they even prepare meals."

"Sounds perfect. Don't wait too long to get in touch with them."

What I hadn't told Frank, or anyone else, is that my end-of-life nursing care was starting on Friday.

XXVII

I'd spent the last two days mired in nightmares about Nicole. Thoughts of her lying in the cold sand, blood pouring from her throat, haunted me. In one nightmare, I was lying on the beach listening to music with ear buds strung from my Walkman, while Nicole was screaming in the dunes just a few yards away. The me in my dreams was oblivious to her cries for help while the conscious me could see that blood was streaming from the dunes and soaking my beach blanket crimson as I slept.

Later the same night, I dreamed I was on the chairlift ascending the mountain at Jay Peak. Riding next to me was Chris Hoffman but he was dressed not in traditional ski wear, but in a bathing suit and was wearing a life jacket. The next thing I knew, he was falling off the chair and when I turned to look at him, it was the face of Nicole spiraling down toward the jagged rocks.

Both nightmares woke me just as they climaxed in those terrifying images. I laid on my bed, staring up at the concrete ceiling of my cell. I tried to imagine I was somewhere else, somewhere safe and warm, but the stark reality of my situation pushed its way back into my consciousness. How the hell did I get here? How do such bizarre circumstances weave their way into one man's life; one otherwise ordinary man?

For the first time in my life, I found myself feeling sorry for myself. Yet, I knew I'd brought this all on myself. I conjured an image of my dead parents, waiting for me at the gates of heaven. Although they were welcomed, they hadn't gone in. They were waiting for me all these years just so they could punish me for what I'd done to my sisters and to make sure I wasn't allowed to join them in paradise.

What kind of a man is so hideous that his own mother and father want him in hell? I focused on that question a moment, and although I didn't think of myself as a monster, it gave me a frightening picture of how others see me. More to the point, how others would see me if they knew all the things I'd done.

And now, everyone would know one of my missteps, ironically, probably the least egregious. Everyone in my life would know that I'd betrayed my wife. And even if they didn't believe I'd killed my mistress, there would always be some doubt.

I found myself crying as the lights outside my cell clicked on at seven A.M. Tears were soaking my pillow. But the garish light rushing into my cell brought me back from my self-pity. The nightmares of my selfish past had to give way to the harsh reality of today. I was in jail. I was confined to a ninety square-foot cell surrounded by concrete and metal bars, much like a zoo animal. That was my present. That was my reality.

It was Friday morning. I'd only been here four nights and yet, I didn't think I could endure four more. Larry Mentz and Bob Colgan, my dream-team defense, were supposed to be here today to begin the process of proving I hadn't technically done what I knew I was responsible for.

At nine-thirty I was brought down to the room where attorneys got to meet with their clients. As in the movies, it was a stark room with nothing more than a cold metal table and four equally unpleasant chairs. Larry was seated at the head of the table. To his left, a sport jacket was folded over another chair and Bob Colgan's brief case rested on the table.

Larry rose to greet me. "How you holding up, kid?"

"I've had better nights' sleep." I replied. I'm sure Larry didn't want to hear about my nightmares. "Where's Colgan?"

Larry finished a note on his pad, then said, "Funny thing. Bob and I got here about thirty minutes ago and as soon as we sat down, Lucas, the ADA, came in and asked him to meet privately with her. He hasn't come back from wherever they went."

"What does that mean?"

"That's a good question. I can't imagine what she had to tell him that they couldn't discuss in front of me."

"Have you seen Annie?" I asked.

"I spoke with her when I got back from my board meeting, yesterday. She said she's doing okay. Her mom's there with her."

"Did she say anything about coming to see me?"

"Yep. As a matter of fact, she's coming today. I think she was planning to be here for the two o'clock visiting session. I gave her directions. I guess her mom will stay with the kids."

That was the first piece of good news I'd had since Monday. But it meant my first conversation with Annie would take place here, in jail. The thought of having this particular conversation in a room filled with other inmates and their visitors, terrified me. How could I tell my wife how sorry I was in front of other people? How could I confess my infidelity with others around? And worse, I planned to beg Annie to forgive me and take me back. How could I do that publicly?

"Also, Michael called me this morning and said to tell you he appreciated the list you made for him. He plans to come here on Sunday. Leo, he's one hundred percent behind you. He wants to talk about some business stuff so, unless you tell me otherwise, I see no reason for me to be here for that."

That too was wonderful news. But my mind was back on Annie and what I'd say to her. How was I going to convince her I never for a moment stopped loving her? What could I say that would right the five-year wrong I'd done? I needed time to think about this, but I wasn't going to get it. Larry had other things he wanted to talk about.

"Leo, we have to start thinking about how we posture in court. We need to spend as much time as the judge will allow, showing you, not as a villainous murderer, but as the good-natured, father of three and pillar of the community that you are. We need a jury to see the boy scout."

"Where do we start?"

"Well, until Bob gets back, let's start with your involvement in Huntington. What, if anything, do you do that would help?"

I thought about that. The truth was, I'd been so busy with MAC Tech and my career, I wasn't involved in our community at all. Except for a "daddy and me" program I took Stephen to at the YMCA on Saturday mornings, I had little involvement with our community. I spent eighty percent of my waking life in Manhattan. Huntington was my home but just as a place to sleep and be with my kids. I wasn't involved in a single civic activity. Larry wasn't thrilled to hear that but understood.

"Okay, how about church. You guys have a church you go to regularly?"

I confessed, "Not really. The last time we were in church was when the twins were baptized. That was at St. Pat's. The kids are sort of young to bring to church and, frankly, Sunday mornings we try to spend doing things with the kids at home. But the truth is, neither of us are very religious anyway."

"I'm one swing away from a strikeout." Larry quipped.

Trying not to sound defensive, I said, "Larry, my life for the past two years has been about helping Michael get MAC

Tech off the ground and helping Annie deal with three infants. There hasn't been much time for the choir or food pantry."

"Okay. I get it. We'll figure out a way to make you look like Mary Poppins at home. Let's talk about…"

But he never got to finish that sentence. And, as it turns out, it didn't matter. Bob Colgan came through the door holding several pieces of paper and looking like the cat who just swallowed the canary.

****

Colgan couldn't wait to give us his news. "Well, Mr. Monday, as much as I would have liked to defend you, collect a huge fee, and get my face on the evening news, I'm afraid that isn't going to happen." Then he paused for a dramatic moment while Larry and I were left confused.

"The DA isn't going to pursue the case against you." He said triumphantly. "You'll be out of here this afternoon!"

To say the least, I was stunned. For a moment, I thought it was some sort of twisted joke; maybe Colgan's way to make the point that defending me wasn't going to be easy.

"How can that be?" I asked incredulously.

Colgan sat down, loosened his carefully knotted tie, and began. "Turns out, they have their killer. They have a guy named Hector Guzman in custody for the murder and have charged Roger Sullivan with conspiracy to commit murder."

"What?" was all I could stammer.

Larry Mentz was a bit more to the point. "The husband? Son of a bitch!"

"I can only tell you what Rita told me a few minutes ago. Frankly, I'm surprised she told me as much as she did. But we go way back."

"What did she tell you?" Larry begged.

"Turns out, Roger Sullivan knew about your affair with his wife for over a year. I have no idea how he found out. Rita wouldn't give me the details, but he's known a long time and had the phone at his home tapped since January. He also had you followed several times. That's how they caught him. They got wind of the phone tap while doing routine background work in preparing the case against you. She didn't tell me, but I assume they we going for phone records that would document calls you made to each other. That way they could document your relationship with the victim. While they were doing that, they happened upon the tap."

"He had us followed?" I asked.

"Apparently so. Rita was light on the details, and frankly, I don't really want to know any more than I do."

"Why's that?" Larry asked.

"Because, in order to expedite Leo's release today, I agreed he would sign this." He dropped a single piece of typewritten paper between Larry and me. "It's a release.

They want to be sure Leo won't sue the county for false arrest. Under the circumstances, Leo, I think it's in your best interest to agree. You probably have nothing to gain with a lawsuit and I assume you want to put this behind you as soon as possible. Also, if they wanted to be pricks, they could drag their feet on the paperwork for your release. Because today's Friday, if they wanted to play hardball, you could be in here until Monday."

"If it gets me out of here today, I'll sign pretty much anything."

"Well, I wouldn't advise that, but I've looked over their release and it's fine."

While the thought of being out of jail and free to continue my life was overwhelming, I couldn't help thinking about Nicole. I had to know more.

"Why did her husband kill her?"

"The husband didn't kill her. He hired Guzman to do it. He paid him a lot of money to kill her and to make it look like you did it. Guzman, as it turns out, was their anonymous informant."

"But why?"

Between what Colgan told us and what I learned by following the case in the news over the next few months, I gradually pieced together the horrible story of Nicole's death. Roger Sullivan had become aware of Nicole's infidelity more than a year before her death. Worried that she would divorce him, he hatched a plan to inherit her wealth rather than fight for it in divorce court. He secretly tapped the phones in their home and had all calls, in and out, recorded. When he would return from his frequent trips, he'd listen to the calls. Using the information from the recorded conversations, he knew nearly as much about our relationship as did we. Each time we would arrange a rendezvous, even for just a lunch, he had Hector Guzman follow us.

Guzman, it turns out, was one of Roger Sullivan's grooms. They'd met years before, after Guzman came to the US from his native Honduras. Sullivan got wind of the fact that Guzman had something of a checkered past with the law in Honduras, so he used him for several nefarious assignments. Among them were drugging the ponies of two of Sullivan's competitors on the polo field, then providing the equine authorities with an anonymous tip, resulting in the disqualification of the ponies and the disgrace of his astonished competition.

Over the years, Sullivan realized Guzman's loyalties could be had for the right price. He was paying Guzman thousands each time he had us followed. Usually, Guzman's report was painfully mundane. But on one occasion, back in April of 1995, Guzman reported that while Nicole and I walked on the beach, I would pick up trash and dispose of it in a barrel near the dunes. Because Nicole and I had the same routine at the beach, it wasn't long before my concern for the environment gave Sullivan his opportunity to dispose of his wife and point the finger directly at me.

Roger knew that if Nicole were murdered, he would be the police's first suspect. He stood to inherit all the money her parents had left her. Therefore, he'd be suspect number one. My affair with Nicole is what provided his chance to divert the suspicion away from himself. I had, in effect, doomed Nicole.

But what Roger Sullivan didn't know was that Guzman had recorded the conversation in which Sullivan asked if, "Ninety thousand dollars was enough to get someone killed?" Guzman said it was.

But shortly after he'd hatched his plan, Nicole and I had a long gap in our rendezvous. Because she became busy with her charity work and I'd been traveling a lot, after our meeting in June, we hadn't seen each other all summer. Roger had a plan and he had someone to carry it out, but he had to be patient. Based on our frequent phone conversations throughout the summer, he knew the affair was still alive. He'd just need to wait for his moment.

Then, when I spoke to Nicole from the airport to arrange our rendezvous for Labor Day morning, his plan was put into motion. He would fly out of town Monday morning, thus providing a solid alibi. There would be ample proof that he was on a flight from Islip MacArthur Airport at seven thirty A.M., and landing in Palm Beach at about the time his wife was to be slain. He'd have no trouble documenting his presence twelve hundred miles from the scene of the murder. Rental car records, hotel registration and a host of cameras throughout the Palm Beach Airport, all supported his well-staged alibi.

Back on Long Island, Hector Guzman knew what he had to do. Following Nicole's car to the beach and parking just a few spaces away, he concealed the rusty knife in a sheath tucked in his cargo shorts. He walked a few yards behind her as she entered the tall grassy dunes, then attacked her from behind when they'd reached the most secluded point. He wore surgical gloves and covered her mouth with his left hand as the knife in his right plunged into her back. He twisted the first wound to ensure enough internal bleeding then, after she'd fallen limp to the ground, stabbed her repeatedly to give the impression a crime of rage had been committed.

He then walked quickly to the trash can, dropped the knife about five feet in front of the can, and put the rubber gloves in his pants pocket.

I didn't know it then, but we actually passed each other as I walked toward the rendezvous point and he walked back toward the parking lot. He glanced back only to see if I bent down to retrieve the knife. If I'd missed it, the plan was to report to the police, during his anonymous call, that he'd heard screams, saw a man running away from the dunes and that the man threw a knife near the trash can then removed a pair of blue gloves. Either way, the false report would conclude with a description of me and my car. The license plate recognition was an extra Guzman decided to add on his own.

I also learned later that when Guzman left Nicole lying in the sandy dunes, she was still alive. According to the autopsy, she died about an hour later, around the same time the police found her body. She'd slowly bled to death.

Excellent police work on the part of the Suffolk County detectives, is what unraveled the crime. First, it was the phone taps at the Sullivan home, then the significant cash withdrawals made by Roger back in June that he couldn't account for. But when an exhaustive search of their home uncovered Nicole's stash of love letters I'd written her, Roger Sullivan's plot began to unravel. Feeling the walls closing in, he quickly conjured a story that he'd been blackmailed by Guzman who'd also fallen in love with Nicole. According to the hastily thought up story, Guzman too had been having an affair with Nicole and demanded ninety thousand dollars to leave her and go back to Honduras. Roger said he'd paid the money back in July, which he had, but that Guzman didn't leave and was determined to have Nicole. When she rebuffed him, he became violent with her. Roger claimed he was concerned enough to report the threats to the police, but his wife didn't want to get Hector in trouble.

So, for a few hours all fingers pointed toward the short Honduran. But when Hector Guzman produced the recording he'd made of Roger offering money for murder, he took Sullivan down with him.

"So, are you saying, I'm completely off the hook? I can leave now?"

"You sign that that and I'll process the rest of the paperwork in ten minutes." Colgan assured me.

And that was it. I was out of jail. Larry called Annie to give her the good news while I picked up my personal belongings at the discharge office, then he drove me home.

Now, all I had to do was explain the last five years to Annie.

XXVIII

I've been feeling sick the past several days and haven't written much. My stomach has felt like it's on fire and anything I eat runs right through me. After two days of the diarrhea, I called my oncologist who called a prescription into my neighborhood pharmacy. Fortunately, they deliver because there was no way I could have made it the three blocks down Fifth Avenue. I'd become so weak from the dehydration, I could barely unbolt my door when Parker, the kid from the drug store, showed up with my wonder-drug. Whatever it was, it stopped the diarrhea and soon after, I was able to eat a piece of toast. Big victory!

This morning I ate two scrambled eggs, buttered toast and a cup of tea. That may not sound like a huge accomplishment, but for someone in my condition, it was. It's the most I've eaten since Christmas dinner at Stephen's. And even that amounted to little more than a slice of white turkey meat, a piece of bread and one glass of water; all done to put my children at ease, not because I was hungry.

Today is December 31st. As the year ebbs, I'm starting to feel like my life on this planet is rapidly coming to a close. Maybe it's my imagination, or maybe it's just all the pain and nausea, but I can't seem to envision anything after January. I know that sounds odd, but that's how I feel-there's a cliff somewhere near the end of January, and I'm going to fall off it into the abyss.

Going to Stephen's for Christmas was difficult but what choice did I have. If I'd lied and told my kids that I didn't feel up to it because of the chemo, which I'm not really getting but they think I am, then they would have insisted on bringing Christmas to me. And, since I'm confident, that was my last Christmas with my family, I didn't want to miss it.

Now that I've typed the words "my last Christmas with my family", I realize how empty those words are. My "family" disappeared the day Annie died. After that horrible day, we were no longer a family, just four adults who shared a common grief. And that's what I have left- four adults who share a common grief, the loss of a mother and wife. That's what connects us.

Don't misunderstand me, I love my three children more than anything in this world, but ever since Annie died, we no longer feel like a family. I guess she was the glue that connected the five of us together. When she was gone, so was the glue.

Anyway, I actually enjoyed about fifteen minutes of Christmas. I really loved watching Peter open some of his gifts- the ones from his two aunts and me. The rest of the holiday season was deeply depressing. I hate being alone and alone is how I've felt after Annie left me. Each Christmas since her death has been the same. Lonely. I can understand why there are so many suicides this time of year. Being alone is so painful.

So, today I feel up to a little more writing and I want to finish my story about Nicole. After the DA determined it was Roger Sullivan and his hired killer, Hector Guzman that were responsible, I was free to leave Riverhead, hopefully forever. Larry drove me back to Huntington and had called ahead to give Annie the good news. At least, I assumed it was good news. I had no idea what to expect when I arrived home.

Mercifully, when we pulled up in front of my home, Daisy's car was not in the driveway. That was a huge relief. Facing Annie was going to be bad enough. I didn't need my mother-in-law adding to the drama.

"You want me to come in with you?" Larry asked as he pulled his Mercedes into my driveway.

"Thanks buddy, but this one I have to do on my own. You've already gone way beyond the call of duty."

"Do you know what you're going to say?"

"The truth. The whole truth and nothing but the truth." "Whoa! Big mistake. Are you crazy? Women don't want that much truth. They just want to be able to trust you going forward. Believe me kiddo, you don't want to share all the gory details with your wife. Not all at once anyway. Just enough truth to explain yourself, but you need to remember, Annie is going to remember this afternoon for the rest of her life. So, be very careful what you say. You can't take shit back once it's out there, even if it is the truth."

I slapped Larry's leg and said, "Thanks Larry. You've been more than a good friend."

Then I stepped out of the car and looked at my front door in a way I never had before. As I heard Larry's car disappear behind me, I felt terror. I was terrified at what the next hour of my life would be like. I didn't know what was on the other side of that door. It could be an angry but faithful wife. It could be a lunatic throwing pots and silverware at me. Or, behind that door might wait a steely silence. That's probably what I feared most.

"This is it." I heard myself saying out load as I approached the front door. For a moment, I questioned whether I should knock before entering. After all, everything had changed. In Annie's mind, this might no longer be my home.

But, before I needed to make that decision, the door was pulled inward and Annie appeared in the gap. She was wearing white shorts and a green NY Jets tee shirt. Her hair was pulled back in a ponytail. Most importantly, she didn't have any potential weapons in her hands.

I knew I needed to speak first. "Where are the kids?" I said solemnly.

"My mother took them to Westchester for the night." She said. "Leo, how are you?"

It sounded like she really wanted to know.

"Can I come in?" I don't know what I would have done if the answer was no.

Annie motioned for me to follow her into the kitchen where she took a seat at the table. She had a half cup of tea waiting for her and she clasped it with both hands. "I just have three questions for you."

"I'll tell you whatever you want to know." I promised.

There was a silence in the room that seemed to last forever. Then, without looking up from her tea cup, she whispered, "Did you love her?"

I thought about Larry's admonition. Might the truth cause Annie more unnecessary pain? Did she really need to know? And, there wasn't a simple answer to the question. I could have spent a thousand words trying to explain my emotions; emotions I didn't actually understand myself.

Instead, I said, "Yes, I did."

Annie held her stare at the tea cup, but I could see her grasp tighten with my answer.

"Second question: were you going to leave me?"

"Never. Never for a second did I think about that." I tried to be as emphatic as possible without yelling. "Please, Annie. Please believe me."

"Final question: why'd you do it?"

I gave her the only honest answer I could, "I don't know. I just don't know. And I know it sounds trite to say it had nothing to do with you, but that's the truth. I never stopped loving you. I didn't love you one bit less. But for almost five years, I was in love with two women. I can't explain it and it wasn't because of anything you did or didn't do. It just happened and I wish it hadn't." I hung my head, filled with shame. I knew those words, the truth, had hurt my wife. I could see the sorrow in her eyes. After all the pain I'd caused my beautiful wife, it crushed me to make it worse.

Annie took a slow sip of tea, then placed the cup carefully on the table. I could sense that the next words out of her mouth would determine our future. I'd betrayed her and lied to her. I'd been in love with another woman and didn't have the strength to deny myself the pleasure of her attention, or the feel of her gentle touch. And now, because of my selfishness, she was dead, and my wife would never know for sure, if she'd always walk in the shadow of a ghost.

Annie pushed her chair back from the table. She stood and faced me. I stood there, ready for whatever was to be my fate. I deserved no mercy, so I expected none.

"Leo, you've brought me an incredible amount of pain and embarrassment. I could hate you for it for the rest of my life. But it's only now that I can understand the hurt you must have felt sixteen years ago. I'm so sorry for causing you this much pain back then. Yet, you forgave me without conditions. Because you believed in us, today we have three beautiful children. How can I not do the same? How can I not believe in us?"

I hugged her so tightly I was afraid I'd hurt her. "I hope you believe I never stopped loving you."

"I do." She whispered in my ear.

"I love you so much, Annie."

We stood in the kitchen holding each other for several minutes. We were both crying. I think we both understood we'd been given a second chance, ...twice.

XXIX

Despite our desire to put the matter of Nicole Sullivan in the past, neither of us were very good at it. And I suppose that was to be expected. After all, Annie had taken a huge step in forgiving me and welcoming me back into our home. I know that wasn't easy for her. To her credit, she tried. But I think the image of me in the arms of another woman was a lot for her to get past. It haunted her. Each time we kissed good night, I could sense something was different. I'd done damage that would not be easily repaired.

And, although my return to work at MAC Tech kept my mind occupied in the weeks following Nicole's death, I was reminded of her every day. I refused to throw out the few trinkets on my desk that were gifts from her; a glass paperweight, a Cross pen, and a small pink shell she'd picked up on one of our first walks on the beach. The ghost of Nicole Sullivan was everywhere in my office. Each time I looked at my sofa, I was reminded of the first day we met. Each time I glanced out toward Judy's desk, the desk that Nicole occupied for a week nearly five years ago, I saw her sitting there, looking back at me. And whenever someone mentioned the word "temp", her face would fill my mind and I would smile. Then, I'd always get sad. I missed her terribly.

And I never got to say good-bye. In the weeks following my release from jail, I learned her body had been claimed by her sister and flown to Sacramento for burial. Roger

Sullivan was behind bars and, once the coroner's office finished its gruesome tasks, Nicole's sister petitioned the court for her remains. I had no idea where she was buried. I would have liked to visit her grave. It seemed like the right thing to do.

But even though I carried a heavy heart, life marched on. We had three young children, enough to keep any two reasonable adults busy full time. Stephen broke his leg falling from a playground the following spring, and the girls started nursery school that January. Our house was a constant tempest. Our plans, those we tried to keep, were inevitably upset by something the kids did, some ear infection they caught and generously shared, or some conflict with their increasingly busy schedules.

When Stephen turned eight, he started playing soccer on a travel-team. That nightmare was one for which I was not prepared. Every weekend for twelve weeks in the spring and summer, our family had to follow him and his team around New England. I never found the game of soccer interesting, so the ordeal was particularly painful for me. But, because our family traveled together, those trips created some wonderful memories and I don't regret any of it.

They also helped Annie and me mend the wound I'd caused. Spending time together and with the kids, reminded us both why we were still a family.

Veronica and Paula got very involved in 4-H, twirling, ice skating and cheerleading. As the years passed and they grew into beautiful young teenagers, our time together was limited to car rides to and from their many events. Fortunately, few of the girls' activities involved much travel away from Huntington, and Stephen gave up travel soccer when he got to junior high in favor of football and baseball. And Annie did her best to try to make dinner time at home sacred. If they weren't involved in a practice for something at school, the kids were expected to be home for our family dinner at six-thirty. To do my part, I needed to plan my afternoons so I could be on a five-fifteen train. It was often difficult, but I loved those meals with the kids.

After Michael was killed in 2001, I was busier than ever at what was left of MAC Tech. We held things together for six more years, but in 2007, at the age of fifty-five, I retired. The kids were all in college and I wanted to use the time to catch up with Annie. I was determined not to take another job. I didn't need to. MAC had left me well positioned for an early retirement. Money wasn't going to be a problem. It was just Annie and me and a big empty house.

We planned lots of travel while the kids were in school.

And, although it took years after Nicole's death, the unbridled intimacy we once shared, was back. In fact, we were closer than ever. We found that traveling the globe sans children, made us feel young again. We were like teenagers rediscovering each other in different places. The first year after I left MAC, we spent a total of eight weeks traveling around Canada, something that had been on my bucket list for years. The kids came home for about a month at Christmas, then we were off to Florida where we bought a modest house on the panhandle. Each year we'd spend more and more time in Florida while the kids were in school. Then, when they all started graduate school, we began to explore Europe. Our favorite place was the Amalfi Coast of Italy.

In September 2011, about four years after I'd retired, we found ourselves at an exquisite resort in Positano, Italy called Le Sirenuse. Our suite overlooked the azure Mediterranean and the terraced white buildings of the town as they cascaded down to the sea. The highly polished marble that was everywhere in our room made me laugh, for I couldn't help think how far this was from the tiny pine lean-to my parents used to rent at Lake George for our family vacations. I wondered if they'd be proud of me. Certainly not, if they knew everything.

Late one afternoon, Annie and I finished a long walk through the cobblestoned streets of Positano, shopping for souvenirs for the kids. We stopped at the bar in the lobby and had a few glasses of Chianti and some cheese, then asked for a bottle we could bring to our room. Lucca, the kid behind the bar was happy to oblige, and gave us a bottle of Classico Reserve. We sat on the bed in our room, sipping wine and looking out the enormous open window at the scenery below. The wine was having its effect on both of us and it was Annie who suggested we take a bath.

"Together?" I replied. We'd never done that before.

"Yes, together. Stupito!" She exaggerated one of the few Italian words she knew. "Did you see that tub? It's as blue as the Mediterranean and looks out onto the side of the mountain. I think it's made of marble too. The view is spectacular."

Before my wine-soaked brain knew what was happening, Annie had filled he tub, added some shampoo to generate bubbles, and slipped from her clothes into the hot bubbly water. "Hey, Stupito! Come join me."

It was the first and only time we'd ever bathe together, but it was memorable, for a lot of reasons. We caressed and made love in the tub, then put on the incredibly plush robes supplied by Le Sirenuse, and recovered in each other's arms on the huge bed, with the slow rotation of the ceiling fan cooling our bodies.

After a second round of love-making, Annie laid back on an over-sized pillow. "Have you ever been so happy?" She whispered.

I wasn't sure if it was a rhetorical question, but I answered truthfully, "Never."

"I mean, we have such a wonderful life, don't we? The kids are all finishing grad school this year, we have a beautiful house and another one in Florida for the winter. We have good health and no money worries. We are so lucky."

I didn't know what brought on this early Thanksgiving but I had to agree. We were lucky. We were lucky just to still be together.   We'd each had a turn at screwing up our marriage and somehow, we survived. I felt very fortunate.

But we were in Italy and the Italians have an odd custom when it comes to good fortune. When an Italian feels very fortunate, grateful for what they have, and someone asks them, "How are you doing?" they respond "Non ce male." The literal translation is "Not too bad."   Italians are superstitious. They think if they admit to being lucky, then their luck will change, or someone will come and take away what they have. So, they always respond, "Not too bad."

And so, as we lay on our thousand-count sheets in a room of marble, over-looking the Mediterranean, our luck was about to change. Just as the Italians believed, you shouldn't revel in how fortunate you are. You shouldn't count your blessings out loud. Someone may come to take them from you. In our case, that's exactly what happened, and it all began that day in Positano.

I was lying next to Annie, gently rubbing her naked back. The cool breeze from the ceiling fan pushed the warm Mediterranean air around the room. She was face-down and purring to my soft strokes. I loved to rub her back. Her skin was so smooth, so soft.   Even at fifty-five, she maintained youthful, almost childlike skin. As my hand slide down her left side, toward her breast, I felt a small bump I'd never noticed before.

"What's this?" I asked, poking at the spot in question.

"What's what?"

"This. This bump."

She reached around and tried to feel the same spot but when she stretched to do so, the bump seemed to disappear. "I don't feel anything."

I tried to find the same spot but, now that she'd repositioned herself on the bed, I couldn't.

"Maybe it was just the way you were lying there. I thought I felt a bump just to the side of your breast. Something I've never felt before."

Neither of us gave it any more thought. We spent two more days in Italy, then three in Paris before heading home for Veronica and Paula's birthday.

But, four months later, during her routine annual physical, the bump appeared again. This time it was picked up on Annie's chest x-ray. At first, her doctor thought it was just a sub-epidermal cyst. Because it was so soft and fleshy, no one was too concerned. Fortunately, Annie's primary care doctor was less casual about it and ordered an MRI. Annie thought so little of the whole thing that she didn't even mention it to me until the night before the test was to be done.

On a bitterly cold January afternoon, Annie drove herself to Melville for the MRI. The technician told her he couldn't give her any information about the bump but that he'd seen hundreds of bumps just like it and they were almost always nothing to worry about. The radiologist would send the MRI results to her doctor the following day.

But that night a major snowstorm hit the northeast and by seven A.M. the next morning, it was clear few people would get to work on time. Eleven inches of wet snow blanketed Huntington. Dr. Raj Patel, the radiologist who was to read Annie's MRI, skidded into a telephone pole on his way to work and broke his collar bone. He was out of work, recovering, for ten days. Somehow, Annie's MRI just sat on his desk, in his in-box and no one bothered to check on it. Because no one called Annie with the results, she assumed there was nothing wrong with her bump, which had now disappeared again. So, she put it out of her head, and we left for our planned trip to Florida on January 26th.

We drove to Rosemary Beach, just west of Panama City Beach, over the next two days. I liked to stretch the drive out over two days. Annie always pushed to drive straight through the night, something I resisted because of my poor night vision. So, we arrived at our house on the 28th and spent most of the afternoon unpacking the car, then food shopping at the nearby Publix.

"Let's take a walk on the beach before it gets dark," I suggested.

"No, you go by yourself. I want to straighten up here and unpack."

"Ah, come on. It looks like we might get a good sunset." I pleaded.

"Leo, we have six weeks of sunsets coming up. I promise I'll watch at least a dozen with you. Just not this one."

So, I look a long barefoot walk on the snow-white sand of Rosemary Beach. I walked east, toward an old pier that stood in the surf like a monument to the past. All that remained of the once utilitarian pier were a few barnacle-covered pilings sticking up from the sand and shallow water. A pelican sat atop one piling, seagulls graced the others. With the sun setting over my shoulder, the vision was a photographer's dream. But I'd taken similar shots in prior years. In fact, one of them graced the wall in our hallway at home.

The wooden relic was also my cue to turn around and head back. The roundtrip walk amounted to just under four miles and I was thirsty. I silently hoped our ice-maker had already produced a few cubes for the gin and tonic I planned to use as my reward for the heart-heathy walk. Better yet, maybe Annie anticipated my need and had two waiting for us on the porch.

But that wasn't the case. When I returned, Annie was sitting on the steps of our porch. She looked upset about something.

"How was your walk?" She bravely asked. I could hear the shake in her voice.

"What's up, honey?"

She drew a long deep breath. "I just got off the phone with Dr. Weiss, my GP. She said there may be a problem with my MRI, the one I did a few weeks ago."

"What kind of problem?

"She said the area around that lump, the one you noticed in Italy, looks very suspicious. At least, that's her interpretation of the radiologist's report. I don't know what the fuck took them so long to get the results!"

It was very unusual to hear that word come from Annie's mouth. I knew she was very upset but trying to hide her fear.

I sat next to her, clasped her hand and asked, "What exactly did your doctor tell you Annie?"

"She said the images had some patterns she was concerned about. I don't know what that means. But she wants me to have blood tests done. She said I can do them down here. She's going to email me the prescription." She put her hands over her face.

"It's probably nothing. The sooner you have the blood work done, the sooner we can forget about it."

"I sure hope so. I'm not going to be able to think about anything else until we know."

And she was right. The email with the prescription didn't arrive until the following day. We both spent hours Googling what the specific blood tests were designed to find and the same words kept coming up on our searches; sarcoma, non-small cell lung cancer, and squamous cell carcinoma. Apparently, the tests were designed to find higher than normal levels of some proteins and gene mutations in Annie's blood which would indicate her body was trying to fight an invader. None of it sounded good.

We drove to a hospital in Destin to get the blood drawn. They promised to send the results directly to Dr. Weiss in New York within forty-eight hours. That sounded like an eternity. How could we think about anything else for the next two days? How could we not focus on the worst?

To make matters even worse, it rained the next two days, so we were stuck inside. We both spent much of the first day on the couch with our laptops. And we weren't playing solitaire. The deeper we searched for information concerning the blood tests Annie had undergone, the more we worried. And the more we worried, the more we each began to think about the future.

On my part, I couldn't imagine a life without a healthy, vibrant Annie at my side. The thought of her being sick had never crossed my mind. I'd always taken her vitality for granted. It was just part of who she was; always filled with pep and willing to try or do almost anything. It was her contagious enthusiasm for life that made us both feel younger than we were. I couldn't picture life any other way.

Annie, as was usually the case, was thinking about me and the kids. How would we get along without her? How would we know where the Christmas decorations were stored? Who would cook Thanksgiving dinner?

Around four in the afternoon on the first day of waiting, she lightened the mood with a macabre joke. "Hey Leo, if I die, who you going after?"

The question caught me completely unprepared. "What?"

"I know you're useless on your own and a handsome stud like you could get anyone you want, so, if I die, who you going to marry?"

"Annie, don't even joke about it."

"Come on. You must have thought about it at some point. You can tell me. Who?"

"I'm not going to discuss this. You're going to be fine and I'm stuck with you for another fifty years."

"Please. Come on. There's got to be someone you've thought about at some point. Someone you secretly lust after but can't pursue because you're married. Tell me, pleeeease." She pleaded.

I could tell she wasn't going to let this go, but I wasn't going to play along. It was just too dark a subject, even if she was just joking.

"I'm not doing this." I protested.

"Look, you have to think about these things eventually."

"No, I don't."

"Well, you should. And I bet you have." She said with an impish grin. "Come on. Who is it?"

Only to shut her up and put an end to this, I decided to turn the tables and lighten the mood. "Okay, I have thought about it. I've thought about it a lot." I lied. "If you die first, I'm going after Vana White!"

"Well, that's good because if you go first, I'm heading straight for Sam Elliot." She smirked and playfully leaned back on the sofa.

"Sam Elliot? The guy with the big mustache?"

"Yep. I think he's really super-hot. And way more interesting than Vana White. You really think Vana even knows how to cook?"

We both had a good laugh and it was nice to have the tension broken, if just for a few minutes. After an awkward dinner at a local seafood place, we polished off two bottles of red wine and took a jagged walk on the beach. The rain had finally subsided leaving a beautiful full moon glistening on the sea. When we returned to our house, we made love. I think each of us knew the next few days may change everything, and this was our last attempt at life the way it used to be. Whatever, I don't think either of us were thinking about Vana or Sam.

XXX

I've felt lousy for three days. My head is pounding, I'm a little dizzy and my stomach feels like I ate a basket of broken glass. And I can't keep any food down- not that I'm hungry. Dr. Romaro sent over a prescription for the stomach pain which knocks me out. But I guess that's a good thing. The more I feel bad, the more I want to sleep to escape the pain. Sleep is good. It relieves the pain, if for only a few hours. In some ways, I'm starting to think about death, not as my enemy, but as the final pain reliever.

I haven't typed anything in two days. I just didn't feel up to it. But, with the help of Dr. Romaro's wonder drugs, I'll give it a shot tonight, at least for an hour or so.

Having just re-read the last thing I wrote, I think it was on Tuesday, I now, not only feel sick, but I've added sadness to my list of maladies. Re-reading about those days in Rosemary Beach when Annie found out she had cancer makes me very sad all over again. It was a hard time- for both of us.

I don't feel up to giving you the long version of Annie's illness. My own cancer is wearing me down. But I want to tell you how incredibly brave my wife was and how she struggled with every fiber of her being, to stay alive. She was ten times the fighter than I.

We got the call from Annie's doctor the next day. She explained that while she couldn't be certain without a biopsy, the MRI and blood work both pointed toward small-cell lung cancer. The biopsy would tell us for certain and would reveal how advanced the cancer's development was. She recommended we get home to do the biopsy.

Not knowing how long we'd need to be back in New York, we threw out all the food we'd just bought and closed up the beach house again. We drove back to Long Island in just under nineteen hours- a new record for us. But it was a miserable drive. Neither of us wanted to talk because the only subject that mattered at the moment was cancer, and talking about it would make it real. So, the ride was unbearably quiet. Annie didn't even want to listen to music. She just stared out the window watching the mile markers roll by on interstate 95. When it was her turn to drive, I was so worried she might be too distracted behind the wheel, that I couldn't get any much-needed sleep.

We crossed the Verrazano Bridge at around noon and, as usual, got stuck in traffic on the Belt Parkway for nearly an hour. When you're so close to home after a long trip, traffic is especially excruciating, and neither of us was in the mood for it.

"Why the hell do we still live here?" Anne loudly asked. "We don't need to be on Long Island any more. We should get the hell out."

This was a conversation we'd had before, just under better circumstances. I could tell Annie was at the end of her rope. It wasn't like her to lash out at me.

"Why don't you close your eyes and get some sleep. At least rest your eyes." I suggested. "We'll be home in about an hour."

"I'm sorry," she said. "I'm just so nervous about the biopsy. What if...?"

But I cut her off.

"Don't even think about it because thinking about it will do no good." I hesitated to utter the word, but it needed to come out. "If you do have cancer, we should feel lucky they found it early, right?

But I was wrong. The biopsy confirmed the NSCLC, the acronym we came to understand stood for non-small cell lung cancer, and that Annie was likely in stage three. That wasn't the worst news we could have gotten but it was far from the news we wanted. Her doctor recommended an oncologist at Memorial Sloan Kettering who seemed to be at the forefront of lung cancer research. She and Annie hit it off because, like my wife, Dr. Wilma Weber was an eternal optimist. She told her patients to make plans for life events ten years in the future. It was her job to get them there.

In February 2012 Annie began an aggressive plan of chemotherapy and radiation that lasted for twelve weeks. She tolerated the treatments surprisingly well and, unlike other women in her group, never lost her hair. Her only problem was the nausea that followed each dose of chemo, and even that only lasted a couple of days.

Three days before Mother's Day 2012 Annie went for another MRI and a series of sonograms and x-rays. The results were encouraging but confusing. The largest of the tumors had shrunk but there was more cancer in the surrounding cells and nodes. Dr. Weber didn't seem overly concerned, but then again, it wasn't her life that was on the line. Nonetheless, her recommendation was for another round of chemo that lasted through the summer and into the fall.

This time, Annie did lose her hair but had less trouble with the nausea. On a hot day in July, we had some fun picking out wigs. She was determined to try a completely different look and I was encouraging her to find a wig that most matched what she looked like before the devastating effects of the treatments. Veronica came along and supported Annie on this one. "Try a whole new look, mom. What have you got to lose? You can always go back to your old style when you're better. Or, maybe not."

So, from that day forward, my beautiful pony-tailed brunette wife became a blonde with a short and sassy do. This might have been a fantasy-come-true for many men, but for me it was one more reminder that I was losing Annie. I hated it at first but kept my mouth shut. Later, I came to accept that if Annie liked it, it didn't matter how I felt.

All the while she was undergoing treatments, we stayed close to home. Annie didn't feel up to traveling and even if she did, the sessions at MSK were scheduled such that any travel more than a day or two would be impossible. So, we spent a lot of time at home that summer and fall. The kids all came home at Thanksgiving and Christmas because they knew their mom wasn't up to a Florida trip.

So, as 2012 came to a close, Annie and I sat on our living room floor watching an old movie and stoking a fire. We both drank ginger ale as our champagne at midnight and kissed a long meaningful kiss. I think we both understood we may not have another New Year's Eve together. We went to bed that night filled with dread about what 2013 would bring.

As it turned out, the new year was a good one. After the second round of chemo, Dr. Weber decided to supplement Annie's diet with mega-doses of certain vitamins and instructed her to try to get back to a normal routine. In many ways, we were trying to pretend she didn't still have cancer, but we'd been reassured by Dr. Weber that Anne's progress toward remission was well underway. She explained that Annie's body now needed time to heal and recuperate from the chemo. The best thing she could do was resume life as usual; shop, go places, plan trips. In short, get back to living.

Maybe we both just wanted to believe so badly, we never questioned the good news. If a respected oncologist from MSK said she was on the mend, we weren't going to question it. We started taking short trips, then planning longer vacations; things we always wanted to get to but never did. We took a cruise to Alaska and a helicopter ride to see Denali which was spectacular. Annie was feeling stronger with each day and by September declared she was "100% back to normal", although I think she was saying it for my sake. The visits to Dr. Weber became less and less frequent, partly because Annie was feeling so much better, but also because she just didn't want any bad news.

We spent a good portion of the winter in Florida and visited Veronica and Paula several times. In October, Stephen and Lilly welcomed Peter into their lives. Annie was ecstatic about her first grandson. He replaced cancer as the center of our lives. We encouraged Lilly to entrust us with the baby as soon as she stopped breast feeding. Annie prepared a room in Huntington just for Peter, the baby's room, as she called it. She was finally excited about something other than just being alive.

I think Peter gave Annie a new reason to beat back cancer. She loved that baby so much, at times I was afraid she didn't plan to return him to his parents. For both of us, it was a rejuvenation. We felt young again, reminded of how life was when our own kids were babies. It felt wonderful.

But it all changed again in March of 2014. Annie and I were in Rosemary Beach. Stephen, Lilly and Peter, now six months old, were coming to visit for a long weekend. I drove to the Panama City airport to pick them up on a sunny warm afternoon. I'd just fitted the car seat in the back of my car when I got a call from Annie.

"Hey love. What's up?" I expected her to remind me to stop at Publix to pick up organic milk.

"Leo, I feel really dizzy. I sat down but it hasn't gone away."

I was about forty-five minutes from Annie and my grandson's plane was due to land in fifteen minutes. I was stuck between the proverbial rock and a hard place.

"Annie, I won't be home for at least an hour. Their flight hasn't landed yet. Try lying down with your eyes fixed on something. That might help with the dizziness."

"I'll try."

"Does anything hurt? Do you have a headache?"

"No. Just very dizzy."

"Okay, lay down and I'll call you back in about fifteen to see how you're doing."

"I will. I hope I feel better by the time the kids arrive."

When I called back, Annie was lying down but still felt dizzy. Fortunately, the kids flight arrived on time and we skipped the Publix stop to hurry home to Annie. On the way, I explained the situation to Stephen and Lilly. Both were insistent I take Annie to the local emergency room.

"Dad, you have to get this checked out. How long has it been since mom's seen her doctor?"

"I'm not sure." I lied. Annie hadn't been to the doctor since before Peter was born.

But when we arrived at the house, the flashing lights of an ambulance were waiting outside. I leapt from the car just in time to see two female EMT's loading a pram into the back of the rig. Annie was on the pram with an oxygen mask covering her face.

"I'm her husband." I said to one of the EMT's. "Is she okay?"

"Do you want to ride with us to the hospital?"

Stephen had come from the car and heard me say, "Of course."

"Dad, give me the car keys and call my cell as soon as you know what's going on. We'll be waiting here at the house."

I tossed him the keys and jumped into the back of the ambulance. The younger of the two medics motioned for me to sit on the bench close to Annie's head. "And please buckle up," she said, pointing to the red seat belt at my side.

The ride to St. Charles hospital in Destin took an excruciating sixteen minutes, lights and sirens all the way. Annie was conscious and answering the medic's questions. I don't think she even knew I was in the ambulance until I grabbed her hand. Then I saw a tear fall from her cheek.

"I'm here honey."

Through the oxygen mask, I heard her say, "Did the kids get in?"

"Yeah, they're fine. They're at the house. Stephen's dying to take Peter down to the beach."

She smiled, but more tears rolled down. "Hey, it's going to be okay. You probably just got a little dehydrated over the last few days from all the wine." I tried to keep things light, but I sensed there was more to it than just a little dehydration.

The medic started an IV line and began giving Annie fluids. I'm not sure what. Then she began asking me a million questions about Annie's medical history, most of which I knew how to answer.

When I told them she'd finished a second round of chemo for NSCLC over a year ago, the two medics gave each other a troubling glance.

Luckily, the ER at the hospital wasn't busy and they took Annie to a room immediately. They quickly gave her another IV drip. This one contained something to stop the dizziness and it did. Within minutes of entering the hospital, she felt remarkably better and wanted to go home. But the attending doctor was more concerned with what caused the dizziness than with the problem itself. When he learned of Annie's history, he suggested complete blood work.

Annie agreed but only on the condition she'd be discharged immediately after.

She rallied the next three days and enjoyed playing with Peter in the sand. He wasn't walking yet but reveled in crawling along the beach, stopping only to put handfuls of sand in his mouth. Stephen and Lilly kept a close eye on Annie when I couldn't. We all agreed she seemed like her old self, the good old self.

But after the kids went back to New York, we got a call from the hospital. Annie's blood work raised suspicion that the cancer was back, maybe even attacking more organs than before. The doctor who saw us at St. Charles recommended another MRI, but since we were due to head back to New York the following week, Annie decided to have the tests done at home.

Once again, we made the drive up interstate 95 with heavy hearts and much trepidation. I wasn't sure Annie had it in her to go through another round of chemo and radiation. She wasn't sure either. The thought alone had her fatigued.

Dr. Weber confirmed our worst fears. The cancer was back and raging in her lymph nodes. It was even in the cerebral fluid on the right side of her brain. The only good news, if there was any, was that the lung cancer hadn't come back and the others were in their early stages so aggressive treatment might prevail. That is, if Annie chose to fight.

"Leo, I'm not sure I can do this again." She said one day as we walked around the pond in the center of Huntington, a place we used to bring the kids to feed the turtles.

"You can't give up, Annie. I need you around for a long time yet. You have to try." I said the words but I'm not sure I believed them. I knew what she went through the first time; the nausea, hair loss and weakness. And for what? Another sixteen months then the same thing again? I wouldn't blame her if she gave up.

But, she didn't. Starting the day after Memorial Day 2014, she began an aggressive program to kill the ravaging cancer that was trying to bring her down. I loved her even more for trying because I knew she was doing it for me.

The girls were both finishing their graduate programs, Veronica in education and Paula in nursing. Annie bravely attended both graduation ceremonies. Then they came home to live with us for most of the summer. It was the best thing that could have happened. Annie thrived on having the girls back in the house. It gave the house a vitality that had been missing. She and her daughters did much together and at least one of the girls escorted Annie to every treatment, along with me, of course.

Annie broke out her blonde wig when she began losing her hair. The girls insisted on weekly spa treatments for the three of them, usually the day before Annie's chemo. In some ways, I don't think I've ever seen Annie so happy. Maybe it was because she could appreciate the lack of time she had left, or the veracity of the love shown her by her daughters. Whatever it was, she was happy and that's all I cared about.

But Veronica had to leave for her new job in August and Paula followed a week later. They were sharing an apartment in West Palm Beach, close to both their jobs. Neither wanted to leave but Annie insisted, promising to visit them often.

She never did.

When the results came in after the treatments ended, the news was bad. Very little change had occurred. The cancer was marching on and infiltrating more and more organs. In September, Dr. Weber told us there was nothing more that could be done. The cancer was just too pervasive. Her best guess was that Annie might have six months to a year left. "And, I have to be honest with you. The end will not be easy. The cancer in your brain will cause some dementia and possibly debilitating headaches. When this begins, I will prescribe something for the pain. Annie, I'd be misleading you if I didn't tell you this. You're in for a rough patch. I'm sorry. I wish I had better news."

I think Annie must have been expecting this prognosis because she took the news far better than I did. In fact, now that the treatments had ended, she felt pretty good. The nausea had subsided and none of the dire symptoms Dr. Weber warned us about had yet to surface. She felt good enough to suggest we travel back to Italy for one last adventure. I marveled at her bravery.

So, we quickly arranged a trip to Milan and Lake Cuomo, two places we'd not yet visited. We went first class all the way; first class flights and a suite at Villa D'Este on the lake. It was as beautiful a place as I've ever seen. Our suite had a large stone patio overlooking the deep blue lake and surrounding mountains which were already capped with snow. We took long walks into town and shopped for knickknacks for the girls.

On our last night in Cuomo, just before we were leaving for Milan, Annie surprised me when she made an unusual announcement.

"Leo, I want to tell you something. This is the most beautiful place we've ever been. I can't imagine, even if I had all the time in the world, I don't think we could top this. It's exquisite. So, I want this to be the last place we ever go together. Let's go home tomorrow."

"Are you sure?"

"I'm sure. I want to remember this the rest of my life. And..., I want you to make love to me here." She said that while we were standing on the patio.

"You mean here, in Cuomo?"

"No, silly. I mean here on the veranda, under the stars. There's something very romantic about it. Don't you think?"

Once again, because my children will likely read this, I'll leave out all the hot details. But Annie wasn't kidding when she said she wanted to try something new. I'll leave it at that.

After our steamy evening on the patio, we laid on our bed, holding hands for nearly an hour. Neither of us knew it at the time, but it was to be the last time Annie and I would ever make love. As soon as we returned to Huntington, she got a very bad bronchial infection and needed to be hospitalized for over a week. The cumulative effect of the chemo had weakened her immune system, making it hard for her to fight the otherwise routine URI.

Her stay at Huntington hospital gave us both a glimpse of what the next few months would be like; much discomfort, a lot of waiting for doctors and nurses, and the indignity of institutional care. Her very first experience with the garish lights and sounds of the hospital determined, in her mind, how she wanted to spend her last days. More to the point, it determined exactly how she did not want to die- anywhere other than at home.

The bronchitis weakened Annie a great deal, a weakness from which she never recovered. When she returned home from the hospital, she spent another week in bed. Breathing was becoming increasingly difficult. I arranged for an oxygen bottle to be set near her favorite chair. With an extended tube, she was able to wear the nasal cannula while sitting but also while she walked anywhere in the living room.

I was startled by how rapidly she had deteriorated since our last night at Villa D'Este. Up till now, I never thought of her as a sick person. Yes, she had cancer, but, up till now, she hadn't shown many symptoms of the wretched disease. She was just another person who had cancer. Now she was sick.

During most of the rest of October, Annie seldom left the house, and when she did, it was only to sit on our rear porch to watch the changing leaves drift down from the towering oaks surrounding our home. "I understand how they must feel." She once said to me. "I feel the same way, drifting slowly toward a fate that has already been determined for me."

Annie had lost much weight. She was down to ninety-six pounds. Her face was pale and drawn. Her beautiful eyes seemed to have sunk into her skull. She had no appetite for food so her doctor prescribed a concoction of nutrients be delivered intravenously until her appetite returned. He inserted a port over her right breast through which life sustaining fluids dripped constantly.

I arranged for a hospital-style bed to be set up in our bedroom after I removed our bed, the bed we shared for nearly thirty years. It was a sad day for me for it marked the point at which I had to accept things were never going back to normal. From that point forward, I slept in the spare bedroom on the second floor.

Then, the headaches started. People whom I've spoken to, who themselves have suffered from migraines, are the only ones who understood her pain. The excruciating headaches came without warning and sometimes lasted for days. They brought Annie to tears and essentially, left her bedridden. Light was painful. Sound was painful. All she could do was lie in bed with her eyes closed, wearing my Bose noise-cancelling headphones.

I had to whisper when we spoke. The only thing that helped was my gentle stroking of her arm and hand, which I was happy to do.

By mid-November, I had to hire a full-time nurse to help out, administer pain meds and stay with Annie when I had to run errands. Her name was Lucille and a more gentle woman has never walked the earth. Lucille was sent directly from heaven. She was about the same age as Annie but the similarities ended there. Lucille was a robust Irish woman who'd buried three husbands and had twelve grandchildren. She spoke with a heavy Boston accent.

Annie was now confined to bed and incontinent. Seeing her atrophy this way, crushed me. I'd never had to watch anyone die slowly before and I didn't know what to expect. With Lucille in charge of Annie's day to day care, I had more free time and used it to read everything I could about caring for the terminally ill. But I can't say anything I read prepared me for what was to come. It was all just heart-breaking.

I would sit with Annie for hours. When the headaches subsided, I'd talk to her about all the wonderful things we'd done together. I held her hand and told her stories, things I'd never told her before, about how much I loved our life together.

"I hope you understand," I said, "... that meeting you saved my life."

"How did I save your life?" She whispered.

"Because, if I hadn't found you that day on that boat, I eventually would have died of loneliness." I teased.

"You're an idiot."

"But I'm your idiot."

"Well, having terminal cancer wasn't bad enough. Now I'm stuck with an idiot." She almost laughed. Instead she coughed at the attempt.

Dr. Weber prescribed a morphine drip to be used when the pain was too intense for the other pain-management drugs. Lucille was adept at its administration and was diligent about when the morphine should be used. She'd been a hospice nurse for several years and could tell when a patient's pain warranted the powerful drug.

Stephen came to visit at least once a week. He, Lilly and Peter lived a short distance away and Annie was always happy to see them. But Veronica and Paula were in southern Florida and had just started new careers. Veronica was teaching third grade, her dream job. Paula was working the night shift in the ER at the Wellington Regional Medical Center. Both my daughters were tortured by their inability to spend more time with Annie. But both were planning to come up for Thanksgiving, just ten days away.

One day, while I was sitting next to Annie's bed, reading her the New York Times, she looked over at me and asked, "Are you my new doctor?"

At first, I thought she was kidding, but it quickly became apparent she was not. For a moment, she didn't recognize me. Dr. Weber had warned us about this- the dementia that accompanies late stage cancer victims, but it never occurred to me that my wife would fail to know who I was.

"Honey, it's me, Leo." I said as calmly as I could, though I was hysterical inside.

She took a good long look at my face, then said, "Yeah, I know who you are." But I don't think she did.

That was the first sign of the dementia that would rapidly get much worse. Within days, she couldn't recall the names of our children and had no recollection of Peter's birth. It broke my heart to see and hear her so confused. I could tell she knew something was very wrong, but her brain wasn't connecting the lines to draw a family.

One night, after I'd sat with Annie until she fell asleep, I made a fire and sat in the living room with a glass of Amaretto. I was quietly reflecting on what the coming holidays would be like. Thanksgiving was around the corner, but you'd never know it by looking at our home. None of Annie's usual decorations were in place. There was no cornucopia, no cinnamon scented candles in the guest bath, and no wreath on the front door, all signs that Annie was no longer with us- at least the way she used to be.

As I warmed my spirits by the fire and with the Amaretto, Lucille came into the room.

Mr. Monday, do you mind if I join you for a moment?"

"Of course, Lucille. Would you like something to drink?"

"No, thank you." She said politely. "But I would like to talk to you about something."

I dreaded what she might say. My fear was that she no longer wanted to care for Annie and was leaving us. Fortunately, that was not the case.

She sat on the opposite end of the sofa and looked me directly in the eye.

"Do you know why I do the work I do? I mean, take care of people who are approaching the end of life?"

"No, but I'm so grateful you do." I had no idea what could motivate someone to do this sort of work. To me, it would be so depressing to watch people die, then go do it again with another family. It couldn't possibly be the money. Lucille charged only four hundred dollars a day.

"I don't do it for those who are dying. I do it for the living, the families who are losing one their loved ones. In this case, Mr. Monday, I do it for you."

I wasn't sure where this was going, I so just said, "Thank you, Lucille."

"I don't think you understand. I see my job as taking care of you. My nursing skills will tend to the sick, but I'm here because there's nothing I can do for the sick other than keep them comfortable. You're the one I need to help."

I still didn't get it and I guess my face showed exactly that. Lucille inched a little closer to me on the sofa.

"Mr. Monday, your wife, the person you most love in the world, is going to die soon. Nothing I do will change that. But I can help you. I can help you survive, because life will go on. It may not seem that way now, but it will. Someday you'll roll around on the floor, maybe right here in front of this fireplace, with your grandchildren. Maybe you'll have a house full of grandchildren. And sure, Annie's passing will leave an emptiness. That's to be expected. But, trust me, that emptiness will be filled by something else wonderful. You'll see. I've seen it too many times not to be true.

"And, here's some good news. The hardest part of your grieving is what you're doing now. The hardest part for someone like you, is helplessly watching her die. The hardest part is watching her suffer. That's the part you're doing now. After her suffering is over, you'll miss her. But the pain of watching her suffer will be over."

I thought about that for a moment, and realized she was right. I knew I'd miss Annie terribly after she's gone but watching her suffer was killing me. This is the part I'm not sure I would survive. This was the hardest part for me. I will be forever grateful to Lucille for sharing that observation with me. Just knowing that my pain wasn't going to get any worse than it was now, was liberating. I could look to the future with far less trepidation. The darkest days were already upon me. Life couldn't get any worse, and, by interpolation, that meant, the future would somehow be better.

Or, so I thought.

XXXI

And this brings me to the most difficult part of my journal.

As I said when I started, my purpose was to give my three children a glimpse of the man I am, the man I have been at different stages of my life. To do that, they needed to see me with all my flaws and weaknesses. They needed to see the far-from-perfect me.

I've confessed my stupidities and my selfishness. I've tried to explain why certain things have haunted me all my life. I tried to get them to understand that I'm human. When I was a child, my foolish behavior ended the lives of my two beautiful sisters, tortured my poor parents and eventually drove them both to an early death. As an adult, my rage cost a man his life. And the damage done by my selfish infidelity haunts me every day; first because of the pain I caused Annie, but also, knowing that my affair with Nicole is what led to her murder.

If there is an afterlife, I'm terrified those six people, my sister, my parents, Chris Hoffman, and Nicole Sullivan will be waiting for me at the gates of hell. Waiting to push me through.

So, if my children have read this far, they now understand how my selfishness, my stupidity, and my weakness caused others to suffer. At times in my life, I failed. And for that, I am contrite.

But, for the deed I am about to share with you, I make no apologies. Although you may see it as the most nefarious, most egregious, I have no sorrow. I would do it again, if some hellish nightmare called upon me to do so. To me, it was an act of love. It was compassion. And it was the hardest thing I ever had to do.

On the Sunday night before Thanksgiving 2014, Lucille and I shared a pizza in the kitchen. Annie had been tormented by headaches all afternoon as she had been the three days prior. She'd finally fallen asleep after Lucille put four drops of morphine in her dripline. The last three nights, it was the only thing that worked. Each time she administered the drug, I was amazed at how quickly Annie's pain seem to leave her. Literally, within sixty seconds of letting those precious drops fall into the saline bag, Annie would be asleep, and the torment was interrupted, at least for a few hours.

Over the last few days Annie had become less and less vocal. She sort of withdrew into the shell of herself. I told her that the kids would all be here in a few days to celebrate Thanksgiving, but the conversation confused her. I'm not sure she even knew the names Stephen, Veronica and Paula any more. It broke my heart to think she didn't remember her children.

When the headaches weren't crippling her, she repeatedly asked who Lucille was. I explained she was a good friend who had come to help me. Lucille had advised me not to be confrontational. Better to go along with her confused state than to say things like, "Of course you know Lucille. She's here every day." That would only confuse her more.

So, each time Lucille came into the room, I would go through the introductions again. She was right. It made Annie happy and less anxious.

The kids were due to arrive on Wednesday, the day before Thanksgiving. Everyone was staying over and, I guess in their minds, intended to somehow be helpful. In reality, I dreaded their arrival. Not because I wasn't looking forward to seeing them. But because I didn't want them to see their mother in this condition. Annie had deteriorated greatly since the girls' last visit. It would shock them to see the extent of the downward slide she'd taken.

Thanksgiving had always been such a joyous time in our house. I can't remember a single holiday when one of the kids hadn't brought a guest home to join us, often someone from college who had no place else to be. We always had extra room at our table and showcasing our family's warmth was something I could tell the kids liked to do. They were proud of our family and it made me proud to see that.

This year would be terribly different and the image of the empty seat at the table, the place where Annie always sat, would be forever etched in their minds. We all understood it would be our last Thanksgiving together, probably our last holiday forever. Annie was unlikely to make it to Christmas. That was the painful reality we all were trying to accept.

Lucille had agreed to stay with us and share Thanksgiving dinner with us. That was very helpful because I promised to pick Veronica and Paula up at JFK on Wednesday morning. But, before that, there was much to do. I needed to shop for a turkey and all the other foods that go into a proper dinner. I wanted to recreate all of Annie's specialties; the garlic mashed potatoes, the string bean casserole, and her famous cherry cheesecake. It all needed to be made from scratch.

But, after Lucille and I finished our pepperoni pizza and I was planted in front of the TV for Sunday night football, I began to hear faint groans coming from Annie's room. I went in to find her turning her head from side to side- a sure sign the morphine drip had worn off and the tormenting pain had returned. The anguished groans seemed to be coming from somewhere deep within her body for I could barely notice her lips moving. They were trembling, but not forming the shape to correspond to the sounds I heard coming from the direction of her body. It was as if someone else was making the sound.

I reached out to hold Annie's hand. It was cold and clammy.

"I'm here honey."

Her grip on my hand tightened. I interpreted that to mean, "I'm glad you're with me." Although, it might have just been a reflexive jerk.

Within moments, Lucille appeared at the door. "She having trouble again?"

"I'm afraid so." I whispered.

Lucille added a pillow under Annie's shoulders then checked the drip bag while glancing at her watch. "It's only been two hours. Too soon for more pain meds."

My heart sunk. Not only did that mean more suffering for my wife but also continued torture for me. Watching Annie suffer was as painful for me as it was for her, maybe more so. When she was in agony, I couldn't leave her side. I felt an obligation to share her misery by staying with her, holding her hand and whispering encouragement. I couldn't possibly leave the room. I couldn't turn my back on her. My hope was that by holding her hand, I somehow halved her pain, some of it flowing directly into my heart.

"When can she have more?" I asked.

Checking her watch, Lucille offered, "At nine. At nine I can give her four more drops. I'll come back then."

That meant another hour and a half sitting at Annie's side, watching her suffer. I decided to read to Annie. Perhaps the sound of my voice coupled with the feel of my hand, might make the next ninety minutes tolerable for both of us. I choose a book I knew Annie loved, one she'd read several times on her own. In fact, she was reading it on our honeymoon back in 1975. Centennial, by James Michener, was one of her favorites, and I began reading somewhere in the middle.

Reading made the agonizing minutes tick away a little faster. At least it briefly kept my mind off our circumstances. I'm not sure if it helped Annie. Her face betrayed no emotion except an occasional grimace. As I read the words about RJ Poteet, one of the main characters, Annie's body seemed to calm, her breathing a little more regular. The story about the nineteenth-century cowboy was completely irrelevant to her current circumstances, but somehow brought her peace. Maybe it was the sound of my voice or maybe it was just the words that were so familiar. Whatever it was, I will be eternally grateful to James Michener for the few precious minutes of calm.

But long before nine o'clock, Annie began to stir again, her head moving back and forth against her pillow. This time, a faint moan followed each twisting movement. I noticed tears at the edges of her sallow eyes. Again, my heart broke. There was nothing I could do to help her. No amount of hand-holding, reading, singing or tap dancing was going to ease her suffering. All I could do was bear witness to it and by doing so, at least I could feel like I was doing all I could. I was with her in spirit.

After what seemed an eternity, Lucille came back in the room. "How's she been?"

"Tossing and turning, at least her head was tossing and turning. Not much movement anywhere else."

"That's not surprising. Often, a patient will stop using hand gestures in an effort to conserve energy. It's as if they're trying to save all their energy for thinking and breathing."

"Annie hasn't moved anything but her head in days." I refused to refer to Annie as a patient.

Lucille prepared Annie for the night. She changed the bed pad beneath Annie as well as her diaper. Both were wet. Then she adjusted the pillows behind her head and shoulders.

Annie let out a muffled scream. Then she turned her head in my direction and looked me directly in the eyes. Her beautiful green eyes were sunken and longing. I may have imagined it, but I thought I saw her lips shaping the words, "help me." She might have been just trying to reach the straw to her water bottle. I'll never be sure. Either way, once again, my heart broke for there was little I could do to comfort her.

But I was glad she saw me. I hoped she gained some solace from knowing I was there at her side, trying to share her pain.

"Hey beautiful," I said. "How you doing?"

She closed her eyes tightly as another round of pain within her skull overtook her. Her body shook. It looked as though she was being electrocuted. Then, just as suddenly as it began, it stopped. Lucille glanced at me with a facial expression that said, "I've never seen that before."

"Can you give her more meds for the pain?" I pleaded.

"I'll do four more drops now and check on her again around midnight. It would be good if we can get her to sleep through the night. Good for her, and for you."

Lucille could tell I was at my limit. I hadn't slept more than two hours at a time in several days. It was beginning to get to me. A severe lack of sleep coupled with the constant agony of bearing witness to Annie's torture, had weaken me. I wasn't eating properly and making up for it with oversized bottles of Chianti. The only thing that gave me strength was the depressing knowledge I wouldn't have to do this much longer. At some point, this nightmare would end and I'd be alone. It was a frightening thought.

I watched Lucille adjust the morphine drip and, just as before, a calm came over Annie almost instantly. Her hands released their clench and relaxed at her sides. Lucille wiped Annie's forehead with a cool cloth.

"You should try to get a little sleep Mr. Monday. Forget about that silly game. You need some sleep."

"Thanks, Lucille. I'll try to sleep a little here in the chair."

Lucille gave me a disapproving glance, but I think she understood that I was trying to spend as much time with my wife as possible. "Okay, but do try to sleep. Good night Mr. Monday."

"Good night Lucille." Then I added, "Lucille, I hope you know how much I appreciate all you're doing for us, especially for Annie. I can't imagine going through this without you."

She smiled and gave me a thumbs-up as she left the room. That was her style; the silent servant. There's got to be a special place in heaven for people like Lucille.

I sat next to Annie and turned on one of those battery-powered candles. It was the only illumination in the room. A real candle was out of the question because Annie still had the nasal cannula pushing oxygen. Her face had relaxed. She was asleep. She looked beautiful. At peace.

I waited until I heard the door to Lucille's room close. I spent several minutes thinking about many of the wonderful memories we shared; the births of our children, our courtship, buying our first and only home. The life we shared together was a rich one. We'd been so fortunate. I was filled with emotions. I loved her so much and my heart was breaking. But I knew it was time.

I put my hand on hers and whispered, "Annie, I hope you've always known how much you were loved. I loved you from the moment I first saw you on that boat. You gave my life direction and meaning. I don't know what would have become of me if I hadn't met you." I paused to wipe away a tear that had run down my cheek. "And you gave me the greatest gift anyone can give. You gave me a family to love. I hope you know how much I love our children. I think you do."

It seemed as though I was talking to Annie's body but I knew she was somewhere else, hopefully somewhere away from the pain. Perhaps this morphine induced sleep would give her the peace she deserved.

"Annie, in a way, you're lucky you know. You'll always be in our hearts, the hearts of me and the kids. We'll always remember all the good times. You'll forever be loved. But I have to somehow go on without you." I choked up at the thought.

"Oh, Annie, how am I going to live without you?" I cried. "I really don't know how I'm going to do this. I'm going to be so sad. So alone."

I took a couple of deep breaths to calm myself.

"Annie, I don't want you to suffer anymore. If I could take all your suffering away and put it on me, you know I would. I know you know that. I wish I could, but I can't."

I tightened my grip on her hand.

"Annie, I want you to be happy again. I want to end your pain. But I don't want to lose you. Please stay with me forever."

I knew it was time. I had to do the hardest thing any man could ever be asked to do.

I stood and faced the saline bag. The valve for the morphine drip protruded from the right and beckoned me. Until my hand was on the valve, I wasn't sure I could do it. But, just then, Annie moaned. I could see in the pale light, her face was twisted in pain. I had to save her. I had to release her from her earthly torture.

I twisted the metal valve and released twenty drops of the miraculous liquid into the saline bag. Then I climbed onto the bed next to her and held her tight.

I didn't want her to be alone.

XXXII

If you're reading this, I assume Lucille was able to get the flash-drive to the printer and that she gave you a paper copy of this journal. You should know that Lucille is one of the most wonderful people who ever walked the earth. Ever since mom died, I've kept in touch with Lucille. I called her two weeks ago to see if she was available to care for me in my final days just as she'd done for mom. She agreed immediately and has been at my side almost constantly. She's taken very good care of me.

Typing on my laptop the past few days has been exhausting, both because of the subject matter and the fact that I have no energy. Just sitting here at my kitchen table, pecking these last few words on the keys wears me out. Telling you about my last days with Annie, took every bit of strength I had.

So, now you know. You know that I took mom's life because I couldn't bear to see her suffer through another night. Maybe I was wrong. Maybe I was weak. But I make no apologies for what I did. I did it out of love.

I know what you're thinking. You're thinking, "Why didn't he wait until we could say good-bye? Why did he have to do it three days before we were scheduled to arrive for Thanksgiving. Couldn't we have had one more visit with her?"

The answer is no. I didn't want my precious Annie to suffer another three days just so you could see her. If that sounds cruel, I'm sorry.

And if you're angry with me for deceiving you about my cancer, too bad. That too, I did out of love. A few precious drops of Lucille's miracle liquid were all I needed to end this nightmare and spare you all great pain.

Finally, I hope you remember that I want to be buried next to mom at St. Mary's. I guess I should have reminded you of that at the start of this. I think I'll just write it on the envelope.

Be kind to one another. I love you more than you can understand.

Good-bye for now.

Dad

Made in the USA
Middletown, DE
17 January 2020